FEVER BURN

RACHEL HATCH BOOK THREE

L.T. RYAN

with

BRIAN SHEA

LIQUID MIND MEDIA, LLC

THE RACHEL HATCH SERIES

Drift

Downburst

Fever Burn

Smoke Signal

Firewalk

Whitewater

Aftershock

Whirlwind

Tsunami

Fastrope

Sidewinder (Coming Soon)

RACHEL HATCH SHORT STORIES

Fractured

Proving Ground

The Gauntlet

Join the LT Ryan reader family & receive a free copy of the Rachel Hatch story, Fractured. Click the link below to get started:

https://ltryan.com/rachel-hatch-newsletter-signup-1

Love Hatch? Noble? Maddie? Cassie? Get your very own Rachel Hatch merchandise today! Click the link below to find coffee mugs, t-shirts, and even signed copies of your favorite L.T. Ryan thrillers! https://ltryan.ink/EvG_

PROLOGUE

MOMBASA, KENYA

THE BOY WAS HUNCHED OVER, digging hard at the ground before him. He wasn't playing. Although, as his mother watched from nearby, she wished more than anything that he would. Masika hung a sheet from a clothesline stretched between two trees. But as was the way of things here, childhood was a fleeting fancy, one stolen by circumstances. It had been over a year since her eldest son had been taken. Zaire, at age twelve, had taken it upon himself to fill the void. His mother looked on sadly as the morning's mist surrounded him and the sun began to rise up beyond the dense tree line. He'd been at it since before dawn. A long line of upturned earth was the result of the last hour of toil.

Masika finished hanging several sheets, spreading them evenly along the line and knotting the ends to the line to secure them in place. The brightly colored cotton fabric flapped in the gentle breeze.

She walked over to the well and filled a bucket. A group of engineers had come to the village some years back and dug it out. It was life changing for them. No longer did they have to make the trek through the pass down to the river to get a drink. Plus, the water tapped from an underground source was much cleaner and therefore better for drinking. They still used the river to bathe and launder their clothes.

The tar-sealed wooden bucket banged into her knee as she walked, sloshing the water and wetting her embroidered kitenge dress. The coolness of the liquid felt good as morning temps began to climb. She knelt on the soft ground beside her son and, using a handmade ladle, scooped out some of the water.

"Drink, my son. It will be hot soon. You need to keep your strength up."

The boy shifted and looked at his mother, his dark hands caked with soft mud.

She brought the ladle close and Zaire slurped it up noisily. The excess spilled out from his mouth and dribbled down his chin. She scooped more from the pail.

Zaire held up his hand. "No more for now. I've got to get back to work. The ground is softer now with the rain, and I want to get the seeds in before sundown."

Light had just broken, and her son was already preparing for an entire day of work. Masika remembered when his days were filled with exploration and wonder. She prayed daily that someday they would be again. With the extraction of most of the able-bodied young men who'd been taken and forced into servitude, the village was left to rely on each member, young and old, to pull their weight. A harmonized synchronicity existed.

Inside their hut, she prepared the morning's meal. The villagers usually consumed two meals a day. Breakfast was done in the privacy of each individual hut, but the village shared a communal dinner after the day's work was done. That meal had been, until recent events, a time of great celebration. When the workday ended, singing, dancing and storytelling took place around the fire. It was a joyous time. Then Dakarai rose to power, and life in the village changed. Wives lost their husbands, children lost their fathers, and mothers lost their children. The village was stripped of its men who were sent to serve a warlord whose purpose was malevolent at best.

Most mornings, Masika served mkate, a simple flatbread. The children liked it when she added sesame seeds. She'd plate it with some fresh fruit. It was easy enough to make and hearty enough to provide energy for the day's work. When feeding her seven children, simple was essential. All breakfasts came with the sweetened Chai tea. Today would be different. One day a week, when she'd gone to the market and had the ingredients, Masika would treat her family to mandazi. It was a deep-fried pastry similar in taste and texture to an unsweetened doughnut.

Masika set about boiling the oil. She knew once the scent of the pastry floated out to her son, it would bring him in. Zaire couldn't resist the treat, no matter how dedicated he was to his chores. As she went to the cabinet and pulled out the flour, she heard the rumble of trucks.

There were two entrance and exit points, one that could be made by vehicle and the other, which was a footpath, led down to the river. Her heart began to beat faster. She hoped the arriving vehicle would belong to Father McCarthy, the priest who served their villages and several others in the area. Maybe he was bringing others with him, which he did on occasion. Humanitarian workers had come to the village several times over the years, delivering food and medicine. One group had put in the well years back. The priest came quite frequently, and they'd come to enjoy his visits, but he wasn't scheduled to be back for another day or so.

Her optimism was dashed as she realized that the more likely reason for the trucks' arrival was the return of the warlord and his men for some reason. And this thought made her panic.

The abduction of her eldest son one year ago left an unfillable hole in her heart.

There were other boys now reaching the age of maturity. Her 12-year-old son was close to being on the warlord's list if he chose their village to replenish his resources.

Masika knew what happened when their men disappeared. They'd heard stories of the conditioning--the psychological and physical tortures they endured. And the drugs Dakarai used to keep them in line and addicted. They were changed. As if their souls had been ripped from their bodies, the men became empty vessels.

She had caught a glimpse of her son six months ago on a convoy when she was in Mombasa town center. He was riding with a group of men in the back of a Jeep. Her eyes brightened at the sight of him, and she waved, hoping he would jump out and run to her. Masika knew her son had seen her. His eyes momentarily locked with hers. But to her dismay, he had no reaction, not even a wink, a secret half smile, anything to tell her that the boy she knew was still inside. He was just a shell of the son she'd raised, his mind corrupted by the warlord who controlled him now.

Masika was determined not to let that happen to her next oldest boy, Zaire, who was out toiling in the field.

She rushed to the door as the roar of the truck engines grew louder. It was the custom that the villagers would greet any and all arriving guests. It was something they'd always done. But now, at Dakarai's decree, all were ordered to come to the center point of the village. The fire pit where jovial gatherings had once taken place was now a place where atrocities were carried out. This past year had soured the affinity of the gathering point.

By Dakarai's edict, everybody was to be out of their huts and in visible sight when they came. It was done to control the masses and to make sure there was no subversion. A few villages had fought back in the early days of his rise to power. The end result carried with it devastating consequences. Her village had heard the tales and offered little in the way of resistance. When time came for a selection of some of their men or the stealing of their food and supplies, the resistance came in the form of a scream or a whimper of protest or simply a tear rolling down a cheek. But no formal attempts to stop the warlord's soldiers were ever made. Bravery was a foolhardy thing at best. Life trumped death, making the decision to comply easy.

Masika stepped out onto the dirt path and started making her way with the others toward the center of the village. With her other children clinging closely to her, she looked around for Zaire. Their scared faces were hidden behind her brightly colored dress. They were young, but they knew the threat.

Her heart sank, as her fear was confirmed. This visit would not be the priest or any humanitarian efforts. Any hope was dashed, as the two-vehicle caravan of the warlord's men moved forward. Guns poked out from several points in their Jeeps with a few men riding high on the top. The second Jeep had a large machine gun fixed to the roof and a man standing behind it at the ready, his eyes bloodshot and wild. She did not like these men. She did not trust them and worried for her village, and more importantly, her family, every time they came. There was no sign of her eldest boy among the soldiers.

Where was Zaire? she thought, frantically scanning, looking for him among her people. She cast a glance back to the garden area where he had been troweling with his hands just a short while ago. His diligent work, churning the soft earth and creating a little repository for the seeds to be sown was evident. She thought of the tender exchange they'd shared as she served him water from the ladle.

But his small body was not crouched where it once was. He wasn't in the crowd. He knew better than to wander off. Whenever the trucks came, he was supposed to find her, to tuck himself deep behind her, making himself small so he wouldn't be worthy of selection, hiding in plain sight. But he was nowhere to be seen, and this worried her.

Without Zaire present, she was suddenly filled with a wholly different prospect. A sense of relief rushed over her. Maybe he had run, taking the back path down toward the river and hiding somewhere down there away from Dakarai's soldiers.

The soldiers rarely went down to the river. On occasion they took some of the female villagers down there for things she dared not think about. Even if that were the case today, they would undoubtedly be too preoccupied, and her son would be safe.

She tried to calm herself and take solace in the fact that he wasn't here. He couldn't be selected if he wasn't here. *Would they notice Zaire's absence?* If they did, she would be punished. They'd need to make an example for the others.

The soldiers exited their vehicles as the Jeeps came to a stop. All except for the man standing behind the mounted machine gun.

The yelling began, ordering the villagers to tightly huddle up. They surrounded them like a pack of rabid dogs. Most chewing khat, the drug

Dakarai used to influence his soldiers. And one that added to their deranged state of mind.

The rifles were used to prod them. The clink of metal and bone and flesh as the elderly and infirm moved slower displeased them. One of the younger soldiers used the butt of his weapon to strike a man using a cane, sending him to the ground.

A young woman ran over to help, and the soldier shoved her from behind, sending her down on top of him.

Laughter amongst some of the men broke out as they jeered the two with taunts. Dakarai wasn't present, but his lieutenant belted out in Swahili for them to stop.

The barrel-chested lieutenant with a penchant for young girls turned his attention to the crowd. "We need three volunteers."

His terse voice and succinct command drew silence from the villagers. Volunteers. They all knew what it meant. And nothing about it was voluntary.

Now Masika was grateful. She couldn't send forward Zaire because he wasn't there. Her other children were far too young to join the ranks. As painful as it would be to watch another family endure such hardship, she was glad this time it wouldn't be hers.

It didn't take long before the soldiers picked their recruits. A tall boy nearby was grabbed by one of the armed men and dragged away from his mother. Masika listened to the anguished screams of the mothers as they made a last-ditch plea, begging for them to stop, trying to remind the soldiers that they were once boys, that they weren't always under the warlord's command.

But it happened regardless of protests as it had in the past and would undoubtedly happen again in the future. These cries for humanity fell on deaf ears.

One of the soldiers went door to door checking each hut, making sure nobody was hiding. Masika could hear the crash of pots. The clang and bang of overturned tables as the man rummaged his way around, sending another message. Don't hide. But no one was hiding. Nobody except her son. *Please be at the river*, she prayed. She tried to calm herself, to remain steady in the face of such danger.

The soldier exited the last hut and shook his head, looking at the leader, saying something to the effect of "nobody's here."

The lieutenant looked at the group, turned to his men and said, "Let's go."

The three boys who had been selected, none of them much older than her son, were shoved toward the awaiting Jeep. In fact, the youngest of the three was only six months older than Zaire, although he was taller and a bit lankier, giving the impression of being maybe a year or two older.

Masika felt blessed her son was born small and that he had remained so as he grew. Maybe he could avoid their interest for another year or two if luck favored? Maybe something would happen to change the course of this current situation and they'd be free from oppression.

As she stood shoulder to shoulder with her people, Masika made a silent prayer that these men would leave and never return. Then movement caught her attention out of the corner of her eye. It was her son. Zaire peeked out from behind the side of one of the huts nearest the Jeep where the young men were being loaded. Whatever she had felt in panic and worry was now giving way to something worse, an impalpable fear. She could taste the bile in her stomach. *What was he doing? Go back to wherever you were. They're leaving.* She willed him to listen, but he wasn't looking at her and she did not want to stare too long in his direction for fear one of the soldiers would notice.

It was too late. He was running now. She held back a scream. Zaire was running at a dead sprint, a large tree limb in his hand. The branch was held at the ready like a baseball player preparing to take the plate. He rushed forward to the soldier putting the last child, his best friend, into the back of the Jeep.

The soldier on the turret, seeing the boy running, yelled something to the soldiers on the ground, who turned and saw the boy. The last to turn was the one forcing the new recruits into the back, and he was the young boy's target. And as the man began to turn to see what the commotion was about, her son swung the stick, like John Henry swinging that mighty hammer. It came crashing down on the soldier's shoulder. If she had to guess, he was not more than 17. The heavy branch struck somewhere between his shoulder and his neck.

Her son was strong. The toil of hard work had made him so. The force with which he struck the soldier dropped the gunman to his knee.

Masika watched in horror as her son jumped on the stunned man's back and ripped free the machine gun that he had been holding. Zaire was swinging it wildly about, pointing it in every direction and yelling. "Go! Leave! Leave my friends! Or I'll kill you all!" he shouted. His voice cracking under the strain.

Tears streamed down her son's face. The look of anger in his eyes was one she'd never witnessed in his twelve years of life. He looked like a rabid dog, loose and unchained.

Several of the soldiers took aim. The lieutenant let out a deep laugh.

Zaire was trembling. These men saw it. They were battle hardened and numbed by the khat. Life and death no longer held the same meaning, as was evident in their soulless eyes. They knew the look of a killer and the conviction it took to pull the trigger. As angry and desperate as Zaire was, Masika had no doubts these men could see that he didn't have it. She knew her son. He was no murderer.

All the effort he had just made was for naught. He couldn't follow through and they were starting to see that. She wanted to cry out.

Several of the gunmen were now taking aim on the villagers.

The lieutenant said, "Drop the gun or we kill everyone here. Your family will die today. Is that what you want?"

Zaire looked to the crowd bearing witness to his act of courage. He looked at his mother. Tears fell more rapidly. His lip trembling in both fear and sadness, his failure immediate as the soldier he'd toppled and taken the weapon from stood up behind him and struck him in the back of his skull. The hard impact could be heard in the silence and it jolted him forward.

Her son's wide eyes, wet with tears, disappeared into the dirt in front of him. His resistance was thwarted as the gun was ripped from his hands.

And then several of the other men surrounded him and began kicking and punching the boy. She wanted to help. She squealed in anguish as a muzzle of a nearby soldier was pointed at her head.

Masika suffered in silence as she watched her son being beaten into unconsciousness by the warlord's men.

The one who had his gun taken from him shoved the others back and pointed the rifle at the back of Zaire's head. Just as he was about to pull the trigger, the lieutenant called out, "Stop!"

He walked over and whispered something into the gunman's ear that no one else could hear, a private one-sided conversation. The weapon was lowered, and the gunman retreated to the truck.

Zaire remained unmoving, face down in the dirt.

A split second later, the soldier who had been embarrassed by the 12-year-old returned with a thick rope. The lieutenant smiled his approval and then several other soldiers grabbed up Zaire. His head hung low.

The lieutenant walked forward toward the villagers, eyeing each one of them slowly and then his gaze came to rest on Masika. He must've seen her distraught look, the pain in her eyes that only a mother could have at a time like this. And then he said, "I am Baako, Dakarai's top lieutenant, and this will be the last time something like this ever happens. You will learn not to resist--not to fight. And this boy," he thumbed to Zaire, who was being supported by his henchmen, "will serve as a reminder."

ONE

FAYETTEVILLE, NORTH CAROLINA

SHE STOOD OUTSIDE THE BAR. It had been a long time since she'd frequented this establishment. Years, in fact. The last time was just before her exit from the Army. Standing here now in early spring, as the heat of the day was already starting to climb, seemed surreal. A deja vu of sorts, yet now she was a wholly different person.

Somebody from the Northeast might feel that it was already summer here, but Hatch knew better. Summer was still months off as far as temperatures went, and by midsummer, the temperature would climb to nearly one hundred degrees with a hundred-plus percent humidity. She'd trained in those conditions, and somehow during that time, had acclimated to them. But after leaving New Mexico, with its dry, cool climate, and making the drive out here to Fayetteville, North Carolina, she was not accustomed to the change, and her early morning run left her pores open as the sweat continued to pour even after the cool shower she'd taken to rinse herself off.

Hatch wasn't exactly sure what she was hoping to find here but figured this was as good a place as any to meet with her former team leader. She wished she could have stayed with the Task Force Banshee and been allowed to be a member of her team a little bit longer, to find some closure and to complete her military service with the men that she had grown accustomed to serving with. But the incident and the fire that crippled the right side of her arm had left her unfit in the eyes of her former team leader. But she needed him now. She needed to sit down with the man and ask him what he knew before she made the international trip out to Kenya. She needed to know what she was up against, and he was the closest thing to insider information she was going to find.

When she had called him, he had been reluctant, to say the least, in agreeing to meet with her. But after some cajoling on Hatch's part, Bennett conceded. He picked the location, one of neutrality, and somewhere there would be others around. She could tell in their brief conversation that he was guarded and wasn't sure how Hatch felt about him. That seemed fair. Hatch wasn't sure how she felt about him herself.

Anger had been the first reaction whenever his name popped into her head. Their last interaction had been less than amicable, and she felt the ties to him had been severed over a year and a half ago when she walked away to start her life as a civilian. She was still feeling out that title. It didn't quite fit her.

He'd said to be there at 11 o'clock. Hatch knew the bar opened at 10, and she decided to arrive at 10:30. She always liked to be ahead of whatever was coming, and in this particular case, a little bit of advance recon of the bar and its inhabitants would give her a leg up if Bennett felt her request for a meeting with him was not on the up and up. Obviously, he was nervous about it, and the fact that he had chosen this establishment proved that. If he was nervous, then her suspicion was raised, too.

Hatch pushed open the door, and although it was bright and warm outside, the bar was warm inside, but also dark. A dankness hung in the air, the smell of old beer and spicy chicken wing sauce struck her nostrils as she entered. The owner and proprietor, Ernie Wenk, had proudly bragged that he'd created a magical hot wings' sauce. He guarded his recipes as if they were the crown jewels. The wings had made him a legend in the area, winning numerous cook-offs. The walls, besides the military memorabilia, were adorned with photos of him in various hot wing cook-off competitions. His broad smile with his apron smeared with hot sauce and a wing in hand appeared in most of the pictures. He'd always told her, when Hatch used to come to the bar, that he planned to market it, sell his secret ingredient sauce to one of the big corporations, maybe Heinz, and make his millions. But as she walked into the bar and did a closer inspection, it seemed nothing had changed since she'd left. His dreams and aspirations of becoming a hot wing sauce household name appeared to have been tucked neatly away, probably in a mental drawer full of other unrealized endeavors.

The bar owner and saucier, for lack of a better term, looked up as Hatch walked in. He gave her a casual nod and a wink. The two had shared many stories over the years and had forged a bond, although it had been some time since she'd seen him. In her world, once out of sight, a person was out of mind as well. But seeing him brought back that comfort and familiarity, that sense of connection to a place, to a time, when things made sense. And in that split second as he poured a glass of beer for a patron, Hatch momentarily forgot that she was a civilian now. She blissfully remembered her time in the service and wanted to stay in that moment as long as she possibly could. She knew as soon as she opened her mouth and spoke to Wenk, the reality of the circumstances that she was just a civilian now, would intrude. She felt that she was a nobody in the world of the military, her service completed and forgotten.

Hatch pushed aside her hesitation as she entered.

Bellying up to the bar, she said, "Hey, Ernie, been a while."

Ernie Wenk pushed his ample girth over the top of the bar. For a former special operator himself, he had allowed the deliciousness of his wings and probably far too many beers over the course of the years to build a layer of bulk, mostly fat, around what used to be rigid, thick muscles.

Pictures on the wall showed him from back in his Vietnam days. A time when he was a lean, thick, strong man, often cutting the sleeves off of his shirts just to expose his rounded shoulders and bulging biceps. But he was no longer that man, although deep inside Hatch knew better than most, rubbing absent-mindedly the scar tissue on her right arm, that outward appearances were not always as they seemed, and people like Wenk and Hatch were always tougher than appearances made them out to be. She knew in a throwdown situation that Wenk would be able to hold his own, and she'd seen him on occasion demonstrate that when tossing out some rowdy soldiers who'd had too much to drink and nowhere to spend that amped up testosterone.

She recalled one time when a young infantry sergeant had finished off a bottle of Jack before coming in and apparently felt the need to test the bar owner by ordering a drink. Wenk, recognizing the condition of the sergeant, refused to serve him and poured him a coffee instead. In a fit of anger, the drunken soldier grabbed a beer bottle, broke it on the counter and proceeded to try to hop over and stab Wenk. As big as he was, pretty much the same size he was now, he had little trouble dodging the attack and knocking the bottle free from the man's hand.

The young sergeant had, for all intents and purposes, tried to stab the bar owner, but Wenk maintained a poise that could only be acquired by somebody who has faced enemy gunfire. He knew, even though the circumstances were intense, that this young soldier was not in his right mind. And instead of treating him like the enemy, he treated him to a quick punch to the stomach.

As the man doubled over, instead of continuing the beating, he caught him before he hit the ground and carried him like a sack of potatoes over his shoulder. He took him outside to the fresh air. Hatch remembered seeing Wenk go back in, get one of the soldier's friends who had been at the bar with him, and kindly ask him to take their friend home. Wenk never called the police. He went right back to pouring drinks for the other patrons as if it had never happened.

That was just one of many times. Hatch saw the bar owner handle an unruly incident with total control. Wenk was not the same size and shape of his youth, but he carried with him a deftness and a depth of character that she found in few others. And seeing him here now reminded her of all that, all those memories, and she smiled back. It felt good seeing him again.

"My God," he said, "Rachel Hatch in my restaurant? And to what do I owe this honor?" He added a pantomimed tip of the hat.

"It looks more like a bar than a restaurant," Hatch said.

Wenk laughed. This was their running joke. He always tried to make his food what people came for, but at Snake Eaters, the drink always outweighed the meal. "What brings you here?" he asked.

"I'm supposed to meet up with Bennett. Hasn't been by, has he?" Hatch asked. She was also gauging whether Bennett had come and done his own precursory recon before the agreed upon meeting.

"I haven't seen Chris in here for a while. Figured he was out saving the world," Wenk said. "Well, look at you, though. You don't look a day out of uniform."

Hatch again rubbed the scar tissue through her shirt. Although it was warm, she still wore a lightweight Lycra long sleeve shirt. She wasn't sure when her self-consciousness would let her expose what was underneath that sleeve, but she'd exposed it to very few and had always been guarded when out in public. As confident as she was, the damage to her right arm caused not only the strange looks, but always brought up the question of how she got it also. That *how* was a very difficult and private thing to share, the resulting damage of which cost some of her teammates their lives. And the image of the mother and girl that had detonated the bomb that burned her flesh still haunted her to this day. She did her best to tuck that memory down deep.

"Well," Hatch said, "I'm definitely not the same person I was. I guess I'm still kind of finding my way in this civilian world. But hell, you know better than me about that journey."

Wenk smiled. "You're right about that. I've been out for thirty-plus years, and I'm still trying to figure it out. So, if you do before me, please let me know how we're supposed to adjust to normal life after the things we've seen."

Hatch appreciated the man for his experience, his kindness, and more importantly, the fact that even since her separation, in his eyes, she was on equal ground with the other soldiers in the bar. Hatch eyed the private section of the bar and said, "I'm going to take my drink over there."

Wenk nodded. "What'll you be having?" he asked.

"Well, it's 10:30, so maybe just a Coke. You know what?" she added, "Why don't you put a little splash of rum in there?"

Wenk smiled and reached back for a bottle of Captain Morgan's and gave a healthy pour, not eyeing or measuring the shot that he put in the drink. If Hatch were to wager a guess, it was probably closer to a shot and a half, maybe two. But her nerves had gotten the best of her, and she figured maybe she'd try to calm them a little bit. Although she didn't typically rely on liquid courage, the meeting with Chris Bennett was putting her in an awkward position.

Filling the rest of the glass with Coke, he slid it over to her.

Hatch reached in her back pocket to pull out her money.

"Not here. Not today, Rachel. It's been too long. This first one's on me." Another wink. "It's good to see you."

Hatch thanked him and took her drink over to a reserved seating area on the right side of the restaurant. In it, there was always one glass set in front of an empty chair at the far end table. Every day, Wenk made sure he poured two fingers of his drink of choice for the day into that tumbler. It was set for the soldier who would never be able to take that drink. Wenk began the tradition when he had first opened the joint.

Hatch sat near the table and, with her back against the wall, faced the door where any moment Chris Bennett would be coming in.

TWO

HATCH SAT and took a slow sip from the rum and coke Wenk had made. It was strong, as she expected, having seen the pour he made into the glass before filling the rest of it with Coke. The soda softened the blow a little bit, but she knew to pace herself. As the liquid hit her stomach, she felt the warmth rush over her. It'd been a while since she'd had a day drink, and although it felt right when she'd ordered it, it also felt out of place and out of character for her.

She was angry at herself, not for deciding to have the drink, but more because she felt the need to take the edge off. After all the things she'd experienced in her life, a meeting with Bennett was unnerving her. Alcohol was seldom the refuge she sought. Hatch had accustomed herself to physical punishment in the way of a hard workout or a long run. Those were the ways she took the edge off or eased her anxiety, or in some cases, tried to forget some of the past. But today was not one of those days, and the workout she had put herself through earlier in the morning hadn't depleted her to the point where the anxiety didn't touch her. So, the drink had now found its way of working a little bit of magic and alleviating some of that stress about her pending encounter.

As she sat there in the bar she had frequented during her years of service, she noticed that one of the soldiers eating a burger in the corner with a few of his friends began eyeing her. At first, she felt maybe he wasn't looking at her directly, but seeing as there was no one else around in the secluded reserved area, it only took a moment for her to realize he was, in fact, giving her the eye. He whispered something to his friends and then stood. Hatch thought to herself, *Well, this isn't going to be good.*

The young man, with his ginger hair tightly shaped in a high and tight, approached in somewhat of a huff. He walked directly to the table she was sitting at, and placed both hands firmly in front of her, jostling the drink, and causing the ice cubes inside to rattle against the glass.

Hatch slowly looked up and then took a sip, silently dismissing whatever this was about.

The ginger looked back at his friends, who nodded, and then turned to her and said, "This is reserved seating. Operators only. I think you might be a little bit lost."

Hatch looked away, back down toward the glass that was still three quarters full, picked it up and took another small sip. This silent defiance seemed to only enrage the young soldier further, as a little vein began to bulge in his neck and his pale face started to redden.

"Hey, lady, I'm trying to be real nice here, but this is a special section of the bar that is reserved for a special type of person."

Hatch set the glass down, droplets of condensation already beginning to pool on its outside in the muggy heat of the room. She pushed back ever so slightly in the chair and readied herself to confront the man. She wasn't quite sure how she intended to address this issue. She was a civilian now, and to try to give her backstory might come off wrong, and most likely, this man wouldn't believe her if she told him. Her experience was unique, not only for the army, but for a female in the army. Few had done what Hatch had. Actually, there was only one other female to successfully complete the selection course, and there had been no other, to her knowledge, that had ever done it twice, male or female.

Hatch folded her arms and said, "I think I'm okay. Thank you." This only seemed to further infuriate the ginger-haired soldier.

He looked back at his friends and threw his hands up, as if to ques-

tion how this girl could be standing up to him. When he turned his attention back to her with his fists balled. Hatch thought for a second that the
soldier was angry enough to possibly take a swing at her. Maybe he'd
been drinking a little bit too long, and his judgment was skewed. It
wouldn't be the first brawl that took place between soldiers.

Hatch had plenty of memories from her time as an MP and the fights
she'd broken up. Many times, the reason was petty. Although she did
understand the ginger's desire to protect the sanctity of the reserved area,
which was set aside for special operators, those who had served not only
in a military capacity, but in some of the most dangerous roles imaginable.
And Wenk, being a former Green Beret himself, found it was important
to designate a space just for them. He always gave them a little bit of
extra in their drink, and comped them some food, typically one of his
extra spicy wing platters, as a way of thanking them.

But what pissed Hatch off was the way this soldier addressed her
from the get-go.

Hatch took a deep breath, exhaling slowly as she stood up. Being
5'10", Hatch was nearly eye to eye with the ginger-haired man standing
before her. And she could see that when he realized this, that her physical stature was comparable to his, he took a step back. His movement was
part fear, but he was also distancing himself and preparing for what
might come.

Hatch didn't make a fist, although she readied herself in case this
young soldier made the mistake of getting aggressive with her beyond his
words. She stepped back with her right foot, just slightly, just enough to
give her balance and put her in a better position to counter anything he
might throw her way.

All of a sudden, a voice boomed. It was Wenk. "Hey! Why don't you
back off and leave her be?"

"But, Ernie, this woman, she's sitting in the reserved section! She's got
no business, you know better!" The soldier pleaded, half embarrassed.
His face turned a blotchy red.

Wenk leveled a stern gaze at the man and said, "She's done more than
you've ever done, or ever will do."

Receiving the admonishment, the red in the young soldier's face deepened. A crease of confusion etched his brow as he looked at Wenk. "I don't understand. What are you talking about?"

Wenk smiled as he pointed toward the bar to a framed article from The Army Times hanging on the wall, surrounded by patches and other memorabilia. The article's caption in bold black letters, "First female to ever complete Army Special Forces Selection Course Twice."

Wenk let the man process what he was reading, and although there was no picture, the message was clearly sent.

The man looked at the article, and then at the woman who stood before him. His eyes ping-ponged back and forth, until they settled back on Hatch. His face was red, but the vein along his neck no longer bulged. The remnants of red peppering his cheeks were out of sheer embarrassment. "I...I just thought that I just... I've never seen...," he stammered.

Hatch gave him a break and decided in that split second that he was, although aggressive and intoxicated, nothing more than a young soldier overeager to enforce tradition.

"Listen, I get it. Maybe next time don't come off as such a hothead. I understand you were looking out for the sanctity of this space, and I never would've sat here had I not earned the right," Hatch said softly.

The ginger soldier said nothing further and turned as if he'd been reprimanded by a principal or parent. If he had had a tail, it would've been tightly tucked between his legs. He walked back to his friends, who were looking at him with dismay and shock that he had been reprimanded, and the woman had been defended by the bar owner.

Hatch turned her attention to Wenk, who was making his way back to the bar area. "Thanks. I could've handled it myself, ya know," Hatch said.

Wenk shot a glance over his shoulder. "Oh, I know. I just didn't want to clean up blood this early on a Tuesday. His blood."

They both laughed as Hatch resumed her seat. She checked her watch and saw that it was nearing 11 o'clock. The little dump of adrenaline from the potential skirmish with the young soldier had mixed nicely with the little bit of Captain Morgan in her system, and she felt a slight weight lift from her shoulders.

Hatch always felt that combat, the potential or otherwise, gave her a sense of calm. It was in those moments of chaos she felt most at peace. She was the proverbial calm in the storm, and she realized that about herself. Ever since leaving the army, she'd sought that connection. It had been severed when the army no longer wanted her, particularly her old unit.

A few minutes later, just past 11, the door opened, and the familiar face of Chris Bennett entered. He eyed Hatch, then he surveyed the bar, his operator training, even in a safe environment, was always on point, as was hers. No amount of time could undo the training they'd been through. Entering any confined space, those with their experience always did a quick check of the surroundings, both of the people and the location.

Satisfied, Bennett moved in. He held up two fingers and nodded at Wenk, who immediately set about lining up two shot glasses. He filled each of them with a Glenlivet whiskey, Bennett's drink of choice.

Bennett didn't hold eye contact with Hatch for long. He walked directly to the bar, grabbed his two shots, and then brought them over to where she was sitting. Before he took his seat, he turned back to Wenk, "I'll grab a Miller Lite too. Thanks, Ernie."

Hatch eyed the two shots in his hands. Ordering a third beverage to wash them down in reverse order meant he was doing whiskey with a beer chaser. Usually it was the other way around.

"I see you're getting a good start to the day. I assume you're not going back to do any range work," Hatch said, eyeing the two shots. Apparently, Bennett was just as nervous about this meeting as she was, as he also was not known for heavy drinking, although on occasion he partook, and this was apparently one of those occasions.

"So, what are we doing here, Hatch?" he asked, downing the first shot and slamming the glass onto the table.

"Well, I have some questions. I told you when we talked that I needed to see you in person, and it's important," Hatch said.

"Okay then, if it's important, get on with it."

Hatch eyed him carefully. The last time they had spoken to each other, she nearly knocked him unconscious. It had been the last time they had faced each other, and it was a heated and physical altercation. But did he assume that she called him out of the blue to set up round two, or was he just awkward around her since that encounter?

"Listen, Chris, I've got a lead on what happened to my father, and I wanted to see if you knew anything that might be able to help me out--point me in the right direction--give me a heads up before I head off to my next destination," Hatch said bluntly.

"And that would be where exactly?"

She thought for a moment about keeping her next stop to herself, but if information was to be exchanged, holding back would most likely result in the same from Bennett. "Africa. I'm heading to Kenya."

"Your father's death has something to do with Africa? That's a dangerous place lately. Not sure you want to be poking about over there right now."

"Let me worry about that," Hatch muttered.

"I still don't really understand what you're getting at," he said. "I remember you saying something about a hunting accident when you were a kid. How would I be able to help with that?"

Hatch sighed. "I've come into some new information. My sister died, well, she was murdered recently, and it set in motion some things when I went home. One of which was I found out a little more about the circumstances around my father's death, and I've been tracking those leads since then," she said.

"Sorry to be so cold, but what does this have to do with me?" Bennett asked. His face was contorted in a look of confusion.

"Nothing, not directly, but I know that you're still in the special operations community, and you have access to things that I don't anymore," she said.

"Wait a minute, Rachel. No way am I going to go pulling black ops folders or digging deep. I'm not losing my job and my career over some wild goose chase you may be on," he said.

"I didn't ask you to do that," Hatch snapped. "I didn't ask you to dig anything up. I wanted to ask you what you know about the Gibson Consortium," she said.

"The Gibson Consortium? I don't know. Well, I know of them. There was a unit of private contractors called that, but that was a long time ago. They changed names and I think ownership. They're known as Talon Executive Services now, TES. I only had a few dealings with them overseas, after you left the unit," he said.

"It's funny that you choose those words," Hatch said. "*Left the unit*. If I recall, I didn't leave anything. My decision was made for me."

"So, you're here to bring that up? We're getting into that now? I thought this was about your father, or are you here to beg to come back? You're a civilian now, Hatch. You're not one of us anymore. I'm sorry that was such a hard pill for you to swallow, but that ended over a year ago," he said.

Hatch took another sip from her drink, this one just a little bit longer than the last. "I'm not looking to get back into the unit, Chris. I know it's over. Trust me. I've already gone down that path. I did what I could to prove my worth to you and it didn't matter. I'm not here to push that issue. Let's drop it for now. I'm sorry I even brought it up," she said.

Bennett threw down the second shot of whiskey as Wenk set the Miller Lite down, collected the two empty shot glasses, and disappeared back behind the bar. He immediately took a pull. The reverse order, whiskey to beer chaser, had been complete. "Okay, so what is it you want to know?" Bennett said.

Hatch evaluated him. She remembered the good times they'd had when the team was whole, when they were out there doing it, getting the job done. They were an unstoppable force, and she had carried her weight and then some. Then, that day happened, and as if the blast wasn't bad enough, the emotional destruction from that moment, for both the team and her, was something that would never be erased. Seeing him sitting here before her now made it hard for her to adjust to the fact that their friendship and comradery had burned up in that blast, leaving invisible scars that both of them carried from that day forward.

"So, what do you know about Talon Executive? What's their deal?" she asked.

"They're like any government contractors. They fill some voids and do some private security work. It's like the former Blackwater. They handle details that aren't tasked to military personnel, but they are all ex-military. I haven't heard anything crazy about them, but I will say this, of all the private contractors that I have worked with, they are the most secretive. They rarely are at any of the combined functions on bases. They keep to themselves and operate exclusively with members of their own unit. They never task out, and never ask for support from us," he said.

"You've never had any negative dealings? You've never heard of anything going wrong outside the wire?" she asked.

"Look, Hatch, I know we've got history so I'm just going to say this. Most of the guys in that unit, in that contractor service, are ex-Delta. These are next-level guys. I knew a few of them, but when they went in, we lost contact. So, really, what I know is limited," he said with a shrug.

"You don't have any point of contact there? Somebody I could reach out to and speak with?" she asked.

Bennett took a sip of his beer and shook his head, and then he leaned forward just a bit. He cast a quick glance, barely noticeable toward where Wenk was at the bar. He was drying a rinsed mug and tending the bar back duties in between orders. "Listen," he said in a whisper. "I do know this, and what I'm going to tell you is just grumblings. You don't have the clearance anymore for the real stuff, but I'll tell you this, they're not a group to mess with. I've heard stories, guys go missing, ops go bad, nothing happens. There's no press, no paper, nothing. Even in our circles, limited details. So, whatever you think you're digging up, you might be crossing swords with the wrong people."

Hatch leaned forward slightly because of his need for secrecy and said, "Why are you whispering? What are you worried about?" she asked.

"Listen, they've got eyes and ears everywhere. They're connected to the military. There's big money in this stuff, you know that. Man, they do some of the stuff that nobody, not even the bigger contractors can handle.

So yeah, I don't like talking about it, especially to you, who's obviously come here on some half-cocked idea that it's linked to your father's death. I don't even want to know why you think that. The less I know about what you're doing, the better off I am," he said, and then pushed back in his seat and folded his arms.

Hatch eyed him. "So that's it? There's nothing else you can tell me? Okay, well I'm not going to tell you where I'm going next, but I've got a long journey ahead of me, and hopefully that next step won't get me killed. Seeing as how I know almost as little as I did when I walked in here, you're definitely not setting me up for success," she said.

Bennett sighed and rubbed his temples, took another long pull from his beer, and kept it in his hand instead of setting it back on the table. He looked over at Hatch. "Listen, Wenk might know something more," he said.

Hatch shot a glance over to the thick bartender and restaurant owner, maker of sauces. "You talking about Ernie? Wenk? Him over there?" she asked, confused.

Bennett nodded slowly but said nothing.

Hatch said, "Why would he know anything about it?"

"Because he was one of the founding members. Eyes and ears everywhere," he said with a wink.

Hatch sat back, absorbing this. The man she'd known for years. She'd come to his establishment, drinking, and eating, and socializing. To think Wenk had known or may have known something about her father or his death, and had held back, sickened her.

Hatch finished the rest of her rum and Coke. The ice had already melted, the remnants in the cup were more water than anything else. She was grateful for it because with too many drinks, she didn't know if she would be able to contain the anger rising up. It was misguided anger and she knew it. She didn't know who she was angry at or if Wenk knew anything at all. But here Bennett sat, laying it all out for her, at least hinting at what potentially could've been right in front of her all along.

"Hey, look, maybe he doesn't know anything. Maybe he was in it early, got out early. I don't know. And I don't know what this has to do with your father's death, but what I can tell you is this--some things are better left buried. Sometimes it's just better that way," he said.

Hatch looked at him, then turned and looked at Wenk behind the bar, who nodded and held up a bottle of Crown and gestured at her glass. She shook her head no, and he went back to his work.

"Yeah, listen, Hatch, I gotta go. I got stuff to do. It was good seeing you," he said.

"Was it?" Hatch asked.

Bennett stood and looked down at her before leaving. "For what it's worth, you were a hell of an operator, and I'm sorry for the way things played out. And whatever it is you're looking for, I hope you find it."

With that, Bennett walked out of the bar, leaving Hatch alone in the private section of Snake Eaters. The lunch wave of people began to trickle in, and tables were starting to fill.

Hatch stood and took her glass over to the bar. She debated on discussing the new information with Wenk right here, right now, but as the man became busy with orders, she didn't want to tip her hand. Hatch decided she would return later, around closing time, and have a little one-on-one with her friend and bartender about the group responsible for her father's death.

THREE

HATCH SAT in a rental car and sipped from a lukewarm cup of coffee she had picked up from a local convenience store. The bitterness of the tepid liquid gave her more of a jolt than the caffeine and was somehow strangely satisfying.

She waited, knowing Snake Eaters closed early. Strange for a business operating outside of a military base, but Wenk kept odd hours. He always had. He liked to open early and close earlier than most other bars in the area. The watering hole became a launching point for most GIs as they set out on their night of drinking. By closing the bar at 11:00, Wenk figured it also prevented some of the fallouts that tended to occur toward the later hours of a bar's night when the drinks multiplied and tempers flared in relation.

Hatch watched as the last group of patrons staggered out into the thick mugginess of the night air. She could see Wenk still inside, working the bar. He was setting up glasses and restocking the shelves of booze. Hatch figured he'd probably be at it for the next hour or two, and she wanted to have a conversation before he was too tired or too put off to fully comprehend her line of questions.

She set the empty cup down in the center console and prepared to exit the rental when her phone began to vibrate. She slipped it out and looked at the incoming caller, Dalton Savage. It was the third time he'd called this week. And it would be the third time she hadn't answered. He left one message out of the three calls, a short, brief voicemail. He had just asked if she was okay and told her that he was thinking about her. *Thinking about her*, she thought. She had saved the message on her phone and listened to it more times than she cared to admit. His voice was the last thing she heard before falling asleep.

Since leaving Hawk's Landing, Hatch had allowed herself to mentally drift back to the place she had thought she'd forever left behind. She was gradually coming to believe there might be a chance at something normal, a life beyond what she knew.

The night she had laid in the motel bed with Savage, nothing happened. But falling asleep to the rise and fall of Savage's chest had left a longing inside her, a sensation she had long since forgotten she was even capable of having.

Hatch knew she needed to call him. She wanted to. She wanted to tell him that she was working on finding her way back to Hawk's Landing. He knew why she was on the move again. And knowing the type of man that he was, she knew undoubtedly that Savage understood. Yet, she couldn't bring herself to answer the phone. Maybe she was more scared that if she answered it, he would say something that would derail the path she was on. Hatch knew he had the potential power to do that, and she couldn't afford to let that happen. She needed to stay the course, focus on the task at hand, find out who was responsible for her father's death, and if possible, make it right. Only then would she be able to really go home and begin taking care of Daphne and Jake, work on the relationship with her mother, and maybe, if she was lucky enough, start a life with Savage.

She let the phone vibrate until the call had gone to voicemail and then slipped it back into her pocket. Exiting the car, she walked across the street and pulled the door open. Wenk popped his head up from behind the bar and was caught off guard by her entrance.

"Rachel? Back so soon? I just closed her down. You know better than most I like to shut things down early before the riff-raff gets out of control." He chuckled. "I'll set one up for you if you'd like?"

"No need. I'm sorry to bother you. I know you're busy getting things set up for tomorrow. I just wanted to touch base on something that's been gnawing at me all day."

He set a glass mug down on the towel he was using to dry it and looked at her, cocking his head slightly to the side. "Why didn't you just ask me when you were in here earlier?"

"I would have, but there were just too many people. You were busy, and it wasn't the right time," Hatch said. "Do you mind?" She eyed a stool.

"I always have time for you, my dear." Wenk rounded the bar and pulled up a seat on one of the stools nearest her. "How about that drink?"

"Not tonight. I'm going unleaded for the rest of the evening."

"Fine by me. I don't partake myself these days." He stared at the empty mug and then to the line of bottles shelved in the backdrop. "Three years sober this month," he said pridefully.

"Huh," Hatch offered. "I didn't know."

Wenk's cheeks pushed upward, creasing the outside corners of his eyes. "It's a strange thing, right? A bar owner on the wagon. I find myself a bit of a hypocrite nowadays. I serve them up all night long but refuse to consume any myself." He continued before Hatch could offer a counter. "Hell, back in the day I used to be half in the bag working the bar. I'm sure I let a lot of money go in and out in the wrong direction. I could barely keep track of things. But after the car accident, I decided it was time I cleaned my act up and got myself together."

"Good for you," Hatch offered, not sure if this was a moment where she should dive deeper into the man's past or let it stay where it was.

"It was really good seeing you today, Rachel. It brought back a lot of great memories. God, I see a lot of your dad in you," Wenk said.

The comment made something ache in a deep place inside of Rachel. That locked fortress around her heart didn't allow for emotion to enter. She kept her feelings contained like sunken treasure at the ocean's bottom. But his comment released a bit of it, and the memory of her father bubbled to the surface.

Hatch felt herself blush at the compliment. "You do?"

"I probably should have told you this before," he said, "but you're the spitting image of him. I mean, I look at you and I remember your father and me, and this goes back years, mind you. We were thin, rugged and headstrong." He lay a hand on her shoulder. "He'd be so damn proud of you, Rachel."

"Thanks. I guess I've always held out the hope that by following in his path I was in some way connected to him. It has been a way to keep him alive, at least the memory of him," Hatch said.

"So, tell me, what brings you back here again? What's got you concerned enough to stop by my shitty little bar twice in one day after not seeing you for, what--over a year and a half now?"

Hatch dipped her head low and gave a soft chuckle. "Yeah, I guess it's been about that long, hasn't it?" she asked.

"So, what gives? What's really going on here? First off, you meet with Bennett and then here you are back again to talk to me. What are you digging at?" he asked.

"It's my dad. I'm trying to figure out who murdered him. Or at the very least--who was responsible," Hatch said.

Wenk reared back slightly at the comment. "Murder? I mean, I know he was killed, but everything I had read or heard about it was in relation to a hunting accident. I mean, that had to have been--"

"22 years," Hatch finished.

"22 years. My God, has it been that long?" he asked.

"Doesn't seem that way to me," she said. "I can still see his face."

"You were there that day. I remember reading somewhere that you were the one who found him. Am I right?" he asked.

Hatch nodded but didn't say anything. To speak of that moment in time was too painful to verbalize. To do so would undoubtedly uncage emotions she had long since kept tucked far away from anyone else. Those private final seconds she shared with her dad as he took his last breath were for her and her alone. She closed her eyes.

She was running. The ground crunched under foot. The steep angle of her descent to the bottom of the running trail forced her into a rapid cadence. Her father disappeared momentarily. Then came the loud crack of the rifle, its origin unknown. Her legs pushed harder than ever before. Seconds later she came to the brook. Her father lay motionless as she ran to him. Her scream shattered the silence, sending a flock of birds high into the sky. Her world forever changed in an instant. Hatch's childhood was stolen as she knelt next to her dead father.

That memory was hers and hers alone, and she would share it with no one.

"Must've been hard for you," he said. "I can't imagine what you went through as a child losing your father like that. But you just said 'murder.' They never found the hunter who shot him?"

"No hunter was found."

"What came of it? To be honest, I kind of lost track," he said sheepishly, offering his apology with a dip of his head.

Hatch evaluated Wenk, carefully studying the family friend who didn't come to her father's funeral.

"Well, that's the thing, Ernie. They had written it up as a hunting accident, but I was recently home again and learned a few things while I was investigating the death of my sister--"

"Your sister died?" Wenk interrupted.

"She was murdered, "Hatch said.

"That's a hell of a thing," he said, shaking his head.

"But I'm not here about that." Hatch now wished she had taken him up on his offer of a drink. "While I was there, I started digging around a little bit. I had access to some old police records, and I found out that my father's death was no accident."

"What do you mean *no accident?*" he asked.

"Listen, Ernie, I don't want to get you in deeper than you need to be. But have you ever heard of the Gibson Group or Gibson Consortium?" she asked.

Wenk's eyes widened a fraction of inch. "I haven't heard that company mentioned in years now. It's an old spec ops contractor group. I mean, if you really want to get down to brass tacks, it was a mercenary group. They forged it shortly after the Vietnam War came to an end. They tried to recruit me. Well, when I say they, I'm going to level with you here, Rachel, it was your father who tried to recruit me."

"My father?" Hatch asked.

"I've told you before, or at least hinted at if not told, during a couple war stories in my more inebriated days, that your father and I served together in Vietnam. Our SOG team was well-feared among the Viet Cong. When I returned home, I was given an opportunity to put my skills to work, and I jumped at it. I tried to get your father to come along with me. A few of us with heavy combat experience were tapped to go and train with the British Special Air Service, the SAS. We were tasked with learning their ways and then developing a variation of it for the Army. The country saw the direction of future warfare and wanted a unit capable of handling the unique challenges," he said.

Hatch looked at him. She knew what he was referring to. She knew the timeframe and time period. Those special operators back in that era were tapped to go and work with the SAS for a specific unit, famous in more recent engagements, but known throughout the world now as Special Operations Group Detachment Delta, or more commonly Delta Force. Hatch's Task Force Banshee had operated on the same Tier 1 status.

"I didn't know," she said. "I mean, I knew you were Special Forces. Obviously, that's pretty much what this bar was designed around, but I didn't know that you were a founding member of Delta," she said.

Wenk smiled. "Well, what kind of special operations group would it be if everybody knew? I mean, I was raised as a quiet professional. I think you understand the importance of that as well as any. Things are changing now, like that young kid from earlier who bowed up on you for no good reason."

"He's SF?" she asked.

Wenk nodded slowly. Shrugged, a bit embarrassed. "I have to say, he's not the face of the organization I had hoped for. But yes. And he's a little more brazen about what he does. I'm sure his Facebook profile tells the world about all the wonderful things in special operations he's performed. It makes me wonder if it still exists now, the true quiet professional," he said quietly.

Hatch only offered a shrug. "I worked with some good people," she said. "We did some good things, and I don't think anyone outside of our circle knew anything about it, which I'm grateful for. I think it always should be that way. It really only matters to the person beside you, especially when the shit hits the fan," she said.

"I didn't mean to go on a long-winded bend. But your father, when they were tapping me to head up and assist with the development of Delta, he wouldn't come. The war affected everybody differently. I can't say I wasn't affected as well. I just poured some of that energy back into the Army. I gave more of myself to the war machine. Your father, on the other hand, decided to separate and go his own way--find a new path."

Hatch looked at the man, and she could see he was digging back into some old memories, uncovering some past he'd probably felt was long buried. And peppered in there was probably a bit of nostalgia as well.

"Tell me more about the path he took," she said.

"Well, he separated from service, and he was picked up by a head-hunter, a recruiter of sorts, who was looking for people with specific skill sets, and in particular the ones that we possessed. Your father possessed them in spades and was one of the best operators I've ever worked with. So, he was an easy mark for contractors, or like I said earlier -- mercenaries. He got picked by the Gibson Consortium. Didn't know much about it. And to be honest with you, at that point in my life, I was focused on my own task. It wasn't long before I was overseas at Hereford with the SAS and lost myself to months and months of rigorous training. And when I came back stateside to start sharing what we had learned, I was hoping that I could bring your father back into the Army, but he was gone," he said.

Hatch thought about that for a moment. Nothing he said seemed to be a lie. She was reading everything from the minuscule gestures in his face, to his mannerisms, to his body's posture, to his breathing. She watched the pulse in his neck. The heavy man's carotid artery thumped in the same rhythmic fashion as it had when their conversation began and never changed. Wenk had no tell, no indication that anything he said was a lie. If he was lying, he'd make a hell of a poker player. And so, for now, she believed him.

"So, you came back and that was it? My father was gone -- off to this Gibson Consortium?"

Wenk shrugged. "That was my guess. We really lost touch after that. I hadn't seen or heard from him till about fourteen years later when I saw that news story and saw him saving that family trapped on the mountain. And then when I went to reach out to your father and reconnect, I found out that a week later he'd been shot in a hunting accident."

Hatch sighed quietly. The memory of that day still haunted her. His summation of the tragedy didn't do it justice.

"Did you know anyone else who joined up with my father at the time? Someone around here, maybe local, something that could point me in the right direction? I have a lead, but it's going to take me far away from here," she said.

Wenk cocked an eyebrow. "How far?" he asked.

"I'd really rather not say. Ernie, I understand, and I trust you. But if what I've learned is true, then anybody who knows what I know really isn't safe. And so, the less you know, the better you are. And I am going to be heading away from here sooner rather than later. But I felt that if I could touch base with my roots, tap into the community and see if some-body knew something, I would at least have a leg up on my next journey," she said.

Wenk looked around as if maybe there was one last patron tucked away in a corner that she hadn't seen when she entered. But there was nobody. Then he looked back and gave Hatch a steady gaze. "Listen, Rachel, what I'm going to tell you can't come back on me. You under-stand? I'm sure you're deft at coming up with a cover story."

"I understand," she said softly.

"But there is somebody local who may know more, somebody who was part of that group at the same time your father was." Wenk rubbed his hands together and then wiped the sweat off on his sauce-stained apron.

Hatch's heart skipped a beat. It was the first bit of good news she'd had since linking up with the man in New Mexico. She hoped this new person would give more insight than the name of the corporation and a contact in Africa. If she were lucky, maybe her international travel plans would be cancelled.

The flip side was she had an opportunity to speak with somebody who at one point had been close with her father. Any chance to know him better, even posthumously, was a rare treasure. Maybe the answer was closer than she realized. And she could bring some closure at least in the knowledge of what had happened to him or who had done it, who had pulled the trigger.

Hatch allowed herself a quiet moment to mull over her thoughts, and then spoke. "That would be great. It won't come back on you, I promise. Who is he?" Hatch asked, the words rolling off her tongue in rapid-fire succession.

"He owns Fat Tony's Tattoos," he said with a laugh. "But don't let the name fool you. This guy's anything but fat. I honestly don't know where he came up with it. But since he got out and returned here to Fayetteville, he's been inking people up left and right. There's a good business for tattoo shops if you've got the right shop and a good reputation. And being a former operator, a Vietnam era operator, owning a tattoo shop on the strip leading to the base was a win-win as far as marketing strategy goes. And he's done pretty well for himself. His real name is Anthony, Anthony Amaletto. A little rough around the edges, but if you break down those tough walls, you'll see he's kind of a teddy bear at heart," Wenk said.

"Okay. Fat Tony's Tattoos. Not too far? You said it was close to base?" Hatch asked.

"Yeah. Take you about 10 minutes, if that, from here."

Hatch noticed the tattoo on Wenk's forearm. It was faded and old. It was a claw with a snake behind it. Hard to tell and make out the shapes. Years of wear and tear on the man's body had taken its toll, aging the tattoo. The ink's fine lines were now blotchy marks, but she could just make out the general gist of its original design.

"Did Fat Tony do that?" she laughed.

Wenk looked down at his forearm and chuckled softly. "Matter of fact, he did," he said. "This was his first tattoo. Hopefully, he's improved since those days. I never really took to the needle. I was a one and done kind of guy. We got it for our old unit. We all did it at the same time. Maybe that's where Tony got the bug or at least the beginning thoughts for pursuing it later in life."

Hatch rubbed her scarred arm and thought of the tattoo she had, the deep meaning behind it. It's the way of some tattoos. Most, she figured, held some significance, some internal connection. Whether it was perceived or real, those markings meant something. If nothing else, they served as a historical marker, a piece of time frozen. A memory etched in the flesh.

She looked at the tattoo and thought of her father and tried to remember, looking back those many years, and she couldn't recall if he had something similar. Her mom hadn't kept many pictures from his days in the Army. None she could recall captured any tattoos. And thinking back to her childhood, none came to mind.

Hatch stood to leave. "I can't thank you enough, Ernie. You've always been kind to me and treated me like a member of the family whenever I came in here. And it means a lot to me. I can't help but wonder where he'd be right now if he hadn't taken the different path," she said.

"If we all knew where the path led us, we'd always make the right choice," he said. "But that's the thing with life. We don't get a preview of what's to come. Well, maybe that's part of the fun of it, not knowing what's waiting around the next bend in the road."

Not knowing. She didn't know where the next bit of her journey would lead, even less where her life and future would take her. Would it take her back to Hawk's Landing, to the family she'd left behind? And Savage? Or would this next step lead her on a path that would send her further into the abyss, drifting from the people she cared about, chasing ghosts.

Hatch turned to leave. And as she made her way out the door, Wenk called to her. "Rach, just do me a favor and remember you didn't hear it from me. He's a crotchety old bastard, so give him a wide berth and let him bow his chest and spread his feathers like a peacock. He'll settle. And once you tell him who you are, hopefully he'll give you the answer you're looking for," he said.

Hatch nodded. "I'll be seeing you," she said. She didn't know if that was the truth or not as she stepped out into the thick, muggy North Carolina night and walked back toward her car. Her next stop, Fat Tony's Tattoo.

FOUR

HATCH WAS CAST in the light outside of Fat Tony's Tattoo Shop. It was as commonplace as any she'd seen, the walls adorned with a variety of prefabricated designs. Hatch knew from her own personal experience if you wanted something made or created by the artist themselves, A, it cost you a bit more, and B, they kept those templates themselves. It made for a more specialized and lengthy process. Most prospective first timers purchased what was known as flash, the pre-made designs. It was basically a paint by numbers operation using the templates. The individualized designs took time and true artistry.

The tattoo on Hatch's arm was not overly complicated, a simple phrase taken from Alice in Wonderland. The words were twisted amidst the web of scars. Although nearly unreadable, the words held more meaning now than when she'd first had them inked into her flesh. *It's no use going back to yesterday, because I was a different person then.*

Hatch entered the shop. It was cooler, but not by much, just enough to keep the moisture off the skin, but not enough to inflate the cost of the electric bill to keep it air-conditioned in the oppressive heat of North Carolina. She could hear the buzz of the tattoo gun working on somebody in the back. The doors were removed from each of the stalls. From her vantage point, she could see the thin hunched body of the artist at work. His long hair was tied back in a ponytail and wisps of gray peppered the darker hair. From the bits and pieces of exposed skin of the artist in his tank top shirt and shorts, Hatch could see he was himself well-inked, and he appeared to be covered from head to toe.

There was an equally inked man with a small cluster of stars in a half moon shape underneath his eye sitting at the receptionist desk. His ears and nose were a montage of studs and jeweled adornments. He didn't offer a welcoming smile. Instead, he eyed the clock on the wall behind her and then cocked an eyebrow in a non-verbal affront to her late entrance to the establishment.

Hatch knew better than to judge a book by its cover. She was testament to that. Many had fallen victim to her natural guise. As a woman, even though she was taller than most, people made the mistake of not seeing her as a threat. With that critical misjudgment, they'd given her advantage. Maybe this guy's look was somehow a mask for some deeper intelligence, or he was a kinder, more tender-hearted person than his exterior exuded.

"Can I help you?" the tattooed man asked softly.

"Yeah, I'm looking for Anthony." Hatch said it loud enough so that if Anthony, or Fat Tony, was the one artist in the back, he would hopefully hear her. The decision to speak loud enough to gain his attention seemed to work because the buzzing of the needle stopped, and she heard the squeak of wheels on tile as the swivel chair turned.

The artist looked over toward Hatch. He eyed her and then gave a dismissive shake of his head. The gesture was not for Hatch. It was for the receptionist.

Not recognizing Hatch, and why should he since the two had never met, the man spun back in his seat and resumed his work. It was, from what Hatch could see from her limited viewpoint, an expansive back piece, some type of samurai slashing bright colors along the large, fleshy tapestry that was the client's back.

It looked like the artist had been at it for a while. Hatch watched him wiping away the client's blood every few seconds after each buzz of the needle. She knew from her own personal experience, as the tattoo gun ran across the surface over and over, pushing the ink into the flesh, the small holes and punctures that were made continued to bleed. The longer the process, the more profusely one would bleed. So, this man, bleeding as he was, would soon be approaching a stop point. With a piece that big, there was no way it could be done in one sitting, and he had only, from what she could see, taken on the back-left quarter of his body.

The receptionist drew Hatch's attention again as he played with one of the studs in his ear. "He's busy right now. Not sure when he's going to finish up. Maybe I can help? Are you looking for something in particular? If not, there's a wall of flash over there. There's some butterflies and fairies over here."

Hatch waved a hand, cutting him off. "I'm not here for any new tattoos, and if I was, I wouldn't be looking for butterflies and fairies."

The man's cheeks flushed, getting a little red just under the bottom-most star on his cheekbone. "Sorry, I didn't mean anything by it. We get a lot of that. You know? People coming in and looking for those types of tats, particularly women. My bad. Force of habit."

"No harm, no foul," Hatch said, dismissively. "You don't know when he will be done? I really have something important I'd like to talk to him about. It's a very personal project," Hatch said, not completely lying.

The man looked at the clock on the wall again and then back at Hatch. "I don't know. I really can't say. He's been at it for quite a while. It's a big piece he's working on. But it's not a one and done. So, if I had to guess, he'll be done when the big boy in there can't take the needle anymore. It's really an endurance test. I've seen the biggest of men come in, and one stroke of the tattoo gun causes them to faint or turn and tuck tail for the door. I've also seen women smaller than you come in and handle an eight hour back piece without wincing."

Hatch smiled. The receptionist understood the disparity between toughness and appearance.

He continued to play with the metal stud in his ear. "I guess it really just depends on the client, and I can't say for sure. But they've been going at it now for almost three hours and it's getting kinda late. Tony doesn't like to tattoo late into the night. He feels that his work begins to suffer and degrades after a certain point. As with any art, there is a limit to the creative. He's going to be heading home after this. Doesn't take late clients," the man said with a don't-bother-finality in his tone.

Hatch looked at him and back toward the buzzing sound from the room where Anthony was hard at work on his masterpiece. "Tell him I'll be back. What time does he open shop in the morning?"

The tattooed man eyed her, and now he seemed to be taking her in a bit more. Maybe he noticed the scar on her hand that peeked out from underneath the sleeve or took better stock of the seriousness in her eyes. Maybe he'd come to the realization that this was not a social call, this was not a girl looking for a butterfly or fairy. This was something else and the man seemed to read that. "It depends," he said. "It depends on a lot of things, but most importantly, Tony. He opens and closes the shop, meaning it's on him. If you come tomorrow and the sign says open, then he's most likely in here. If it's closed, then maybe he took the day off or he's coming in late. The hours say 11 to 11, but rarely do we keep those. Kind of the nice thing about owning your own business and one of this variety where clientele can be scheduled in advance. I can say stop by at 11, but you might be wasting your time. I could say stop by at 2, but again, I don't have the answer for you. Do what you feel you need to do. Check in tomorrow. Here's a business card. You can call if you don't want to waste the trip."

Hatch took the card and tucked it into her pants pocket. She gave one last look back toward the room where the potential link to her father's past sat hunched, oblivious to her and engaged in the crafting and design of whatever art he was making.

She looked at the clock on the wall. 11:45. If what the man said was true, then Tony would probably be coming in later tomorrow since he stayed later today, and who knows how much longer he'd be working on this man's ink job. Frustrated, Hatch turned and walked out the door.

She walked down the street and climbed back into her rental car. Hatch was about to drive away. *He's here now. The man who may hold an answer to her father's death is literally less than a block away from her. A* few buildings, in fact, separated her from the potential answer she was now wholly desperate to find. And one that, if she had it, might result in her not having to make an international flight all the way to Africa to hunt down a man, who by word of mouth was a reformed special operator and mercenary turned Catholic priest. That trip did not seem as appealing as finding the answer stateside, maybe getting the closure she deserved, her family deserved and then heading back to Colorado, back to Hawk's Landing. To Daphne and Jake, and maybe, if fate favored-- Dalton Savage.

Instead of turning the ignition, she did the opposite and pocketed the key. Hatch sat back and reclined the seat slightly, keeping the tattoo shop's storefront in her side mirror.

She laid back but didn't close her eyes. Instead, she allowed herself to absorb this semi supine position and take a moment of deep relaxation. She learned during her time in special operations that sleep was a gift, and it was one that sometimes did not come for an extended period of time. When the opportunity to relax and decompress came, you seized it. One never knew when the next opportunity would arise. It was like a meal. More important than a meal. It allowed the operator to mentally reset.

She had no idea what was in store for her in her encounter with Fat Tony. She'd been warned that he was hot headed and standoffish, something she was concerned about. Their meeting might result in confrontation. Unnecessary, most likely, and hopefully it wouldn't lead to something further. But she wanted to prepare herself. The better she was prepared mentally and the calmer her mind and more relaxed she was, the easier those decisions under duress could be made.

Now, she waited. She waited to see either the light turned off, or the man exit, an indication he was done for the night. She would seize the opportunity now rather than wait for the morning. In her life, the here and now is where you had to take the advantage because sometimes it didn't present itself again.

AN HOUR HAD PASSED before Hatch saw the tattooed-faced receptionist exit, holding the door open for the large man who had received the samurai tattoo on his back. The two shook hands and then the receptionist handed the burly man a Dr. Pepper. Hatch knew the soda's sugar helped steady the nerves, especially when someone was completely depleted after being under the needle for several hours. It worked the same way with combat stress after the human body was in an adrenaline dumped or hyperacute state; the simple sugars helped to provide balance.

The receptionist slipped back inside in for a moment, flicking the light off and then locking the door. He left. No sign of Fat Tony. He wasn't anywhere to be seen. There must be a back exit, as most businesses had, and she realized Tony must've taken it. Hatch exited her vehicle and hustled down a tight alleyway between a restorative hardware store, now closed, and a billiards hall that was filled with a variety of soldiers playing an inebriated late-night game of pool. She could hear the laughter of the men inside and the bass from the stereo reverberating through the thin walls as she made her way past to the back side of the strip of businesses containing Fat Tony's Tattoo Shop.

Rounding the backside, she saw Tony walking toward a purple Prius. She found it odd and laughed to herself. The ex-Special Forces operator who had some connection to her father, just exactly what, she didn't know yet, ran an apparently lucrative tattoo parlor and was tattooed from head to toe, but drove a Prius--a purple one. A subtle reminder for Hatch not to judge a book by its cover.

Tony pressed the fob and the taillights flashed.

Hatch quickened her step, wanting to catch up with him before he entered the car. As she closed the distance, he must have heard her coming, which showed that his skills were, even if unused for a while, still relatively sharp.

He spun, and in doing so, he withdrew a small caliber pistol from the back of his waistline. It was aimed at Hatch. She stopped less than six feet away. The tattoo artist eyed her warily. He was staring down the front sight post of the weapon, which was aimed squarely at her forehead.

Hatch brought her hands up slowly and said, "I don't want any trouble. I just need to talk to you."

The man did not move. The gun remained leveled right at the center of her forehead. She knew what the shot would do if fired. It would enter through her prefrontal cortex and scramble her brains like a whisked egg. A kill shot, undoubtedly. And the man had her dead to rights.

"Listen, Anthony, I need to talk to you. It's about my father."

His head cocked just slightly, and she saw a slight twitch in his non-dominant shooting eye. "Your father?"

"My name is Rachel Hatch. You knew my father years ago."

She saw a slight flinch of the weapon. It was a minute tell, but whatever she had said, some piece of it, had rocked him slightly.

"Did you say Hatch? As in Paul Hatch?"

"Yes."

"Who the hell runs up on a guy in a dark alley?" He huffed.

Hatch shrugged. She relaxed slightly as the man seemed to be reevaluating her level of threat.

The gun lowered slightly, but not all the way. It was not pointing at her face anymore, but it was somewhere between an aimed shot and a low ready. It would take nothing for him to pull the trigger and hit something vital. She remained still, with her hands right about shoulder height, showing that she was unarmed, which she was. She had no weapon on her. The only weapon she had right now that could be deployed to diffuse or stop this situation from getting out of control was her mind, and one she found to be the most dangerous weapon of all.

"Listen, Anthony, I'm just here to get some questions answered. I only recently found out that my father's death was no accident."

He lowered the weapon further. "And where'd you learn this?"

She couldn't tell if his question was one of fear or genuine interest. "While I was in Colorado. Some things didn't add up, and I started poking around."

"And what did you find?" he asked.

"I found that they never found the hunter who supposedly shot my father. Without revealing my sources, it was readily apparent that he was murdered. And I think whoever you used to work for was responsible."

Now the weapon raised slightly. "How do you know who I used to work for?"

Hatch looked at the gun and could tell he was again teetering on the edge of pulling the trigger.

"Listen, I'm not divulging my sources, as you wouldn't do yours, but in light of everything, you knew my father. I can tell you knew my father. And if you worked with the people that he worked with, then I know how dangerous this conversation could be," she said.

"Then why are we having it?" the tattooist said, as a long wisp of salt and pepper hair fluttered in the breeze. "If you know the risks, why would you risk coming here and exposing yourself to me?"

Hatch thought about that for a minute. She was definitely putting herself in harm's way. She wasn't sure what allegiance or alliances this man had with the company. She doubted he still worked for them, but his reaction made her uneasy. She'd seen a similar fear in the old man in New Mexico. He had warned her about how dangerous this group could be.

Hatch needed to figure out which side Tony was on.

The gun wavered slightly and then the tattoo artist lowered it to his side. He exhaled slowly as he tucked it into the back of his waistline. He looked around the back alley. "If you want to talk, let's step inside."

FIVE

HATCH FOLLOWED Tony to the back door of the tattoo parlor. His sleeveless vest exposed his inked flesh. Not one bit was left colorless. Tattoos disappeared up his neck behind his salt and pepper ponytail. She imagined the artwork continued up onto his scalp but had long been covered by the mess of hair. The man unlocked the door and escorted her inside. He guided Hatch over to a back office, meagerly furnished with stacks of unopened boxes of ink and equipment.

The room had a medicinal smell. Rubbing alcohol and bleach stung her nose. He must've just finished cleaning, and although Tony himself looked a little slovenly, she surmised he ran a fairly tight ship when it came to the health inspectors, which was always a game that must be played carefully, especially when poking needles into people's skin for a living. One bad health rating could shut a shop like his down. The fact that he had apparently managed such a business for a considerable amount of time and amassed a steady flow of clientele made her realize he must have a rigorous cleaning protocol before departing each evening. It reminded her a bit of a hospital's scent, although the room's lack of organization made her think it lacked a woman's touch.

Tony sat with a huff. He set the gun atop a sketchpad and folded his large arms across the table and leaned in. He then pointed at a chair across from him but said nothing. Hatch took a seat and leveled a steady gaze at the person who, only moments before, had leveled a gun at her.

"So, what is it you really want to know? Why are you here to see me?" Tony asked.

"I just need to know as much as I can about Talent Executive Services. I believe you know it better as the Gibson Consortium," Hatch said.

"You rush me in an alley and start asking about a company you shouldn't know anything about--and what? I'm supposed to just start spilling my guts?"

"It's all related to my father's death."

Tony's face reddened and his brow furrowed, creating deep creases. "How am I supposed to know what happened to your father? That was twenty-some odd years ago. In my world, that's a lifetime ago."

Hatch gave a barely perceptible smile. The man had tipped his hand and given up the fact that he had obviously worked within the group and personally knew her father. This was one step closer to getting something in the way of valuable information. Although she already knew this before coming in, having him say it confirmed Wenk hadn't led her astray.

"Let's not beat around the bush. My father was killed. It was no accident. I know that for a fact. I'm guessing it had something to do with the company. I'm also guessing it had something to do with what he had done or the people he had worked with. You were one of those people. So, if you weren't involved, maybe you can point me in the direction of who was," Hatch said, taking a business-like tone. It was her turn to lean in, pressing her forearms hard against the rigid armrests of the uncomfortable seat like a tiger ready to pounce.

Tony didn't look the least bit intimidated by her, and his gun still rested on the table. He caressed the curved butt of the revolver with his index finger. Whether this was meant as a threat or just an absent-minded gesture, Hatch didn't know. Either way, she didn't like it.

"Whatever I say in here stays. Do you understand that? Before we talk, before I give you anything, you need to agree to that. And if I find out that what I've said comes back on me--if I live, you won't," Tony said. His voice was icy cold, his eyes never wavering from Hatch's.

Hatch was not one to be intimidated, but she understood his tone. Based on everything she had learned up to this point, and how much these men feared their former employer and the reach the company still had, it made sense to be guarded. She nodded and said, "Anything you say will be between you and me. I'm the only one looking into this. I'm not involved with any government organizations, and I'm here of my own accord."

Anthony Amaletto didn't appear to be wholly satisfied with her answer, but it seemed to be enough to open the gates of conversation because he started speaking. "Your dad and I served together in Vietnam. We did a lot of things operationally, though they were never fully documented. We earned our place within the special operations community," he said.

Hatch read between the lines. The black ops missions he was talking about were probably carried out deep inside the Cambodian border, which at the time of the Vietnam war was considered a zone in which combatants, at least US military combatants, did not go. She knew this history, having been a part of the special operations community herself, and could figure out exactly what he was talking about. Her father had been in operations that remained classified to this day.

"I understand that," she said, interrupting him briefly. "I know my father was Special Forces, and I understand there was a lot that happened in those smaller unit operations in Southeast Asia. But what I don't understand is why he transitioned to the Gibson Consortium, and what happened that caused them to come after him over twelve years after his leaving?"

Tony looked away. It was the first time he had broken eye contact since they'd entered the room. "Listen, when we first got out, we were lost. We came back to a country that didn't want us. And beyond that, we were special ops guys. We were the Green Berets, the Snake Eaters, the ones out there in the jungle doing some of the Army's dirtiest work. And the country wasn't ready for us, and to be quite honest, we weren't ready for it. So, guys like your father and me, we looked for work that was similar to what we knew how to do, basically a way to put our skills to work. And we found a group that was looking for men like us."

"The Gibson Consortium," Hatch muttered.

"Yes. And once we were recruited, we were given specific assignments and areas of responsibility. Your father and I partnered on more than one occasion. What we did for them, I will never tell you, because that would completely compromise the contract I had with them. And to break contract with them is a guaranteed death sentence." Tony let the words hang in the air and Hatch absorbed them.

"Does that death sentence still hold today?" she asked.

Tony nodded slowly. "I don't know how they do it. To be honest, their reach and their ability to find out who has betrayed them is alarming, to say the least. But there's been more than one person to have a tragic accident since leaving the group. I don't want to make that list."

"But you've managed to stay alive this long," Hatch offered.

"Well, there's something to be said about being a good soldier."

"How did you steer clear of any fallout from them?" She asked.

Tony gave a soft chuckle and leaned back in his chair. He picked up the revolver and placed it in the top drawer of his desk, removing the threat and tearing down the final barrier to their conversation. "Well," he said, "it's really quite simple. I never went against the company, and until this moment, I've never spoken about it with anyone."

Hatch leaned back a little bit herself, mirroring the man's movements. "So why now? Why talk to me?" she asked.

Tony eyed her, not in an ogling fashion, but just surveyed her intently. Then he said gruffly, "You're Hatch's kid, and that means something. Paul Hatch's life mattered. And what happened to him was a tragedy. And maybe one you can make right."

"So, help me make it right. Tell me what happened. Why would they come for him twelve years later? What could he have done to upset them that they came and hunted him down?"

The memory of her father and seeing him dead on the ground on that trail in Colorado came flashing back. And although she thought of it numerous times, every time she spoke about it, a surge of visceral anger combined with the ugly pang of anguish. She felt her heart rate increase slightly, something she didn't like. Her sense of control was paramount. Losing it, physical or otherwise, put her at a disadvantage. Even though Tony had put the pistol away, she didn't allow herself to let her guard down. Hatch pushed the image of her father back into the recesses of her mind.

"Like I said," Tony said, "when you break the contract, it's a death sentence. There's no expiration on a kill order with this group."

"What did my father do to break the contract and sign his death warrant?" she asked.

"We were operating in Libya at the time. I'm not going to say exactly when or what the target was, but I will say this, it was a high value target. But the hit wasn't the norm."

"How do you mean?"

"The target was outside our normal parameters. But once an assignment's been given, we're on the hook. Your father was tapped to take the shot. When it came time to pull the trigger, he hesitated and missed his opportunity."

Hatch heard the words and knew her father, and it didn't jive. "Hesitated?" she asked. "My father? You're saying my father hesitated. I don't believe it."

"Don't take what I'm saying personally. You asked and I'm telling."

"I remember my dad clearly, and hesitation was something I never saw from him," Hatch said with more emotion than she'd intended.

Tony seemed to stir slightly in his seat. It was either awkwardness from the confrontation of his explanation or something deeper. Hatch didn't know.

"Listen, when I say hesitated, I'm just saying ... How can I put it more bluntly? He didn't take the shot. Maybe it wasn't hesitation. Maybe a better word would be frozen. When it came down to doing it, he decided that he couldn't. He couldn't pull the trigger and the target got away."

Hatch thought about this for a moment. She envisioned her father looking down the scope of a rifle at whatever this potential target was, and in the moment that he had to pull the trigger, something had stopped him. And Hatch understood the million thoughts that flooded the brain before taking a life, having done so herself. She also knew the fallout from the time she hesitated, and the damage that it carried, not only physically in the form of the shattered and scarred arm of her right side, but the death of her friend. And hearing her father had also made a similar choice made her feel even more connected to him.

"Who was the target?" Hatch asked.

"I can't say," Tony replied.

"Give me something. Help me understand my father. Help me understand why a man who was as capable as he was didn't complete his mission. Help me see the truth, so that I can better understand the rationale, so I can figure out why they would come for him," Hatch pleaded.

Tony let out a long slow hiss, like the air being let out of a tire. "It was a child. The target was a child. It was the son of an up-and-coming leader. He was deemed a necessary ally to the US operations in the area, but he was not cooperating. It was decided at levels well above my pay grade that a message should be sent. Kill the son and gain control of the father. There were big things at play at that time. This was Libya in the '80s. You've got to understand it was a volatile time, to say the least. And not taking that shot had as many shockwaves to follow as if he had pulled the trigger," Tony said.

Hatch thought about this. Her father couldn't kill a child, and the thought of that pleased her, even though she now understood it was that decision which ultimately took him from her at an early age. His resolve to stand his ground, knowing the potential fallout from not completing the mission, was impressive. The courage it took to do something like that is rare at best. And the fact that she was of the bloodline of a man of such valor pleased her greatly. Hatch silently beamed with pride.

Hatch looked at Tony, who now looked despondent, as if calling forward the memory had saddened him.

"So, where were you during this? How do you know so much about it?" Hatch asked.

Tony fiddled with a loose thread on his vest. "I was his spotter. I was the one who called the shot, and I was there when he didn't take it."

"But nothing happened to you. They didn't come for you."

Tony continued to keep his eyes downcast. "I wasn't assigned the trigger. They didn't fault me for your father's actions. I was absolved."

Hatch looked at him. "What happened to my father? Why didn't they kill him right then and there?"

"He was able to escape. He escaped the country and then he went dark," Tony said flatly.

Hatch looked at him. "You were his spotter. I know a thing or two about snipers and spotters. You were right there. So, you didn't try to stop him from running?" she asked.

"I would have," Tony said with a distinct resignation in his voice, "but, and I don't say this about many, your father was a better operator than me. Before I was able to stop him, your father rendered me unconscious."

Hatch tried to hide the grin fighting its way to the surface.

"I take no pride in the fact that I would have held your father until the Consortium deemed what they wanted to do with him." Tony gave up on the bit of thread and began twirling the ponytail draped over his shoulder. "Anyway. I made a move for him, he knocked me out. I woke up several minutes later, and I was bound and gagged. It took me quite some time to undo the restraints your father had put me in. And by then, he was long gone."

"He escaped. And was able to disappear off the radar?"

"Like I said, Paul Hatch was the best operator I've ever known. And he became a ghost. The Gibson Consortium was unable to track him. I know they searched extensively, putting a lot of assets in play."

"I understand operational security. I've never heard of this type of sanitation after a compromised mission. What am I missing?" Hatch asked.

"They've deemed him a liability, a security risk. If you were to know anything about the contracts that we handled, security risks were terminated quickly. There was zero tolerance for anyone who stepped outside the line. The compromise that could come from your father being loose after failing to commit a mission and the knowledge he alone held made him an absolute risk." He leaned forward, his facial expression deadpan. "Hear me well, Gibson Consortium reaches to the highest levels of government, then and now. Your father became number one on their list, and I imagine if you keep poking around, you'll get their attention soon enough," he said.

Hatch listened carefully. She heard the warning, the not-so-veiled threat Tony had just delivered. Their reach was powerful twenty years ago and apparently still was.

"But he was off the grid. No one ever came for him, not for 12 years." Her voice cracked slightly. Her twelfth birthday and the day of her father's death were forever intertwined. The two days blended into one. It was the moment in her life where the fork in the road had been chosen for her and her path was cut, an arduous journey ever since.

"It was that news story. You're right. Paul was completely off the grid. We never would have found him," Tony said. "I don't know how he pulled it off for so long, but he did. Like I said, he was a better operator than me. He disappeared. Disappeared into the mountains of Colorado, that small town of yours where you grew up, not even a blip on the map. His footprint was completely wiped away until he saved that family in the mountains. When that story went national, his image went up. I'm going to be honest with you, they have programs scouring the internet for intel. Over the years, your father had fallen off the grid, but he never dropped off their list," Tony said, a little more emphatically than he'd been thus far.

Again, another subtle message to Hatch that if she continued to push this, she might very well make their list. For all she knew, she may already be on it. Hatch had dug the file out in Colorado, she had the conversation with the old man in New Mexico, and now here she was in North Carolina, poking around, likely alerting Talon Executive Services, formerly the Gibson Consortium. But she didn't care who she pissed off if it meant getting at the truth. The only thing she cared about now was bringing to justice the people responsible for her father's death.

"So that was all it took. My father saves a family in the woods. A news camera gets a quick still shot of him, and it ends up on national news. A software program picks him up using facial recognition, and boom, a bell goes off and my dad is dead a week later?"

"You hit the nail on the head," Tony said. "That is exactly what happened."

No good deed goes unpunished. "And they were able to cover it up with the locals?" She felt foolish asking. She already knew the answer.

Tony grumbled a little bit and said, "Come on, now. You seem like a smart girl and I can tell you've been in the business long enough to know money buys everything. Everybody has a price, and we just found the price of the sheriff. It was an easy buy. Poor towns like the one you grew up in, it didn't take much to convince him. And then they always take an insurance policy. This group is thorough."

Hatch thought for a moment. "Then all I need from you now is the name of the person who pulled the trigger and we'll call it even steven."

"Even steven?" Tony asked, cocking one eyebrow.

"Yeah. You were going to turn my dad over right after he didn't take the shot. You effectively turned on him. So, we're going to make it right now. Make things even. You're going to tell me who shot my father and then I'm going to leave."

Tony gave her a hard look. His fingers drifted over toward the drawer that held the firearm, the invisible barrier to this interrogation going back up.

"Listen, I told you I got out. I left shortly after the incident with your father. I walked away. I'm compromising everything by talking to you now. I don't know who pulled the trigger. I just know that's how it works. They find people, they always find the people they're looking for. It may not be immediate, but they always come. I'm not so sure I didn't just make their list because of this conversation we're having. And you better take heed, little Miss Hatch, because they very well could be coming for you, too."

Hatch sat quietly for a moment waiting to see if there was anything further. She read the man's body and tried to decipher if he was telling the truth, but he was hard to read. And so, for the moment, she had to take what he said on face value.

Hatch stood. "If I find out different, if I find out you had a hand in this, you'll see me again. And next time, I won't be so nice."

Tony looked like he was about to utter an angry response, but before he did, Hatch let herself out the door and disappeared into the hot, muggy night air.

SIX

HATCH SAT IN THE DINER. She had received a call earlier from Bennett wanting to meet. She hadn't expected to see him again so soon after their conversation yesterday. She hadn't expected to see him again at all, if ever. She put a dash of sugar and a touch of cream into the coffee to remove the bitter taste. It was hot, and it was caffeinated, and perhaps that was good enough. She was never one, even in the heat of summer, to drink an iced coffee. She couldn't remember where, but maybe it was something she had read or heard, that if you drink something hot on a hot day, it did something to regulate your body temp. So, Hatch always drank her coffee hot regardless of the temperature, and today was looking to be a scorcher. But by the time it really hit the high temps, she would be airborne.

Bennett had picked the meeting location. Because she didn't completely trust the man as much as she used to, Hatch decided to arrive early to ensure it wasn't a setup.

She'd been seated in the booth for over twenty minutes and had started in on her second cup of coffee when Bennett entered. He took a seat across from her, and before speaking, flagged the waitress and ordered a cup himself.

"Well, Chris, I didn't expect to see you again so soon," Hatch said.

"Listen, Hatch. I was thinking. Maybe I was wrong," he offered.

"Maybe?" Hatch said. "About what?"

"About everything," he said, taking his spoon out of the wrapped napkin on the table. "About the way I treated you after your second evaluation, after you completed the selection and went through the gauntlet. I turned my back on you, and I'm sorry. I was in a bad place then. Maybe I was looking for someone to blame, and I guess it was easier to just blame you. What happened that day, it still haunts me. It has stayed with me. And for what it's worth, I know it wasn't your fault."

Hatch looked down at her coffee, swirling it with her spoon before taking a sip. "I never thought I'd hear you say that, Chris. I thought it was a grudge you'd always hold."

"Me too," he said. "I really just didn't know what to do. I mean, we lost some good people that day. I also know if it hadn't been for you, I'd be dead. What you did that day was nothing less than heroic, and instead of punishing you, I should have awarded you. But I didn't, and I'll probably regret that for the rest of my life."

"So, that's what this is about, this meeting? Offering an apology? A way to clear your conscience?" she asked.

"Look, Hatch, I don't expect you to accept it right off the bat. I just want you to know it's how I really feel. The other guys on the team feel the same way. I'm sorry we gave you the black ball treatment. There's not much I can do about what happened in the past. I'm just trying to make it right now. But no, that's not the reason I asked you to meet me today. Well, it's part of the reason, but if you're going to Africa, like you said, if you're really going after these people, then I want to give you something."

Bennett reached into his pocket and removed a small business card, blank, except for a name and a phone number written on it, and he slid it across the table. Hatch took a quick scan of it. She saw the number and recognized it as international. One name on the card, Jabari.

She looked at it and then looked back at Bennett. "What's this?"

"It's a contact I have in the Mombasa area. He's a good guy. He's like us. I've worked with him in the past, recently actually. All you have to do is tell him my name. I haven't called him and told him that you'll be coming that way, but if you get in a bind, he's a good guy to have on your six. And trust me, he can keep you safe. If you find yourself in circumstances that are dangerous, it's a lifeline."

Hatch slipped the card into her pocket and looked at him. The waitress came over and gave him a cup of coffee with steam floating from the deep black of the liquid inside, even in the warmth of the cafe. The restaurant's air conditioning unit was running full tilt in an endless battle against the heat and humidity. He took a sip without putting anything in it, and his face contorted because of the bitterness.

"You might want to add a little bit to that." Hatch slid a glass jar with granulated sugar across the table to him. "The coffee here is not great."

Bennett gave a soft smile, putting a spoonful of sugar in and stirring it gently. "I should have known better. I eat here every once in a while. The coffee is less than desirable, but the food is good."

"So, that's it, huh? A name and an apology."

"I don't know what else you want from me, Hatch," Bennett said.

She thought for a moment, and she didn't either. Hatch had come prepared to argue with him. She was not expecting an apology and she sure wasn't expecting a favor offering. "It's just a hard pill to swallow. It's been a long time coming. But the fallout had a heavy toll. It was not an easy transition to civilian life."

"Better late than never," he said.

She accepted it. "I guess you're right," she said.

"When do you leave?" He asked.

"A couple of hours. I've got to get there soon. It's an international flight, so security is going to be a pain in the ass."

Bennett nodded. "Do you have somebody there you're going to meet with? Do you know where you're going or are you just going on a blind hunt?" he asked.

"For somebody that doesn't really want to know what I'm doing, you're asking a lot of questions," she said.

"Force of habit, I guess. Just want to know that you're going to be okay," he offered.

"I'll be fine. Can't be any worse than the places we've been," she said.

They both gave a soft chuckle at that.

"You're right about that," Bennett said. With that, he drained half the cup and stood. "You take care of yourself, Rachel Hatch, and don't be a stranger."

Bennett said nothing further, and Hatch offered nothing in return. He turned and walked away, out into the stifling heat of the day.

Hatch finished her cup of coffee and flagged the waitress. She came over with the tab. Hatch left a ten-dollar tip. Her father had always taught her that the breakfast servers got dinged the most when it came to tip percentile. Meals were cheaper, and therefore any percentage of the meal, even twenty percent of a cheaply priced meal, meant for lower tips. He had always told her to tip heavy in the morning and that it goes a long way. *The small kindnesses are the best ones and easiest to do.* So, she did. She left a ten-dollar tip for her four-dollar cup of coffee and walked out the door.

Steam rose from the concrete walk as remnants of an early morning shower evaporated with the temperature beginning to climb. Her skin moistened as she walked over to the rental car. She looked at her watch. Three hours until takeoff. She headed for the airport. Next stop, Africa.

SEVEN

THE TEDIUM of nearly twenty-four hours of air travel had come to an end with the bump and skip of the jolted landing. She recalled her father telling stories of international travel back in the '70s and '80s, and how they used to allow smoking on the planes. He described how the upper third of the plane's fuselage would be coated in a plume of cigarette smoke. She was grateful that was no longer the case, and that regulations had since changed.

She slept a little on each leg of the journey, but only fitfully. Comfort just goes so far when crammed into an airplane seat. Hatch had traveled light, packing only one bag. She got off the plane and merged into the hoard of people making their way through the customs checkpoint.

After clearing customs, Hatch exited the airport. There was no one there to greet her. And it only took a moment before she managed to hail a cab. She had an idea of where she was going since she knew the PO Box where the priest received correspondence. During her research, Hatch had learned the particular post office where that mail was received. She had done some site research and found a small cafe with a room for rent above it. She directed the cabbie to take her there.

The roads were congested. Mombasa was a thoroughfare of cars and people, the pedestrian traffic matching that of the vehicular in density. The heavily populated coastal city seemed to be in a perpetual jam. What should have been a thirty-minute drive from the airport to the cafe took nearly double the time.

The cab's air conditioning, working at full blast, did little to beat back the heat. What she thought was warm in North Carolina was nothing compared to this. *I guess that's why they call it Africa hot.* The thick humidity and the overwhelming heat index mixed with the diesel fuel of the cars and buses. She had the window down, even with the AC running, in an effort to get some much-needed air flow in the car. In no time, Hatch was slick with sweat.

Arriving at the brightly colored cafe, Hatch paid the cabby, and stepped out. The kind man who spoke broken English offered to assist in getting her luggage, but Hatch had already retrieved it. He gave her a toothless smile before parting ways.

She shouldered her travel bag, the same duffel she had carried with her when she had returned home to Hawk's Landing. Hatch had stream-lined her life in such a way that everything she needed could be stuffed into it. She had enough essentials and clothing to last her a week before needing a wash, maybe longer if she stretched the limits.

Hatch stepped inside the cafe. She barely noticed a temperature change from the outside. But once inside, the smell of food overwhelmed her, and she realized how famished she was. Even though they had served food on the plane, it was a meager offering and didn't really suffice in satisfying her hunger. Hatch had also been awake for most of the past day of travel, so her metabolism was on overdrive.

She pulled up a seat at a vacant table and plopped her duffle bag on the chair next to her. A man approached wearing a brightly colored short-sleeved shirt, the vibrant yellow and orange shapes blended in a unique pattern. He had kind, welcoming eyes. But what caught Hatch's attention most was his skin. The dark tone of his face and neck was peppered with light cream-colored spots, almost like looking at a negative of a leopard. It took only a second for Hatch to discern that the patches were burn marks. They extended from the left side of his face down his neck and disappeared into his collar. Hatch suddenly felt embarrassed at her need to hide her damaged arm. Even in the heat, she was wearing a long-sleeve Lycra shirt. And yet here was this man coming toward her who did nothing to hide the damage to his skin. *Maybe it's time I didn't either.*

He came over and gave a pleasant smile. "Good afternoon, I am Khari. And this is my cafe. May I get you something to drink?" he asked, his English remarkably clear.

"Tea will be fine, but I'll be needing some food, too. Any recommendations?" Hatch's stomach rumbled loudly as if to punctuate her appetite.

"I know just what you need," he said. "It's a cafe specialty."

He retreated and spoke in Swahili to a woman behind the counter.

Hatch looked out the window of the cafe. Across the street, she could see the front doors of the post office. It was the other reason she had chosen this location, a perfect surveillance point, a place where she could sit, watch, and wait. The only thing she had was the PO Box, so she needed to wait for the priest. She didn't know how long that would take, or how frequently he got his mail.

Khari returned a short time later and laid down a plate of food. On the plate was a small cluster of deep-fried potatoes, golden brown. A thick dark brown sauce accompanied them, a sweet and sour aroma wafted up and pleasantly greeted Hatch's nostrils. A small piece of blackened chicken rounded out the platter. Khari then set down another plate with a round flatbread. "I think you'll enjoy this," he said. "If not, please let me know and I can get you something else. Did you want your tea with ice, or would you like it hot?"

Hatch looked at him and smiled. "I'll take it hot, please."

He poured her a cup, leaving the pot there with her. "How long are you in town for?" He asked. "Are you visiting? On vacation?"

He asked a lot of questions, she thought. But he did it in such a way that was cordial and very friendly. Hatch discerned no underlying intentions, although experience had left her guarded. "I'm here to see an old friend. It's been a long time, and I'm just trying to surprise him if I get the chance."

"Oh, wonderful." He seemed giddy with glee at hearing this. "I love surprises," he said. "Will you be needing a place to stay?"

"Actually, yes. I saw you have rooms for rent. Is one available?" Hatch asked. Hatch actually already knew this. She had done her research before coming and she knew that, right now, there were two rooms still available. The one overlooking the post office was the one she hoped to get.

"As a matter of fact, I do," he said. "It's not too expensive, either. Not as much as those fancy hotels that offer the Safari trips. And you'll get fine dining. Breakfast, lunch and dinner are served down here in the cafe. All part of the cost, if that suits you."

"It does and thank you." The man's smile was infectious, and she couldn't help but like him.

"After you finish eating, I will show you to your room. Do you have any other bags?"

"No. Just the one here." She patted the canvas bag resting in the chair next to her.

"I can bring that up for you," he offered.

"No, that won't be necessary," she said. "I've got it."

"Very well. Please let me know if there's anything else I can do for you. If you need a map of the place or you want to know some of the sights to see while you're here, please don't hesitate to ask. I'd be more than happy to be your unofficial tour guide," he said pleasantly. "And let me be the first to welcome you to Mombasa."

"Thank you."

"As I said before, my name is Khari."

"I'm Hatch."

"Hatch? Is that a first or last name?" he asked.

"Well, it's Rachel Hatch, but people just call me Hatch," she said.

"I like that. Hatch. It sounds like thatch. Like the roofs." He kept mumbling it to himself with a smile on his face as he walked back to the woman behind the counter who was serving another patron at the bar area. It wasn't crowded. There were only a few others in the cafe, all of whom seemed to be indigenous to the area. She did not see any Americans, which she was glad for. The last thing she wanted was a chatty tourist to talk her ear off.

Now the waiting game began. Hatch watched the post office as she devoured the food in front of her. It was delicious. Khari wasn't wrong. She ate every last bit on her plate and finished a second cup of tea before signaling to him.

He came over quickly, smiling the same smile he had when he first met her. "Please, Miss Hatch--correction--Hatch," he said with a chuckle, "let me show you to your room."

"Thank you."

"You must be exhausted. Did you just get in?"

"I did. I came straight here."

"Wonderful, wonderful," he said. "You're in for quite a treat. We are in the rainy season, mind you, and so you are going to get some heavy downpours. I hope you brought a raincoat or poncho."

"I didn't," Hatch said. She had a lightweight parka that should suffice, but nothing heavier.

"Well, if you need one, again, I can get you anything you need. All you have to do is ask. There is nothing you should want for while you're here visiting our beautiful country."

"Thank you." He escorted her through to a back stairwell that went behind the kitchen area. It was narrow, and although it was small, she noticed that everything was neatly kept. The wooden stairs that led to the second story had been recently swept, and there was no evidence of dust or dirt anywhere she could see. Khari obviously took great pride in the restaurant and the living area of his makeshift bed and breakfast.

He took her to a room and based on her understanding of the layout of the place, she realized he was putting her in the room that faced away from the post office.

"Khari, would it be possible if I took the room that overlooked the city street?" she asked.

He cocked his head and shrugged. "Sure. I don't see why not. I think it should be clean. We had somebody depart unexpectedly earlier today, but my wife said she took care of it. Let me check before I let you in. I don't want to send you into a dirty room."

"It's really no trouble," Hatch offered.

"Please allow me to check." Khari unlocked the door, leaving Hatch in the cramped hallway space with her bag over her left arm, her undamaged side.

Khari slipped inside and closed the door. A minute later, he popped out with a smile on his face.

"It looks good. My wife is a wonderful cleaner. She is amazing. She keeps this place in ship shape. I don't know how she does it. I, on the other hand, am a bit of a slob, but we work well together," he said with a laugh.

Hatch had already grown fond of this man. He was a genuinely kind person and his obvious love of his current profession as restaurateur and head of the bed and breakfast seemed to fit him. He'd put any Walmart greeter to shame.

"Here you go. There's only one, so try not to lose it." He handed her a key with a plastic diamond shaped keychain attached. It reminded her of the motel where she stayed in New Mexico. At that moment, she thought of room two and the girl who had died there. The flashback to the charred shadow of the girl she had tried to help was brief, but powerful. And for a moment, she thought she could smell the burnt flesh.

Shutting her mind to the memory, Hatch took the key and then shook Khari's outstretched hand. In doing so, the extension of her arm exposed part of her scarred wrist. She could tell he noticed.

"Ah, it seems you and I are not so different," and he patted the damaged flesh along his cheek bone. "I got caught in a fire long ago, a terrible story. Maybe one I'll share with you over breakfast one day while you're here."

"Fire got me, too," she said, but offered nothing further.

"Both of us were baptized by the flame. How interesting." Khari pressed no further. "Well then, how about I let you get situated? Looks like you could use a rest."

"That's the plan."

"If there's anything you need, don't hesitate to call. My wife and I are down the hall. See that room right there? It has the red door?" He pointed down the hallway to the brightly painted door. "That is where we live. So, if we're not downstairs in the kitchen, then we're in there. We don't go out much these days. This place requires a lot of tending, and so if you don't see us, that's where we'll be. Any time, just knock," he said.

"Khari, thank you very much for your hospitality. I shouldn't be much trouble. You'll probably hardly notice me here," she said.

He smiled broadly, his teeth showing their bright white. "I hope that's not the case, Hatch. I hope that I get to know a little bit about you. I like to get to know all our visitors. Each one has their own story to tell. Each one brings something to me, and I hope when they leave, they feel I have given them something in return as well. That is the way of things here. This is a magical place, Hatch. The people are amazing. This country is wonderful. I love it, and I want to share as much of it as possible with you while you're here, whether it is through food or story. I'm here to entertain you, as much as I am to take care of you."

"You're too kind," Hatch said.

She released the handshake and slipped inside the room, closing and locking the door behind her.

The room was small, but not so much so that she felt cramped. The sparsity of furnishings made it appear slightly bigger than it was. The room had one bed, one dresser, and a chair placed by the window. There was nothing but the basic necessities, a place to sleep, a place to watch the post office, and downstairs, a place to eat. Regardless of how long it took to find the priest, she at least would do so in relative comfort. There was a ceiling fan that was working overtime, oscillating with a rhythmic hum. The fan motor made a clicking sound as it turned, but the metronomic fashion of the clicks had a soothing effect. Although the wind generated did little to stifle the heat, it did bring about a sense of comfort.

No air conditioning. Hatch opened the windows to let in what little breeze there was. She smelled a hint of rain in the air and remembered Khari said they were in the rainy season. She would have to make sure to shut it every time she left.

With a full belly coated by the warm tea coupled with the whirling of the overhead fan, Hatch took one last look at the post office, which appeared to be closing for the day, and decided it would be a good time to rest.

She felt more tired now than she had in a very long time. Hatch also felt a great sense of relief from Bennett absolving her of any wrongdoing. She felt that an invisible weight had been lifted from her shoulders. She could finally fully rest.

Hatch slipped off her boots and flopped back onto the bed. It was firm and comfortable. The linens smelled fresh, most likely washed and then air-dried on a clothesline. There was a hint of lemon or some citrus scent she couldn't quite place. But all of it mixed together like a spa on steroids, and within a minute, she was sound asleep.

EIGHT

HATCH SAT at the same table she had used for the past four days. She had grown quite fond of the tea Khari served. It had a unique sweetness with an almost floral aftertaste. She had it with every meal, partly because she didn't completely trust the water unless boiled. She was adjusting to the climate, to the food and the conditions of her surroundings. She had occupied her time between eating and watching the post office, venturing out infrequently.

During business hours, she maintained a relatively steady focus, rotating her time between the cafe down below and her room overlooking the street. On rare occasions, she would stroll around the marketplace, always keeping an eye out in hopes of seeing the priest.

But with the past four days as a predictor, she wasn't confident today would be any better. She watched Khari as he prepared her mid-morning meal. He took great pleasure in surprising Hatch with the meals. He brought her something new and different each day, and she found herself secretly looking forward to each culinary adventure. Today he did something different. As he set the plate down in front of her, Khari took up the seat across from her.

They had been engaging in small talk in the days since her arrival.

The conversations were kept light. Hatch maintained her distance, as was her nature. It made it easier for her to keep moving, or disappear, should the circumstances dictate. Without creating a connection, her mind was much clearer to do such things. But she'd found herself softening in that regard. She did not want a repeat of New Mexico.

In Luna Vista, she had become close with Manuel Fuentes and his family. Connecting with people inevitably meant caring for them, and with that came complications. She didn't want to bring any unnecessary problems down on Khari and his wife, Josefina.

As he pulled up a seat across from her, his smile broadening, his white teeth shining against his dark complexion, Hatch could see he was intent on making her decision to remain disconnected much more difficult.

"Hatch. Are you ready to hear a story? I want to tell you a little bit about me, and maybe in sharing some of my personal life, you will share some of yours with me. In doing so, in that exchange, we will become closer. That way when our two paths part, I will feel that I have somehow left you with a piece of me, and in turn you will do the same for me as well," Khari said. His deep voice boomed even when trying to speak softly.

Hatch had trouble saying no to the man, although her first inclination was to dismiss his offer and retreat to her room. She knew it would be socially awkward to do so and downright rude. She had no intention of humiliating a man who had been so hospitable over the past few days since she'd been a tenant in the apartment above the cafe.

"Sure, I wouldn't mind the company," Hatch lied. All she really wanted to do was stare out the window, eat her food, and drink her delicious tea while waiting for the priest. *A little conversation couldn't hurt,* she thought. *At least it will pass the time.*

"I grew up in a small village, not too far from here. Mombasa always seemed like a big city to me as a young man growing up. But those were troubled times, and back then, there were rival gangs fighting for power, trying to overthrow the government. It was a dangerous time to say the least."

Khari spoke English with a heavy accent, but in the past few days, Hatch had grown accustomed to it and hardly noticed. She was able to understand most of everything he said. Every once in a while, he would stumble on a word and holler to his wife. They would speak in Swahili for a moment and she would give him the word he was looking for. According to Khari, Josefina was more fluent in English, but was shy and didn't speak much.

It was a unique dynamic. The woman could speak perfect English but refused to talk. And as Hatch watched over the last few days, she saw that Josefina hardly spoke to any of the patrons. She focused entirely on cooking and cleaning the cafe and the rooms that were used for boarding visitors. Khari was the face of the business, and Josefina was the engine keeping it running.

"One day, a group of soldiers came to my village. I'd seen what these men were capable of, and I didn't like it. And me being the oldest in my family of eleven brothers and sisters, I decided to stand up to them."

Hatch cocked an eyebrow. "Khari, that couldn't have been a good thing."

He laughed. "Oh, absolutely one of the worst decisions I've ever made, hands down. To this day, I think to myself, *Khari, what were you thinking?* But at that moment, I was filled with so much anger, you know, a teenage boy can be quite a...what is the...?"

Khari called back to his wife and spoke to her in Swahili. She answered and then he turned back to Hatch and said, "I had mixed emotions. I was filled with them, and I was learning about myself. I felt that since my father had died, I was the man of our house, and it was my duty to stand as protector."

Hatch listened. She respected his rationale for its simplicity and the fact that this man, even as a young boy, felt the compulsion, the drive, to stand up for something he felt was right.

In that short introduction to the story, he had endeared himself to her.

"So, I set a trap. I was worried they would take one of my brothers or sisters or hurt my mother. I was always fascinated with science." Khari gave a mischievous smile. "I rigged our door and made a trip wire, so to speak. I took some fishing line and set it up near the entrance to our hut. When two of the men came into the room, they fell. I tried to jump on the back of one of the men. I don't know what I was thinking at the time. I thought maybe I could get the rifle. If nothing else, I hoped to beat them in a fight and scare them off."

"It was foolish, and I paid dearly for it. We live in a beautiful country with beautiful people, but even in a place like this, there are those who see nothing but hate and power and all the corruption it comes with. So, the only thing I could figure to do was to fight and–"

He stopped himself. Hatch reached across the table. In doing so, she pulled back her sleeve, exposing more of the damage to her arm and put her hand gently across his, "You're very brave. You have an innate kindness. I see you around the cafe. And the way you treated me when I first arrived speaks volumes about you as a person. It's amazing that after whatever it was they put you through, that you were able to rise above it. And I'm glad you stayed. I'm glad Africa still has Khari. I'm glad that you are the first person that I connected with when I came here."

His eyes watered ever so slightly. He looked down at her damaged arm and then he smiled, not as broadly as before, but more a smile of understanding. She let go of his wrist and he continued.

"They decided to teach me a lesson. Well, more to make an example of me to the other villagers. That's the way it works. Sometimes killing somebody isn't as effective as hurting them." Khari touched the cream-colored blotches on his face. "I became a visual reminder to all my brothers and sisters, to my village, that standing up against them would leave them marred. They dragged me out of my house and in front of everybody, they lit a fire and they let it burn until the logs were white hot ash. Several men held me down. The ash and rock were smoldering, and they pressed my face and body into it. I tried to fight back, but they held me there, stepping down on my head and back until my flesh put out the fire. I can still remember the man's boot pressing against my face, pushing it against the hot coals."

"I'm sorry," Hatch said. "That sounds absolutely awful. I know pain, and I can't fathom what that must've been like. I was an adult when I was burned. I can't imagine going through it as a child."

Khari shrugged, "But see that's the thing, Hatch. Through the pain, I saw what mattered. As I lay there burned, I saw my family through my tears. I saw something beyond the fear in their eyes. I saw a deep pride, a sense of respect in the eyes of my younger siblings, and I knew at that point that I would survive. I didn't know how. The pain was so intense that at some point I passed out. But just before I did, I thought to myself, if I live, I will fight in a different way. I will be a good man no matter what the situation. I will honor my family through acts of kindness."

Hatch was silent, blown away by the story.

"I picked kindness in that moment of anguish and pain. It was my fork in the road and my decision afterwards forged the man I am today."

Hatch absently rubbed her arm. The raised bumps of the spider-webbed scar arced up past her elbow and shoulder. The damage, the pain, the anger. She looked at it, then looked at this man, and then she thought, *He took a different path. I haven't quite found mine.*

In that moment, she didn't understand why he told her the story. It just felt like he was put in this particular place at this particular time. They were meant to meet. He was there like a mind Sherpa, someone to guide her forward. And the first thought she had was of Daphne and Jake and then of Savage. Maybe she could live a good life. Maybe she could push past the pain of that moment and the fallout thereafter. Maybe this was that time for her, an invisible fork in the road. Maybe once she finished what she came to Africa to do, she could go back home. Maybe she could choose to be happy.

The thought filled her with a mixture of fear and, if she were to be wholly honest with herself, unbridled excitement. Hatch felt her body warm, and not just due to the sweltering heat passing through the open windows of the cafe. It was a warmth from inside, radiating from deep inside her heart. She felt like the Grinch listening to the Whos singing after waking up to find their presents stolen. Lost in thought, after a moment, Khari interrupted.

"So, Hatch." He said it almost as if he just didn't tell her a tragic story.

His demeanor had flipped like a switch, and he was back to a full smile. "Tell me about you. Give me something from your life. A piece, a rare gem, something that I can take. A personal story from you that will make me feel, when you leave, like a piece of Hatch is left here in my cafe with me."

Hatch thought for a moment. *What should she share?* He obviously would understand the story of her arm, but that story was complicated for a variety of reasons. Maybe she could tell him about her sister, her death, and coming home and trying to figure it all out. *Would that be too long? Too complicated? Too unnecessary?* It was still so raw and fresh. Maybe she could tell him about New Mexico. Every story was a different level of tragedy.

As she pondered what she could share with the cafe owner that wouldn't expose her too much, something caught her eye out on the street. An olive drab faded green Jeep, weathered and beaten by the harsh conditions of the African sun, pulled to a stop on the street in front of the post office.

The door opened and Hatch watched as the driver got out. He was wearing the all black cassock of a Catholic priest. He was here. Four days had passed and here he was.

The priest looked around cautiously, obviously a man of his background, still checking his surroundings. He paused for a moment, but only briefly, smiled at a passerby who nodded their head in a slight bow. The priest then made his way toward the post office's entrance.

Hatch suddenly realized Khari was still waiting, his eyes pleading for her story.

"Khari, I'm truly sorry. I've got to go. Something has come up. I think I see my friend."

He looked behind him, expecting to see somebody on the street nearby and seeing no one of interest, turned back with a contorted, confused look on his face. "I'm sorry, Hatch. I didn't mean to keep you. My stories are a bit long."

Hatch knew the timing of her departure couldn't have been worse, but she was secretly grateful for the reprieve from having to reveal something personal.

"Please don't take offense. I would love to talk more. When I'm done with what I have to do, after I meet with my friend, I'll come back. I promise. We'll finish this conversation."

His eyes lightened a little bit and he smiled. "Of course, Hatch. Of course. I don't mean to keep you, and if you'd like, I can keep your things for you. You said when you come back. Are you planning on leaving?"

"Not sure. It shouldn't be long if I do."

"I don't mind keeping your room available."

"That would be great. I'll pay you through the week. If I'm gone longer than that, feel free to store them somewhere else so that you can put somebody in my room if you need to."

"It shouldn't be a problem. We haven't had many visitors lately. Besides the one that left just before you arrived, you're the only person we've had here this month. But the restaurant keeps us busy enough," he said with a laugh.

Hatch nodded, took one last sip of her tea, and then slipped out the door. No time to grab her belongings. She wanted to make contact with the priest but didn't want to do it in the open air of the marketplace, so she formulated a plan on the fly.

Sometimes the best plans are ones that weren't truly laid out. It was simple in design. Get him alone. *But how?* She saw the Jeep. It looked old. She crossed the street quickly. As she did, Hatch could see through the glass windows of the post office. The priest was in line behind a heavy-set woman with a large woven basket in her hands and three children circling her feet.

Hatch quickly made her way to the Jeep while the priest's back was turned away. At the rear passenger door of the Jeep, she pulled the handle. It was unlocked. She looked around, carefully surveying the foot traffic. Nobody seemed to notice her, although she did stand out in a crowd at just under six feet, slender and white. She was definitely an anomaly to the area, but it wasn't wholly unique. Foreigners visited quite frequently. People passed by, but nobody paid her much mind. She waited for an approximate two-second count before opening the door fully and slipping inside.

The windows in the back had a heavy tint. In fact, all the windows did, including the front windshield. The level of tint would be considered illegal stateside but was essential in a region like this where it was necessary to shield yourself from the brutal rays of the sun. Hatch was grateful for the obscurity it provided because it gave her additional concealment as she manipulated herself into position. A tattered blanket was on the floor, along with several odds and ends.

Hatch wiggled herself down between the back of the front seat and flattened to the floorboard. Using the blanket, she covered up as best she could. It wasn't an optimum level of concealment, but it would have to do for the moment. The camouflage would be for naught if the priest opened the back door. Hatch hedged her bets and hoped luck favored her today.

As she waited with the blanket over her in the heat of her enclosed metal hiding place, the Jeep's lack of air flow quickly began to take its toll. Hatch began sweating profusely. It was a staggering heat, like being inside a furnace. It had only been a couple of minutes, but the combination of the moist, thick, humid air had a suffocating effect. She guessed the interior temperature to be over one hundred degrees. Hatch found herself taking shallow breaths, trying to conserve her energy. She worked to relax and slow her heart rate.

Her plan was simple. Wait until he pulled away and was out of the town center and then she would try to address the priest without startling him. She hoped that whatever tactical training he had gone through had long since softened during the years of religious servitude. But as she knew, and from what she had seen in Tony just the other day, those skills die hard.

A few minutes later, the driver's door opened. She felt a slight whoosh of air and then the dip of the vehicle as the poorly maintained shocks absorbed the weight of the driver. Without hesitation, the priest started the Jeep and drove away.

With his window down in the front, the air started to circulate. The wind fluttered the blanket Hatch had over her. She lifted it ever so slightly to let in more of the air to alleviate some of the oppressive heat.

The Jeep rumbled along, shaking violently as it bounced over the road's uneven surface. She noted the priest had left the hard pack of the city streets and now was traversing a rural, unpaved trail. They'd been riding for approximately forty minutes.

Hatch realized they were definitely far away from the town center by now. However, she didn't know their exact location or the priest's ultimate destination.

Hatch moved the blanket aside. She allowed a few seconds to pass. She now had a visual of the priest. His hair was snow white and his unkempt curls blew wildly in the wind from the open window. There was no reaction from the priest, and his eyes remained focused on the road ahead.

Hatch edged backward and propped herself up against the right passenger door. Her tall frame filled the space between the backseat and the front passenger seat. She then slid herself into the gap between the back of the two front seats, making herself visible in the rear-view mirror.

The priest, seeing her, slammed on the brakes, jerking her forward. He turned and shot his right hand in the direction of the glove box. Hatch grabbed his wrist before it arrived at its intended destination. The priest was older, a little bit slower, and certainly not as strong as Hatch. She was able to stop him, and because of his twisted position, he was unable to counter with his left hand. He was effectively trapped in a modified armbar.

She didn't want to hurt him, at least not yet. Hatch just wanted to talk to him. She knew he was scared. She could see it in his eyes. He had no idea who she was, and the quicker she could deescalate the situation, the better off they both would be.

"I'm not here to hurt you," she said rapidly. "My name is Rachel Hatch. You knew my father, Paul. I'm here to find out what happened to him."

He seemed to be trying desperately to connect the dots.

"I got your name from a friend in New Mexico." She felt the tension leave the man's arm at that.

The priest's posture went slack. Any resistance seemed to dissipate. "I won't go for the gun. Just let me go. I'm going to put the car in park now." He spoke softly, calmly. He was a man familiar with confrontation, and he was handling it much better now that he had settled somewhat.

"Okay," Hatch said. She released her grip on his right wrist, and the priest did as he said. He put the transmission into park and then shifted slightly in the seat so he could better face her. "Say the name again."

"Rachel Hatch."

"My God. I never thought the day would come."

NINE

"WHY DON'T you come sit up front with me? Feel a little bit like a chauffeur with you back there." The priest's voice was kind, his eyes equally so. He was soft-spoken, even after having been surprised by Hatch.

Hatch hesitated a moment and weighed the consequences of climbing into the front passenger seat. It would be her first test with the man. If she exited the vehicle and he proceeded to drive off, then Hatch would know he was a threat. It would bring her back to square one. But she would undoubtedly find him again. Although, should he leave her stranded, the walk back to the city's center would be brutal, especially in the heat of the day.

It was a risk she was willing to take. A first gesture of trust, one that would take time to establish, and one she knew might never come. So, Hatch slid herself over to the back right passenger door. Standing outside the Jeep, she eyed the priest. He remained unmoved. No second attempt to go for the glove box.

Hatch entered the vehicle and the seat's leather, burning hot from the relentless sun, penetrated her cargo pants.

Even though the roadway they were on was covered by overgrowth of the trees above, nothing seemed to shelter the land from the oppressive African sun. The priest didn't put the car into drive right away. He remained facing her. A half smile was etched on his face, but there was an underlying depth she hadn't noticed before. His smoke gray eyes held a deep sadness.

"What happened to your father was an absolute tragedy. I had heard he had a family. I wish there was something I could have done either to stop it or to help you in the aftermath, but I was a different man then, and it was a different time." The priest began absentmindedly rubbing the sweat from his hands on his thighs, wiping at the never-ending flow from his open pores.

Hatch surveyed him. Even under his clothes, the loose-fitting black of his Catholic priest ensemble, she could see the outline of a man that at one time must've been physically tough. Although the years out of civilian life had undoubtedly left him softer.

His jawline was not pronounced, but she could tell it had once been. There's always a look, that piece of an operator that never dies, no matter the age or circumstance. It's an intangible "it" factor they possess after going through the rigors of training and the missions that follow. It never leaves a person. Hatch knew this firsthand.

"So, you feel bad about what happened to my father?" she asked, "Bad enough to tell me who did it?"

The priest closed his eyes briefly, either deflecting or recalling, she couldn't tell.

"Listen, it's far more complicated than you realize. You being here now tells me that there has been a massive leak, and there's only one way the consortium stops a leak," he said.

Hatch understood the message. She had heard it from everyone involved. Truth lives in consistency. And one thing was for certain, the former members of the Gibson Consortium had been nothing if not consistent in their warnings about the company's deadly reach.

"It seems an old friend in New Mexico has been speaking more than he should," the priest said with a slight shake of his head.

Hatch winced slightly at hearing this, knowing that the man who had first passed on the information about the priest's location was probably the only person he had kept in touch with. Her being here now compromised that information. But the man in New Mexico knew she would be coming and so must have, in turn, accepted his fate. It seemed as though many of the men from her father's old unit were accepting their fate. Whatever the hand they had in his death, enough time had passed that the guilt of the circumstances left them needing to rectify it. Even though, in doing so, they were exposing themselves to great danger.

"Rachel, you shouldn't be here," he said softly. "The fact that you are means our friend is most likely already dead. If they're not here in Africa yet, they'll soon be coming for you and me, and anyone else you've talked to about this. I don't think you understand the Pandora's box you've opened and the lives you've put at risk," he said.

Hatch looked at the priest, studying his features. "Lives I've put at risk? This could have been resolved years ago when my family lost our father, when whoever was responsible for pulling that trigger was dealt with properly. But from all that I have gathered, nobody has paid for the hand they had in his death." Hatch's face reddened as her temper began to flare. "So, I am the unforeseen consequence. I'm here to make things right. And I welcome anyone who comes to stop me."

The priest gave her a once over and a slight nod. "You remind me a lot of him. Your father had the same stubborn will. Not to mention a fearlessness to take on all comers."

Hatch shrugged but said nothing.

"But more importantly," he continued, "it's your willingness to do the right thing in the face of the utmost danger and that, my young girl, is exactly what cost your father his life. His first mistake was when he didn't pull the trigger twenty-plus years ago. I don't know how much you know about what happened, but obviously you know enough to find me here, so I can only gather that you've probably surmised the circumstances around his death."

Hatch was about to stop him but figured it couldn't hurt to hear the priest's take.

"There was a tasking in Libya. The company was looking to destabilize a country by gaining control of one of their political rising stars, and to do so, they had to send a message. And that message was to be sent by way of a bullet through his young son's head. A bullet your father was supposed to fire but didn't. His moral compunction stopped him from taking the shot, and in turn, set in motion things that are still unraveling to this day.

"But what I will say is, him not taking that shot was probably one of the bravest things I've ever seen. And it was at that moment that I decided to take a different path myself. He showed me that we can still do good. That even in the face of the pressures surrounding us, that we can find another way. And in him not pulling the trigger, I found the strength to take a different path. I found myself here, doing God's work. I changed my name, and I obviously am not the same person I used to be. I can trace all that back to your father.

"And the next time he risked everything to do the right thing, whether you know it or not, was when he went out and saved that family stranded on the mountain. That decision got him unpredicted national exposure, which ultimately brought down the hammer from Gibson Consortium."

"I believe they're called Talon Executive Services now," Hatch said.

The priest nodded. "They are. I keep tabs as best I can. My circle of intelligence is somewhat limited in my current position. But there's a lot happening here in Africa, and when there are things in turmoil, countries in flux, groups like Talon show up and get their piece of the pie. I'm sure they're here now, and it's only a matter of time until somebody from them comes for me and most likely you. Your father risked his life to save that family, and not just in the challenge of finding them on that icy mountain. No, that was an inherent risk, but one he knew he could face. The deeper threat was the one that nobody knew except for him, and that was the knowledge that any type of publicity could expose him. For him to step out of the shadows and save that family, putting himself in the media spotlight, was a dangerous move.

"As a man of the cloth now, I've seen the sacrifices people make, and each is unique. Few would have done what your father did. I think of him often as I falter in my own life. I want you to know, I'm a better man for having known him."

Hatch listened to the priest, absorbing his words. They were heartfelt and genuine. Hearing his thoughts affirmed her belief in her father's character. Given the perspective offered by Father McCarthy, her father had risked his own life, not only in the rescue that brought back the family, but in the fallout and aftermath that came. She now knew he must have been aware that they would be coming for him. Maybe that's why on that infamous day he went on his run without her.

Hatch and her father had always run together. It was a tradition he had started and one she now carried on solo. In those early morning runs, she felt her father trekking along with her. On rare occasions, she would hear his voice.

Her father must have had a suspicion that associates of his former employers were in Colorado, and he didn't want them coming to his home. He didn't want her with him, if and when they came for him. He isolated himself to protect her, to protect his family. One final sacrificial act in her dad's selfless service to country, to community, and to her. She loved her father now more than she ever thought possible.

McCarthy began speaking again. She didn't hear the first few words he uttered, as she was lost in thought. She was back in Colorado, down by the brook where the water bubbled as it navigated the rocks breaking the surface. A sound that for most people would be considered calming caused Hatch to shudder, a reminder of when she found him face down in a pool of his own blood.

The priest's words came into focus. "Please, why don't you come with me?" he said. "Come to one of the villages I care for. My mission work has me servicing several, but one of them is in a dire situation and needs as much help as it can get. I promise you, while we're there, we'll talk. I'll tell you everything I can. Maybe point you in the right direction for wherever it is you need to go. And hopefully by the end of this week, if you and I are still both alive, we can do something to make this right. It's the thing I've prayed on most, beyond all others. I've prayed that I could bring about a resolution for the untimely death of your father. After being a part of the group that took his life, I should somehow make it right before I leave this world."

Hatch considered the offer for two distinctly different reasons. For one thing, it was her code. Help those in need. Secondly, she wanted to decide what this former operator turned priest knew and why everybody she encountered pointed in his direction. "How far is the village?" She asked.

"Not too far. Would have already been there by now had you not jumped out and surprised me like a Jack in a box." He gave a wink.

Hatch gave a soft chuckle, barely perceptible as the priest started up the engine.

"So, how about it? Will you come with me? Will you help me do a little good? I really could use someone like you. You'll see what I mean when we get to the village."

Hatch nodded. "Sure. It's not like I've got anywhere else to go. You're kind of the dead-end for me in whatever journey this is that I'm on."

The Jeep rumbled forward. The rocks and pebbles of the uneven surface of the road shook the boxy 4-wheel drive as they headed deeper into the jungle.

TEN

AFTER TWENTY MINUTES of the Jeep's loud rumbling, the dense jungle foliage opened up, and Hatch saw the makings of a village. As they snaked their way through the final leg of the journey, smoke rose from their destination. On first thought, Hatch assumed the villagers might be having some type of pig roast, but with the windows down, her sense of smell dispelled that notion. The air didn't carry with it any of the familiar hints of spiced meat cooking, nothing like the fragrant notes of the food provided at Khari's cafe.

Once the Jeep rounded the final curve and the first huts came into view, Hatch was able to realize the exact source of the smoke. To her dismay, the billowing gray came from several of the huts in the back. The embers still glowed orange. The frames of the huts were barely visible, like skeleton bones reaching up angrily at the sky, completely blackened with ash.

There were several members of the village meandering about, most of the men were old, above the age of seventy, if Hatch were to guess. A group of young children were playing with a goat tethered to a frayed rope tied to a piece of rebar protruding from the ground.

It was sad and picturesque at the same time, as if a National

Geographic magazine had popped open in front of her. Had she been able to erase the imagery of the damaged village in the backdrop, it would have been beautiful. The brightly colored clothing of the villagers stood in stark contradiction to the sadness of the people wearing it. A solemnness was visible on each face she encountered as the people toiled, rebuilding after whatever had happened. Hatch looked at Father McCarthy as he pulled the vehicle to a stop. The engine's loud cacophony of noise ceased as the old Jeep's interior rattle subsided.

"What happened here? What happened to those homes? To these people?" Hatch asked with great concern. It was in her nature that when a person was wronged, someone should make it right. To fix it somehow, or at least understand it. Find out who was responsible, if possible.

For all she knew, the damage could have been caused by a lightning strike. African weather patterns were unique and at times violent. It was very possible that one of the storms that she'd encountered over the last week could have easily caused the damage, but something told her that was not the case here. The people in the village had a familiar look, something about their body language. It told her that there was more to this story, and now she better understood why the priest wanted to bring her here.

"They were attacked," he said. "I was out of the area, servicing another village. The rebels came through. They were seeking male enlistments. Totally unlike any draft process the US has ever seen. They go from village to village and grab able bodied men and boys and recruit them into their militia.

"The warlord that runs the group is a brutal man, to say the least. Not that I could have done much to stop it even if I had been here. Most likely I would be somewhere in one of those piles." The priest pointed to the burning rubble at the back of the village.

"How many did they take?" Hatch asked.

"A handful," he said, rubbing the tension along the bridge of his nose. "Six men. Well, if you want to call them men. Most were under the age of seventeen, but here in Africa that makes you as much of a man as you're going to see anywhere else. The responsibilities these young boys take on would shock most of their US counterparts."

"That's awful!" Hatch said. "Is the government doing anything about it? What about the UN? Do they know?"

"Yes." He sighed. "Both are involved. Both are battling for position. But there's been much in the way of political meanderings. No formal commitments to bring things to an end. The warlord, Dakarai, is well-protected, well-financed, and there are some who believe the government is feeding him financially because they want him in power. One thing's for certain, somebody wants him in a position of authority."

Hatch had been in enough destabilized regions of the world to know that whenever it occurred, there were lines of people jockeying for control. Much of it was done by using brutal warlords to hammer down on the commoners. Even the United States had used them to their advantage, either by financial aid or military support, until they were no longer needed. It sounded as though this was one of those cases, and it seemed like it was rapidly getting out of control.

"What is it you think I can do?" Hatch asked. "I'm not here to get in the middle of a civil war."

"Well, for starters." McCarthy pointed toward the damaged huts. "Maybe you can help us rebuild. We need somebody strong to help with the work since most of the able-bodied men have been taken. The women here are strong. They work hard and can handle much, but somebody like you would make a big difference in what we're trying to do rebuilding this village. The faster we get this back into order, the faster they can begin the spiritual journey of making things right."

Hatch nodded. Hard work and physical labor were something she was accustomed to and didn't mind at all.

"There's something else," the priest said, "that makes this attack worse than most I've encountered recently."

Hatch focused her full attention on McCarthy. "What's that?"

"There was a young boy, not twelve years old. He tried to stop them from taking any more of his villagers. He fought one of the men, jumped on his back and was able to take the soldier's gun."

Hatch closed her eyes, picturing the scene and understanding the sadness in the priest's tone.

"The soldier wasn't harmed, minus his pride. But the warlord's men couldn't let it stand. After the boy was disarmed, a message needed to be sent."

Hatch swallowed hard. She thought of Khari and the story he had told her, from years back when his face had been pressed into the hot fire leaving the deep burns as a constant reminder. She scanned the crowd of children swarming around the Jeep now, looking for a burned or injured child, hoping that's where the story ended. But seeing none, she feared the worst.

McCarthy cleared his throat and continued. "They hung him from the branch of the big Fever Tree." The priest pointed back to the large domed canopy of the tree. "It was a message to everybody not to cross them, and it broke this village like something I've never seen. If you had come here a few days ago, you would have heard the laughter of children and families singing. The mass that I'll be giving today will be one of the most solemn I've had to do since coming here. I hope you'll attend."

Hatch thought about his request for a second. It had been a long time since she'd attended any type of religious service, but under the circumstances, she felt compelled to agree.

ELEVEN

HATCH SAT on the soft earth, listening as Father McCarthy delivered his sermon. The villagers had ceased their work and surrounded the priest in a semicircle. One woman sat in a cluster of small children and was braiding the blades of a palm into what looked like a small doll. She was a vacant shell, her eyes empty, and her movements were trancelike. The children sat nearby quietly listening to the priest, but their eyes were filled with tears which streamed down their dark faces, making a line through the light coating of dirt.

Hatch didn't understand a word that McCarthy was saying. Not because the sermon was too complicated or overwrought with Christian overtones, but because he delivered the entire mass in Swahili, something she never predicted. Now that she came to think of it, the man had obviously spent numerous years in the country and would need to be fluent in the multiple languages from the various dialects in the region. If he was to be an effective leader of the churches in those villages, he needed to be able to speak to them in their native tongue.

She found it fascinating. Although she didn't understand the words, she could see the conviction with which they were conveyed, and she could see that whatever he was saying resonated deeply with the members of this village. It was a powerful moment for her, one which she had not expected when she had first met the priest. She watched him as he delivered his sermon, his hands animated, and his face serious. McCarthy moved slowly back and forth, not in the traditional manner of the priests of her youth that would stand behind the altar and deliver their mantra, the repetitive phrases, and ceremonial up, down, kneel that she had been indoctrinated with but had grown apart from in her adult life.

He was directly interacting with this community of villagers, in his words, in the way he moved. He was an enigmatic character. McCarthy reached down and rubbed the head of the child nearest him as he spoke. He moved around the circle, never staying in one spot for too long, and it felt as though he had individually addressed every member of the village with his words and his subtle gestures. Seeing this, Hatch found it difficult to picture the priest in his former role in life as an elite operator turned contract killer.

Hatch found herself impressed, not an easy thing by her standards. Her preconceived notion that this man had somehow been responsible, if not by action then by association, for her father's death seemed implausible under the current circumstances. She found herself conflicted, wondering how this kind man, now a priest, could have been involved with the murder of her dad.

McCarthy seemed to be truly devout to this new principled way of living and to the people he served. She wondered if the trip to Africa had been for naught. Had the journey halfway across the world to find an answer to her questions been a complete waste of time and energy? Hatch now found herself in a totally unforeseen predicament, in a village suffering at the hand of a ruthless warlord, not unlike the community she had left in New Mexico. Although different in nature, the critical fundamentals of power and control and the abuse of the innocent were the same.

Hatch felt herself drawn to this small community of tormented villagers in the same way she had felt in Luna Vista. It was the same, just a different gang, a different measure of control, this one seemingly more violent and more volatile. There was obviously no attempt by any type of law enforcement to help the villagers. Hatch wondered if she had just stepped out of the frying pan and into the proverbial fire once more. She hoped that whatever the priest could provide as far as answers would give her enough to move on before she got herself entangled again. But she already felt the tug, the draw of the people around her, the desperate need for somebody to stand up for them, to protect them, to keep them safe. Her code.

She was only one person, and obviously this feudal war went well beyond what she had faced stateside. Hatch questioned whether she was the right person for the job, and then she thought of Bennett and the contact number he had given her. She kept it in her pocket for fear that if something did happen, she would need to access it quickly. But now she wasn't entirely sure, maybe his point of contact, Jabari, was somehow involved with the warlord. She wasn't sure what kind of alliances were struck in this part of the world. She hadn't spent much time in this region during her time in service, and so she really didn't know the players. She was better versed in regions in the Middle East. But she was a quick study and was confident it wouldn't take her long to figure things out. One thing was certain. These innocent people were caught in the crossfire and needed help.

The sermon ended and the group of villagers quietly got up. One by one, they lined up in front of Father McCarthy, who blessed them individually, making the sign of the cross and kissing them on their forehead, a ritual she had never seen in her childhood. It was a sweet gesture, one of true kindness, true connection and devotion. Each seemed to be less burdened when they walked away to return to the duties and responsibilities of rebuilding their village. Although they were not smiling and tears still flowed from many of their eyes, they seemed somewhat lightened from the burden of the last few days, the trauma that they had faced, and the death of the young boy which had obviously rocked them all to the core.

After the last child had come before the priest, McCarthy turned and looked over at her. Hatch stood, dusting off her pants. He walked up with a slight smile on his face.

"So, what did you think?"

"I'm impressed. That was definitely something I never expected to see, an Irish priest giving a mass in Swahili."

Father McCarthy laughed, but not loud enough for any of the others to hear.

"I wish you had seen this place a few days ago. My sermon would have had a much more festive tone. I had planned to talk about the growth of the coming months, with the rainy season upon us, and the time to sow our seeds. But I had to change my sermon kind of off the cuff, of course, to deal with the tragedy that has occurred," he said.

"It seemed to resonate with each one of them. I couldn't understand what you were saying, but it seemed quite powerful. You have a way with these people. They truly adore you."

"Well, it has been hard-earned," he said, rubbing at a curled tuft of white hair. "Things like this don't come easy. I've been here for a very long time. Some of the villages still don't want me in them, but every once in a while, I approach them again and try to bring the word of God to them. Years ago, when I first tried to reach out to this village, I was met with an unfriendly reaction. I was looked upon as an outsider coming to push his religion on them. It was not well-received, but over time, the small gestures I made brought about a change. I can't force myself. I can't force God into their lives, just like I couldn't force it into yours or anyone else's."

"How'd you do it? How'd you win them over?"

"I came each day and did something for them, something small, simple. I'd help somebody carry a basket, help somebody wash clothes in the river, or bring some food. Fastest way to a person's heart is often through the stomach."

"I couldn't agree more," Hatch said, thinking back to Khari at the cafe in Mombasa center. She then thought of Harry and the diner in Luna Vista, New Mexico. Food was definitely a way to Hatch's heart.

"The more I did, the more they came to trust me. And the more they came to trust me and talk to me, the more I learned about them and a connection began to establish itself in the natural course of things. And then one day it happened. I was asked if I wanted to share, and so I did. The group attendance was small at first, only a few that were interested, and again, I didn't push. But as time went on, it grew. And the message I was spreading was well-received. Before long, the entire village was my congregation, as are many others in this area."

"Winning the hearts and minds. I guess your previous life experience helped in that regard." Hatch knew the foreign internal defense, or FID, was a critical mission with the Special Forces, and skilled operators learned to navigate the delicate balance better than most.

McCarthy winked. "Trained by the best." He took a deep breath. "This isn't the only village in need. Many others are facing similar strife. You've come at a strange time, and you're witnessing firsthand a major political change. And I don't know what the end result will be."

Hatch looked at him and then out toward the villagers. The woman who had been folding the palm fronds into the shape of a doll was still seated on the ground. She was putting the finishing touches on it. The doll's arms were stretched out like a gingerbread man. Hatch was impressed with what she created with the simplest of materials. Upon closer inspection, Hatch noted the doll was intricately designed. It had a wicker basket complexity in the twined bits.

"Who is she?" Hatch asked, gesturing with her hand to the doll maker.

"That's the mother of the boy who died."

Hatch's heart sunk. "What's that she's making?"

"An offering. Some of the superstitions remain. Masika will leave it at the foot of the tree. It's been made with bits and pieces of the tree in which her son was hanged. She wanted to make something beautiful out of the ugliness that happened."

"That is one strong woman."

"Well," he said, "she needs it. All those little ones around her need their mother. She can't allow herself to fall apart in a village like this where everyone has to pull their weight. There is no time for grieving, no real opportunity to sit back and cry and allow things to fall apart around you. The process is different here. You grieve in your own time."

Hatch understood. She'd been grieving for her father in her own way for a very long time.

"I hear her at night, crying to herself after the children have gone to sleep. I stay over there, in my hut. I've got a hut like that in most of the villages I serve. It's important for me to be able to watch over my flock, especially after a traumatic event like this. And each night since I've been here, I hear her cry in the quiet of the night."

Hatch listened and then thought about the strength of this woman, the strength of this village and how different things were here.

"I want to help," Hatch said.

"Good. I was hoping you'd say that. Maybe you understand more Swahili than you admit." He winked again. "I mean, my sermon was about rebuilding, about finding strength in tragedy, about pushing through the pain and finding joy in the fact that life still abounds."

Hatch looked at him, looked at the life of the people that were left in the wake of tragedy and realized the truth in what he said. Life was meant for the living. The dead had no place among them. When tragedy strikes, it's a setback, but life eventually moves on. Day turns to night, night becomes day, growth continues, rain falls, people laugh, and the world continues to spin. This was a hard concept for Hatch to grasp at age twelve when she lost her father. It was no easier in her adult life, in the years of turmoil that came with the loss of many friends overseas. But with each death, she kept moving forward, never allowing herself to stop. Life does continue, albeit often on a different course.

"So, Hatch, you want to help?" he asked. "Let's start over there. We need to break down the rest of that smoldering ash, and we've also got to clear a path because we have to rebuild. We need to get rid of the destroyed huts, bring the debris into the center of the village, burn off the remnants of the wood that is no good and then start setting up and rebuilding the homes. There's three that were severely burned. The rest require minor repair."

"That's not what I meant," Hatch said, folding her arms. "I mean, don't get me wrong, I'll help you here with whatever you need. I'll help these families rebuild. I'll put in my day's work. I don't mind good hard labor. But I have a very special set of skills, and I can help these people in another way, maybe one that makes it so that they never have to live in fear again. I want to help so no more homes are burned, and no other children are enslaved. That no mother ever again has to see her child hang from a Fever Tree."

The priest stopped and looked at Hatch, and then the softness of his features hardened. She saw the underlying operator buried deep beneath the soft edges of his face. "What you're talking about is suicide. That's not what I meant when I said I needed your help. I'm not sure what your skills are, but many people have tried and failed. And when I say people, I mean small militias. These villagers didn't initially bow down to the warlord's demands. Many of the men fought back. They lost and paid with their lives. That's how it got to this point of minimal resistance. There's been a lot of death and a lot of tragedy here."

"I'm not afraid."

"That's not the point. I'm not sure what you think you can accomplish as one person. But I can guarantee you this, if you set out to face off against Dakarai, you're going to be buried here in Africa. And I, for one, would hate to see that happen."

Hatch looked at him and didn't waver. "I appreciate your concern, but I can take care of myself. And like you said, I've got a little bit of my dad in me. And if you knew him as well as you say you did, then you know I cannot sit idly by and put up the side of a house when I know there's someone who's terrorizing another village around here, killing innocent people and destroying these good, hardworking families. It just isn't in my code. It's not in my genes. I've got no other choice. Do you understand that?"

Father McCarthy lowered his head and shook it side-to-side. He seemed saddened to hear her rebuttal. It was obvious to Hatch now that he never intended to bring her here to be the village savior. He obviously thought she would just be a little extra muscle to get things back up to status quo. But in her mind, the status quo was unsatisfactory. These people needed somebody to be their champion, to take them under their wing to protect them. And who better than her?

"Well," the priest said, "one thing is for damn certain, you're as stubborn as your father. That's for sure. I couldn't reason with him either." He laughed. "Maybe that's a good thing. If there were more people in the world like you, maybe we wouldn't have incidents like this. Villages destroyed, families ruined and children dead."

"All I need you to do is point me in the right direction. Tell me where I can find Dakarai, and then I'll figure out the rest from there."

"Let's start here, with these people. Dakarai can wait. In what I've seen in my life, vengeance brings more pain than solace."

TWELVE

HATCH WATCHED as the groups of people made their way into the village, all of them on foot. Each face painted in the pain and horror they had just experienced. Sadly, she'd seen this scene, or ones similar to it, numerous times during her time in service. The look of desperation, anguish, and loss all rolled into a swirl of unimaginable despair. The macabre procession moved in a slow shuffle. Members of the village who were still recouping from their ordeal rushed over to assist in any way they could.

Hatch watched for a moment, took in the scene. Some of the new arrivals carried the wounded and some carried the dead. A woman in her eighties collapsed to the ground and Hatch ran to her. Slipping her shoulder underneath the frail woman's armpit, Hatch gently hoisted her up into a standing position. Hatch was taller than the village elder and had to stoop slightly so as not to put her further off balance. She shuffled alongside as she brought the injured woman into the village's center.

Father McCarthy and some of the other villagers were already fast at work preparing a fire. A recent deluge of rain left them soaked to the bone, and although it was warm, wet clothes on damaged skin only caused future problems as they dried. Plus, they would have to provide medical treatment for some of the wounds. Needles for suturing would have to be field sterilized, and that meant they needed fire. Hatch knew this and apparently so did McCarthy, either from his prior life experience or his current one. The priest set small irons along the rocks outside of the fire, heating them, prepping them to be used to cauterize the wounds if necessity dictated.

A field hospital in this remote part of their world was nothing short of a throwback to times before modern medicine. McCarthy would undoubtedly reach out for aid, but in the interim, the villagers, McCarthy, and now Hatch would be the sole providers of first aid until more formalized help arrived, if at all.

Hatch sat the older woman down on a flat rock near the fire. The damp wood threw a thick gray swirl of smoke into the air. She stared up at Hatch for a brief moment. The deeply wrinkled skin of her face held no expression, an empty vessel. No words were exchanged. The only form of communication came in the form of a slow, deliberate blink which Hatch took to mean thank you.

Hatch held the woman's hand in hers for a brief moment before turning her attention to the others in need.

The newcomers were guided toward the warmth of the fire so they could dry themselves. Hatch knew without question the next series of tasks would be arduous ones. The treatment and care would be carried out by a group who had just suffered their own loss. This unforeseen complication would compound the problems they were currently facing in rebuilding their own community.

Hatch had only arrived at the village the day before, and the work had been tireless. The mending of the damaged huts and working to get the people back to some semblance of order. And now this new edition, the twenty or so villagers who had staggered in. Apparently, the warlord's campaign was getting more aggressive.

These two communities would quickly have to join together in building additional living quarters for the new arrivals. But the immediate focus would be on tending the injured, triaging those who needed outside medical care first, and then working their way down the list to dealing with the infirm.

Hatch walked over to McCarthy, who was righting himself after gently sitting a child by the fire and giving him a bowl of water.

"My God, how often does this happen? I mean, I just got here, and you said that—"

McCarthy looked out at the group and stepped a little further away so as to be out of earshot. "I've never seen it like this. Something must be happening. Somebody must be pushing Dakarai into action. I'll have to reach out to some of my connections and see what's really going on here. But there's definitely a power play being made. I've never seen back-to-back assaults like this. They used to happen with more frequency years ago, but it had died off and they were very localized.

"Once a raid would take place, we wouldn't hear or see from Dakarai or his men for a much longer period of time than this. But for two attacks of this nature to take place so close together, it must mean they're making an aggressive move, pushing for control or someone's pushing them to make these moves. Regardless, these are unsafe times. Hatch, I asked you to help here, but I've got to be honest with you, I think it may be too dangerous. Maybe it is time for you to cut your losses and head home."

"You're kidding, right? I wanted a piece of Dakarai and his goons when I first saw what happened before I arrived. Now, I'm seeing more of it and more of a need for my assistance. Now you tell me you think I should go, that it would be safer for me, that it's not my fight. Is that what I'm going to hear next?" she asked.

McCarthy looked out at the injured and wounded circle of new arrivals scattered about the fire and then back at Hatch.

"Look at them. It's not your fight. You've got no skin in the game here. These are my people and as awful as this is, it will happen again. It always does. I do my best to mend the damage and then pick up the pieces and rebuild. But for you to stand up for them seems reckless. You don't live here, Hatch. You can go home."

He was right. She could go home, but she also knew after witnessing what she'd seen the other day compounded by today's events, she would never be able to live with herself if she chose to walk away. She offered one last bit of resistance, figuring it might resonate with the priest.

"What would my father do?" she asked.

McCarthy closed his eyes and hung his head in resignation. Hatch had her answer.

"I'm going to put my personal agenda on hold for the time being. Do you understand me? But you're going to owe me. You're going to tell me everything I need to know. But right now, what I need to do is find a way to help these people," Hatch said. "And I think I have an idea of who can help me, or at the very least point me in the right direction. Will you take me to the cafe in the Mombasa town center?"

McCarthy nodded.

"And one more thing," Hatch added. "Do you have access to a satellite phone so I can make a call?"

McCarthy began walking toward his quarters. "Follow me."

Hatch followed him into the hut. She was surprised to find he had no lock on the door. He apparently trusted the people of the village completely. The reformed operator seemed to have an open-door policy within the community, allowing the villagers to have access to him day or night.

It was a meager existence, to say the least. A dirt floor, military-issued style cot on the ground, a couple of wicker baskets where he kept his clothes, and a small table and chair where he could dine or read by candlelight. On the wood plank wall was a handmade cross, similar to the doll she'd seen the old woman make, intricately woven. Hatch wondered, looking at the complex weaving of the palm fronds, if the bereaved mother had made it as well.

Inside a wicker basket, under a pile of clothes, McCarthy pulled out a thick sat phone that looked more like an old school walkie talkie and handed it to Hatch. "You should get a decent signal in here, that way the villagers don't see it. I use this for emergency purposes, and after you make your call, I'm going to need to call the hospital and have them bring in several transport vehicles to get the worst of our injured into care. The hospitals aren't great, but they are better than we can provide here."

Hatch nodded.

"I'm going to leave you. The less I know about what you plan to do or who you plan to meet with is better for me in the long run. I'm out of the game, Rachel, and I don't want to accidentally fall back in. Do you understand?"

"I do." She looked at the phone and thought of the card in her pocket. "And call me Hatch."

"Uncanny." A thin smile crossed his lips. "You're definitely your father's daughter."

Hatch herself had left the official game of spies and counterspies, secrets and secrets upon secrets, and deadly covert missions. Yet it still seemed to find her. Although she'd been trying to find her way out of that game, it was one she continued to play, albeit by her own rules now and not those set forth by any government entity. She was still finding her footing on the terrain of this new and uncharted territory.

As McCarthy left, she pulled the card from her pocket and punched in the numbers that Bennett had given her in that cafe in North Carolina. She waited and listened for the connection to be established. Unlike a conventional phone, there wasn't the traditional ringtone. Instead, there was a series of three clicks followed by a beep.

She waited patiently, and after several seconds and several more clicks and beeps, she heard a connection established. Though no one spoke, Hatch knew someone was now on the other end of the line.

"Jabari?" she asked. Nothing. He obviously did not recognize her voice, or the number she was calling from. The fact that he still had not answered her after she had said his name meant that Bennett had kept his word and not given any forewarning of her arrival in Africa and the possibility that she might need to reach out to him.

It was going to be even harder for her to finagle and establish trust on a satellite phone in a village in Africa connecting to someone somewhere in the country who she had never met. But she'd had some experience with these things and continued.

"My name is Hatch, I'm assuming this connection is secure. We have a mutual friend. Chris Bennett told me I could reach you if I needed any assistance." Hatch offered nothing else, and quietly waited for the man to process the information. The ball was in his court now, and it was up to the man on the other end of the line whether this conversation would continue or not.

"I'm listening," the voice said. Curt and direct.

"Can we meet somewhere in Mombasa town center?"

"Fine," he said flatly.

"Do you know the cafe across from the post office?" Hatch asked.

"I do."

"When can you meet me there?" she asked.

"I'm close," he said. "Tell me what time and when, and I will make my arrangements to be there."

"Let's say three hours. I've got some things to tend to first," she said.

"Fine, three hours it is." There was a pause, and she did not hear the click of the disconnect on the other end and knew that the man was still there.

Unlike the clear cell reception one would experience on a cellphone, she couldn't hear the man breathing or any background noise. But the connection was still established; she knew that much, so she waited.

"May I ask where you are?" he said.

It seemed only right the man would be somewhat curious as to where she was. It might give him some bit of insight as to why she was contacting him. But she thought better of it until they could establish contact and meet face-to-face. Both of them came from worlds of subterfuge, and espionage and she knew trust was a precarious thing at best. So she offered an answer that would hopefully suffice. "I'd rather not say. It could put some peoples' lives in danger. But I'll be there in three hours, and we can talk more about it then."

"Three hours it is then," he said.

And now Hatch heard the distinct disconnect between their lines of communication.

THIRTEEN

MCCARTHY HAD DROPPED HATCH OFF. He said he needed
supplies at the marketplace and that he could get them on his own. He'd
said he'd be back in approximately an hour and asked if that would be
enough time for her to meet with whoever it was she was set to meet.
Hatch felt it would be more than adequate.

She went inside the cafe, just avoiding a torrential downpour of rain
as she entered through the hand carved wood doors. The windows were
open, allowing the droplets to spatter onto the sills and trickle down to
the tile floor, pristinely maintained by Josefina.

Hatch saw Khari before he saw her. But as soon as he turned, a broad
smile curled up on the man's scarred cheeks. He rushed over and took
Hatch's hands in his.

"Hatch, so good to see you," he said. "I wasn't sure if or when you'd
come back. I hoped it would be soon. And the fact that you left your stuff
here, I imagined it would be sooner."

Hatch smiled. The cafe owner's large hands swallowed hers in his
hearty grip. The scars of his tragedy stretched from his face down his
body to the discolored blotchy patches of white and light pink over the
deep dark mahogany brown of his hand. Hatch normally offered her

left hand to people, but with Khari, she felt no need to hide the scars. The raised flesh peeking out from her sleeve was smothered in the gentle warmth of his grasp. The smooth flesh of his palm now covered Hatch's.

"It's truly great to see you," Hatch said.

"I'm glad to see you, too. I miss our talks. Where have you been?" Khari asked rapidly, almost giddy.

"I've been in a village, a little way out of here." Hatch wasn't sure how much she should say about her most recent adventure.

"You look sad, Hatch," he said.

"Not sad. Pissed off maybe. There's been some awful things happening in Kenya lately."

Khari nodded and released her hand from his embrace. "I've heard. I'm sorry that you've had to see the ugly side of our beautiful country, but remember, what did I say? You choose how it affects you. You decide what it does to you, and how you come back from it. There is beauty here. I promise you that."

She realized then how much she'd missed Khari's insightful wisdom in the days she'd been gone. The way he could turn the ugly upside down, and make things seem normal and right. He had an uncanny ability to find the silver lining under the direst of circumstances.

She thought about his reaction to her comment. He mentioned having heard of the troubles in the jungle. Hatch wondered if this was a community thing, a family thing or something else. She started to wonder a little bit more about the friendly innkeeper and cafe owner. Maybe there was more to his story, maybe a couple pieces had been left out.

But either way, right now without peeling back the layers of that onion, she was content to call him her friend. She hoped the day would never come when that would change.

"Would you like me to make you something to eat, Hatch?" he asked.

"Absolutely, I'm famished. The food in the village was great, but nothing compared to what you make here," she offered.

A big smile grew on his face, and the whites of his teeth shone bright. "You make me and my wife very happy when you say that, and I have a special treat for you today. I'll get back to it and you have a seat. Some of the tea while you wait?"

Hatch nodded. "What meal would be complete without it? I think you've got me addicted to it. I found myself missing it."

He gave a loud boom of a laugh. "It does have that effect."

"You'll have to tell me what blend of tea that is so that I can pick it up when I'm home."

He laughed again. "You won't find this anywhere in the United States. It's a blend that my wife makes by hand. But I'll tell you what, whenever it is that you're ready to leave, I'll package some up for you to take home with you. If you can get it through customs."

Khari then disappeared back to his wife, and they spoke in rapid Swahili. Josefina nodded, but as was her way, never came over to speak to Hatch.

Josefina set about the cooking, and Khari assisted her. They worked seamlessly together, complementing each other at every turn like a culinary samba. Seeing them together made Hatch think of Dalton Savage, and the balance that his level-headed-ness had provided her during their short stint together in Hawk's Landing. She found herself thinking of him more often than not these days. Hatch regretted not calling him before she left for Africa. She'd meant to, but for some reason talking to him scared her more than anything else. Something about him weakened her. And Hatch was not comfortable with weakness.

She shook off the thought, mentally clearing her mind. Hatch was here to meet with Bennett's contact, a man she'd never seen before. She needed to keep her wits about her. Not the time or place to be thinking of Savage. If she found her way out of this mess, Hatch vowed to sort out those feelings.

Hatch took a seat, facing the entrance. A moment later, Khari returned with a teacup and the kettle. He poured her a glass of the piping hot tea and set it on a hand-painted plate. He smiled. "I'll leave you be for a moment, Hatch. I've got to take care of a couple of things. Josefina needs my help." He walked away, chuckling to himself.

Hatch blew softly at the tea, sending the steam away from her and cooling it just a bit. Then she took a sip. The warm, fragrant liquid hit her empty stomach and it grumbled noisily in protest. She was hungry. It'd been a while since she'd had a full meal. In the physical and mental stress of the village, she hadn't realized until that moment how hungry she was. It didn't help that the restaurant was filled with fragrant aromas from the kitchen. A few of the patrons seated nearby took bites of their food, making her mouth water.

Hatch scanned the crowd outside, looking for Jabari, but not knowing what she was looking for, it was a wasted effort. She sipped her tea and waited.

She looked at her watch. She had gotten here earlier than the agreed meeting time. Several minutes passed, and nobody came in. Hatch looked out toward the street, looking for anyone out of place, for somebody paying a bit too much attention to her. But nobody fit the bill.

Khari came from the kitchen area with a plate of food. Hatch noticed a man she'd never seen before following closely behind. The man was shorter than Khari, shorter than Hatch. She guessed him to be five-foot-seven at best. He was thinly built, dark-skinned, and wore a bright Hawaiian shirt and khaki pants. The man's shirt looked like something Magnum PI would've worn.

Hatch eyed the two men as they came to her. Khari set the plate of food down. His smile was still present, but a little more subdued. "Here you go, Hatch. You're going to love this."

Hatch smelled the food but didn't break her eye contact with the man standing just off to the right and slightly behind Khari. "Who's your friend?" Hatch asked.

He stepped aside and said, "I think you already know. You called him, didn't you?" Khari laid a gentle hand on her shoulder and then retreated to the kitchen.

The short Hawaiian-shirt-wearing man took a seat across from Hatch. He did not smile broadly like Khari did. Jabari had an intensity to him, which made sense. If he was who Bennett said he was, then he was combat-hardened. He looked battle-weary, something Hatch was familiar with.

"It seems we have a mutual friend, Miss Hatch," Jabari said, seriously.

She caught a glimpse of Khari in the background. He was watching the meeting. Hatch realized there was more to the kind-hearted cafe owner than met the eye. He was not just a survivor from a village attack, not just the eternal optimist who had turned the other cheek and opened a cafe and B&B in Mombasa town center. He was a freedom fighter, a militiaman, maybe ex-Special Forces or something.

Hatch focused her attention back on Jabari, now seated across the table from her. "Khari has been good to me since I've been here. Funny that you two know each other."

He lightened a little bit. "This is Africa, Miss Hatch. There's still a lot you need to learn. You've only been here a couple of days, less than a week. How is it you would assume to know what really happens here and how things work?"

Hatch knew he was right. There was no way she could. No way she could understand the complexities of this environment. She had just dipped her toe in the water of a massive pond, but she was a quick learner.

"So, you understand what's going on? You know about the village attacks," she asked.

Jabari nodded. "I do. It's been a very bad week for us, and I can't see it getting any better anytime soon."

"I want to help," Hatch said. "I think I can. Correction, I know I can. I just need to be pointed in the right direction and I need a little bit of assistance. I came here with no materials for such a task."

"Why did you come here, Miss Hatch, to Africa, to Mombasa, to the village? What are you doing here?" Jabari asked.

Hatch looked at him and understood why the man would be concerned. He was probably more concerned she was operating on behalf of a government entity, or worse, a government contractor. And that he was getting himself tied into some deep cover CIA operation. "I'm not here for anyone but myself. If that's what you're asking."

He cocked an eyebrow and gave her a sideways glance. "You just showed up to Africa and started poking around in some of the villages.

While a series of attacks suddenly start happening the same week you're here, and boom, my satellite phone rings, and you need my help. Please tell me if there's something I'm missing, Miss Hatch. Sounds to me like a little US government involvement is now underway, and I, as leader of the rebellion, should have been made aware of this and aware of your arrival prior to your arrival."

"You're wrong. I'm here because of something that happened two decades ago."

Again, his face was a blend of interest and confusion. "I don't understand."

"My father was killed over twenty years ago. I have information that may lead to whoever did it, and it brought me here. I came here on a fact-finding mission, nothing more, nothing less. It just happens that the person I was speaking with about it was in the village at the time of the attacks."

"The priest?" Jabari asked. "You came to ask the priest about something that happened twenty years ago. The man never ceases to amaze me. He has been a great ally to me and to our cause and to the villagers who love him, but I always knew there was something more to him, for a man like him to survive the things he survived out here and to do it with such grace and poise. Funny, he never mentioned his past, though. His mission work was always priority number one. He has been a good friend to us here in Africa, and we greatly respect him, but it sounds as though I should regard him a little more carefully."

Hatch felt as though she'd somehow betrayed McCarthy, but she needed to get some headway with this man. Without being open and honest with him, the likelihood of his assistance would be minimal at best, especially if he believed she was a deep-cover CIA operative working now in this region and looking for some type of alliance.

"Okay, let's say everything you're saying is true," he said. "Let's say you really are here to find out about what happened years ago to your father, and you happened to be in a village just after an attack and then in between another attack. And let's just say by happenstance you come to Khari's cafe, an old friend of mine – and I think you know what I mean by old friend – and that's where you decide to stay," Jabari said. "A lot of coincidences lining up, Miss Hatch, that makes me slightly more than concerned to provide any assistance to you if, in fact, you are not who you say you are."

Hatch understood it couldn't look stranger, and now that he laid everything out the way he did, she realized that it was.

"Listen," Hatch said. "I need your help. I didn't know what I was getting myself into when I came here. I knew there was civil unrest, but I didn't know that it was this bad, and I didn't come here looking for a fight, but sometimes the fight finds you." Hatch paused. Jabari nodded and Hatch continued, "I'm not asking for you to come along with me into the village. I need some equipment and to be pointed in the direction of Dakarai, the one who is responsible for all this, for the two village attacks, for killing that young boy. I need to know where I can find him."

Jabari seemed intrigued. He leaned forward, pressing his thin arms against the table and pouring himself a cup of Josefina's special tea. He sipped it as he gave Hatch a pensive look.

"Miss Hatch," he began.

"Hatch," she interrupted. "Just Hatch is fine."

"Hatch," he continued. "You mean to tell me you want me to give you some weapons and a map and point you in the direction of one of the most dangerous men in this region and wish you well. Is that what you want? Are you crazy?"

She shrugged. "Maybe, but it doesn't seem like anybody else is doing much about it. I think I could make things right. Who knows? Maybe turn the tide. I've got a list of items I would need if you want to help me. If not, I'll look elsewhere." She actually had no idea where else she would look.

Jabari took a sip of his tea and continued to eye her carefully. Then he turned and said something to Khari. The gregarious cafe owner was standing near Josefina and pretending to wipe down a plate, obviously trying to listen in on the conversation as best he could from a distance. Khari responded in Swahili. She couldn't decipher any of it. She actually wished McCarthy was sitting with her now. He could at least translate what was being said.

Jabari nodded and then turned his attention back to Hatch. "Khari said all you've done since you've been here is wait for the priest. That was it. You didn't make any phone calls. You didn't bring anything with you. There was nothing in your stuff that you left behind."

At that point, Hatch realized the man who she trusted had rifled through her things and done a little bit of investigative work. Although she couldn't blame him, now knowing his position and under the circumstances, he obviously knew Jabari and worked within some type of intelligence network. Hatch didn't believe the cafe was a front. During Hatch's time overseas, she had used several people, business owners and villagers alike, as sources in the intelligence chain. And it appeared that Khari was one of those.

She did not fault Khari for rummaging in her bags and looking for anything suspicious. In light of everything, he was probably also checking for weapons and potential bombs. Leaving a duffle bag behind in a bed and breakfast café that also doubled as an intelligence center in Jabari's network would have been an ideal way to cause some damage. She saw Khari raise his hands in an apologetic *I'm sorry.*

"So, let's cut to the chase. I told you what I've come here for. I stumbled upon these villagers. And I'm telling you I can help."

"How can you help us?" Jabari asked. "How can you do anything that we haven't already done?"

"Fresh eyes," she said

"Fresh eyes," Jabari repeated. "What does that mean?"

"It's something we used to say in my old unit. When you're looking at a problem, you can look at it so long that you can only see one solution. When you look at it with fresh eyes, someone else's perspective, somebody who doesn't know as much or maybe is a true outsider, they might see something that you don't and in doing so you might find a solution."

"Fresh eyes," he repeated again, this time softly and more to himself. "I think I like that. So, Miss Hatch--excuse me, Hatch. You'd like to provide me with fresh eyes? You want to see the problem and then what? Me, give you a rifle and you can go and kill the warlord yourself."

"How about this? How about you explain it to me. Show me where the problem lies, and I'll see if I can provide any assistance. Is that fair? A compromise of sorts."

Jabari sipped his tea and thought. She watched and could almost see the gears inside his head turn. He gave a barely perceptible nod. "Tell you what, Miss Hatch. You come with me to my compound. You meet my men and maybe we'll let you look at our problem with your fresh eyes. Then you tell me what you think. And I'll tell you if I can help you. Does that sound fair enough?" He asked.

"It does and thank you."

"Don't thank me. You have no idea what you're asking for."

Hatch's stomach rumbled.

"There's one more thing. You can't see how we get to the compound. My people are very guarded, if you understand what I mean by that."

"I understand."

"And when you get there, there'll be a test. Nobody comes into our group without being tested." Jabari paused. "It's hard, and you're a woman."

"What does being a woman have to do with anything?" Hatch asked.

"Please don't take offense. We've never had a female in our compound. I just thought I should warn you. These things you must know before you agree to come with me," he said.

Hatch leveled her gaze at the man. She thought of the tests she's been through, the gauntlet that she'd run would rival all others. *How bad could it be?*

"Don't worry about me," she said. "I'm ready for whatever test you have."

FOURTEEN

THE TRUCK HAD RUMBLED for what felt like maybe an hour or a little bit longer. She was blindfolded now, and the dark, double-bound handkerchief which covered her eyes and part of her face was moist with her sweat. The windows were open just enough to let some of the warm air circulate around the inside of the vehicle. It wasn't in much better condition than McCarthy's Jeep.

She had no idea what she was in store for, but if history, her history, was any prediction, it would be a test of endurance, strength, or will. Hatch fancied herself qualified on all three fronts and looked forward to the opportunity to prove herself worthy and to move this forward.

The truck came to an abrupt stop. The slight skid of the tires across the uneven, rocky, dirt surface beneath kicked up a plume of dust that circulated inside the open window of the truck, causing Hatch to cough briefly as it tickled the back of her already dry throat. She sat still, waiting for the next command to be given by Jabari. She was on their turf now and would be under their rules. She did not want to say or do anything to jeopardize what she hoped to be a prospective alliance.

"I must apologize for taking you to our village this way," Jabari offered. "It is essential that I keep our location and our route here as much of a secret as possible. Trust is hard-earned around here, and Dakarai has eyes and ears everywhere. Until you've proven your worth, precautions must be taken. I hope you understand, Hatch."

Hatch nodded, and her door opened. She then felt his hands guiding her out of the truck. As the man leaned closer to assist her, she smelled a distinct blend of lemon zest and eucalyptus, sweet and refreshing. She wondered how he maintained the fragrant bouquet under such hot, oppressive conditions. Hatch was slick with the sweat. The hard work and labor of the morning coupled with the long, poorly air-conditioned ride to her current location gave her a much less pleasing personal aroma.

Jabari gave a slight tug at the knotted end and lifted the handkerchief blindfold from her eyes. Sunlight penetrated through her closed eyes. She slowly let the light in, blinking rapidly against the sudden injection of sunlight after the dark of the last hour of transport. As her surroundings came into focus, she saw that she was in a small clearing surrounded by high trees. The road which led in was barely a path, and she was impressed Jabari was able to navigate the truck through the winding passage.

There were several small huts and a larger building set back from the rest. It was solidly built, a bunker of concrete cinder blocks and mortar.

"So, this is it?" Hatch asked. "This is your compound?"

"It's not much, I know," Jabari said. "But it suffices for what we need, shelter and training ground, and a weapons cache. Right now, we're in the midst of a civil war brewing, one that has humble beginnings. But if we don't act, it will leave the people of this region at the mercy of Dakarai and the puppeteer who controls him."

"I assume you know who is doing the controlling, who is egging him on, driving him forward?" Hatch asked.

"We have our ideas. Nothing confirmed yet. To be quite honest, it's why I was so guarded with you," he said.

Hatch listened, thought for a moment. "So, you think it's a westerner? You think it's military?"

Jabari shrugged. "We'll talk more later. First, there's some things you must go through before I can really allow you to settle in here. If things don't work in your favor, and you don't earn the trust of my people, then I'm sorry to say, Miss Hatch, but this will be the last you see of us. And I will return you to the café. We are selective in who we allow in. There is a test that everybody must pass. Does this make sense to you?"

Hatch nodded. She knew exactly what he was talking about. They needed to know she could carry her weight if she was to work with them. She needed to prove that she could hold her own. Hatch understood, having been through several such situations herself. She knew it was vital to gain their trust.

She knew the question about her father's death and solving that piece of the equation might die here in Africa. She wasn't sure what McCarthy planned to share with her. She hoped it would be enough to at least give her some closure. And who knows, maybe when all was said and done, when she had the answer, she could return home and to the potential of the life she left behind.

She leveled a gaze at Jabari. "I understand. I'm ready for whatever it is you need me to do to prove my worth to you and your men," she said.

"Please wait here. I'll be right back," Jabari said.

Hatch stood still. A slight breeze came through but didn't help much in alleviating the sweltering heat surrounding her. The trees, although they provided some shade, also blocked most of the wind and stymied the circulation of air.

She looked on as heads popped out from some of the huts. Five men joined Jabari when he returned to her. There was a large man with him, well over six feet tall and thick with muscles. He was dark as night and had a raw intensity to him like a caged animal released into the wild for the first time.

If Hatch was a different person, she might even be intimidated. She steadied her nerves, not knowing what was coming next. The men stood back at the center of the compound. Jabari continued to where Hatch stood. The smell of lemon zest and eucalyptus entered her nostrils again as he closed in.

"Are you ready?" he whispered.

"As ready as I'll ever be," Hatch offered, not quite sure still what the plan was, but willing to go along. She followed Jabari back to the men who were standing in a haphazard semi-circle.

"This is Dubaku. He's our strongest man. And he's your test."

Dubaku began rolling his shoulders and loosening his neck.

"You must grapple him. Time to show us what you got," Jabari said.

Hatch gave the large African closer inspection. There wasn't an ounce of fat on the man. He was a towering figure, maybe 6'3" or 6'4" if she had to guess, pushing somewhere in the range of two hundred seventy-five lean pounds of muscle. And unlike the large biker she had dealt with in New Mexico, this man looked combat-seasoned and capable.

Dubaku said nothing. He gave a respectful nod like a boxer before a match, touching gloves. Hatch did likewise and stepped forward.

Dubaku took a step back and planted the ball of his right foot, bringing his large fists up to chest height.

Hatch assumed a similar stance but kept her hands loose and open.

They were now about six feet apart. Hatch knew there'd be no announcement. It wasn't a sparring match. This was the kind of fight where rules, points, and referees didn't exist. Winning would come at a cost, just as losing would. She braced for what was coming.

Her strategy was simple: wait and counter. Learn her opponent and see how he moved, get a feel for him. She hoped it wouldn't prove to be a mistake. Hatch hoped if he landed any punches, she'd be able to withstand the blows.

Hatch guessed the larger man would see her thin, wiry frame and the fact that she was female, and miscalculate his attack. Actually, she was banking on his underestimation of her, at least at the onset, in those first few seconds of the bout. Hatch knew once she moved and countered, he'd realize he was in for a real fight.

Dubaku's moves were quicker than Hatch expected them to be. As large as he was, she expected him to be more telegraphed, more pronounced. But he wasn't. He stepped in quickly and shot his hand out in a jab that caught her in the upper shoulder. She slipped it just in time to miss the intended target, her jaw. Instead, it impacted her damaged right shoulder, sending a tingle down to her fingertips. It was a hard blow. Had it connected with her chin, highly likely she would have been knocked unconscious or at least staggered to a point where a secondary blow would have ended it. *Not the way she wanted this match to go*, Hatch thought. A knockout in the opening seconds of the challenge wouldn't be much of a way of proving herself to the group.

Unacceptable. Hatch was angry at herself. *I'm not going down that easy. Not today. Not ever.*

The big man followed through with an overhand right accompanied by a left elbow strike. His moves were quick, crisp, and concise.

Hatch saw them coming just a split second beforehand, allowing her to parry the blows. Dubaku's thick elbow grazed her cheekbone, another blow that would have rendered her unconscious if not shattering her jaw.

His near miss exposed the side of his neck. Hatch struck hard with an elbow of her own, slamming her forearm into the man's trunk-sized neck. Her left elbow and forearm crashed into the soft, thick meat between his jaw and trapezius. The blow was hard but not hard enough. It staggered him, but Dubaku immediately righted himself.

He actually paused long enough to give Hatch a smile. She could see he was happily surprised he had an opponent in her, that this wasn't going to be a one punch knockout. Hatch smiled back, determined he wasn't going to have an easy victory, if a victory at all.

Smile still on his face, Dubaku dove at her and tried to swallow her up in a bear hug. Hatch sidestepped, jumping just out of reach. His arm snagged the thin, long sleeve of her Lycra shirt and tugged it. She fought against his forward momentum and used a two-hand grip to apply a wrist lock. Hatch then kicked hard with her right leg against the outside of his shin near the ankle. Hooking his leg, she jerked him back toward her and used his locked arm to give her additional leverage and control in the takedown. Spinning the large man off balance, he collapsed on his right side.

Hatch realized she only had a split second to capitalize on her advantage and moved around behind him. He still held on to a bit of her shirt, which started to separate and stretch. She used it to her advantage, and she wrapped her sleeve around his neck. Hatch then hooked her legs around his body, mounting his back.

Dubaku had effectively created a noose with the Lycra material of her sleeve. Locking her body tight against his, Hatch took his back and now controlled him.

She arced back, pulling with her damaged right arm with the heavy scar tissue. The movement cinched the sleeve tight around his neck, effectively cutting off his oxygen.

Hatch pulled it tighter and Dubaku, now desperate for air, started reaching up and trying to separate his throat from the material. It was too late. The shirt sleeve was deep-set, biting into his flesh. The more he struggled, the tighter it went. His fingers clawed at his throat as he gasped for breath. Hatch's legs constricted, pushing against his diaphragm. Hatch knew when his oxygen was deprived, a rapid descent into the unconscious approached.

She could feel the large man begin to panic. He began to buck wildly, arcing his back, kicking his legs against the ground he was pinned to. Somehow under enormous effort and physical strain, miraculously, Dubaku pushed himself up from the ground. He was now in a staggered, half-hunched position.

Hatch was still tightly latched onto his back. Her legs tight around his mid-section, she squeezed her thighs together, hoping to squeeze out any last bits of air, increasing the pressure on his diaphragm. At the same time, she pulled the Lycra shirt tighter around the man's neck. She attacked his capacity to breathe. He spun wildly and flailed his arms.

She heard a raspy squeal escape the big man's throat, but it was barely audible over the grunt of exertion from Hatch as she leveled all of her strength into maintaining her position.

His hands reached to his midsection and Dubaku tried desperately to separate her feet hooked together at the ankles. He was looking for any way to try to relieve some of the pressure, either on the diaphragm or the throat, but finding no success on either front.

She felt the grip on her ankles weaken. He was strong, but his reserves were waning. Dubaku staggered again. This time forward, down to one knee, then the other. And then his body lurched forward, like a tree after a final blow from an axe. His hands shot out at the last second, catching his body's weight, slowing himself enough not to land face first into the dirt below. Hatch remained on his back with her weight pressing down at the center of his shoulder blades.

Dubaku succumbed to her assault and collapsed into the ground, unmoving.

Hatch immediately released the Lycra binding from his throat and separated her leg lock, although it took some wiggling to get the big man's heavy bulk off her right leg. She pushed herself off and then rolled him onto his back and checked his pulse, faint but there. She felt the slow ragged breath return. The autonomic nervous system kicking back into play. Oxygen would soon be returning, and he would begin his recovery.

Dubaku inhaled loudly and clasped at his throat, his eyes wide. He half sat up and then collapsed onto his back, still recovering from the restraint recently removed from his neck. He spit into the dirt and rolled to his side. Still clasping his throat with his left hand, he brought himself to his knees. He looked around.

Hatch sat on the dirt next to him. Seeing her, even in his painful condition, he managed to give her a nod and a wink.

"Well done, little lady," he said through raspy breaths.

Hatch shrugged, not knowing exactly what to say.

Jabari then grabbed Hatch by the arm, hoisted her up to a standing position and took her hand in his. "Hatch, that was truly impressive," he said. "Duke is not a man easily bested. To be honest, nobody has ever managed to do so. I have to say, I did not expect to see that from you."

"So, how about it then? Are you going to work with me, help me get what I want?" Hatch asked.

Jabari gave a soft smile. "I think you would be a great asset to us. Maybe once you hear our plan, you'll see that we already have some things in motion, and we could use your help if you'd be willing."

Hatch let a slight smile cross her face.

FIFTEEN

HATCH LEARNED Jabari's men had a tradition in their small unit. Once one's worth was proven, they celebrated with a small, hearty feast prepared by the loser. As big as Dubaku was, Hatch wasn't surprised he was an impressive cook as well. The goat was seasoned in lemon juice, garlic, and other spices Hatch wasn't familiar with before being slow roasted over the open flame of the fire pit. Vegetables stewed in a cast iron pot on the indirect heat.

Hatch took in the smells encircling the small camp and salivated as Dubaku plated the dish and served her first.

"Winners eat first," Dubaku said, handing her the aluminum plate.

"Thank you, Dubaku," Hatch said.

"Call me Duke," he said.

"Oh, here we go again." Jabari laughed.

The rest of Jabari's men joined in the laughter.

"What'd I miss?" Hatch asked.

"Dubaku is a huge fan of John Wayne films and tries to get everyone to call him The Duke," Jabari offered.

Dubaku, apparently numb to this chastising, continued serving the group their food without any rebuttal.

"Well, I for one like it." Hatch gave big Dubaku a wink and smile as she forked a mouthful of the goat and vegetables into her mouth. "And this food is absolutely amazing," she offered as she swallowed.

Duke smiled, either at her defense of his nickname or her compliment of the food. Hatch wasn't sure which. What she was sure of was that this meal would rival Khari's offerings at his café, but Hatch would keep that to herself. She did miss the man's tea as she took a sip of beer.

Jabari's soldiers and Hatch sat around the fire as evening began to give way to night. The joking subsided as the group turned the topic of discussion to their plans for taking down the warlord. Jabari laid out what they had as far as equipment, weapons, and personnel. Right now, his small militia force really consisted of a total of seven men, now eight with Hatch, should she choose to join. Each member of the group had specific taskings, as it would be with any Special Forces operation group. This was an essential piece for any small unit tactics, each person was assigned areas of responsibility that were task specific and would come into play should the need arise.

Jabari's men had been planning an assault raid on the warlord's operation for quite some time. They had conducted small raids on various outposts and caravans, grabbing weapons, destroying transportation. But they'd never made a formative assault on Dakarai's compound. Jabari said an attack of that nature might be possible, but it would most likely be a guaranteed death sentence for any who tried.

Hatch learned Jabari's unit had amassed a detailed amount of information about the warlord's compound. Jabari, although he didn't disclose his source, had a decent level of intel within Dakarai's organization. It was the bread and butter of any military unit: They required and thrived on intelligence. From what Hatch could gather, it appeared Jabari had created a formidable network, although his unit's numbers were low and, therefore, he'd never tried to take the warlord head on.

But in looking at the problem, Hatch saw that they were thinking of it in terms of numbers of men as the major factor. Dakarai had many more and therefore was deemed untouchable. And although their style of warfare was guerrilla in nature, they hadn't quite grasped the concept of force multipliers. Hatch listened to the discussion quietly, building up enough mental ammo for her arsenal when she was to counterpoint some of their tactics.

When Jabari finished laying out the details of the compound and the plans for their next raid, which was supposed to be an ammo cache, Hatch decided to ante in.

"Do you mind if I speak, Jabari?" Hatch knew that by asking permission rather than asserting herself, she would allow the unit's leader to save face should she call into question any of the tactics or plans being discussed. There was always a political aspect to any operation, to any unit. She knew that better than most, having just had a confrontation with Chris Bennett for his treatment of her in the wake of their team's disaster overseas. Hatch knew the delicate balance of these units, the leadership and the men, or women, who served in them. All were alphas in their own right, all jockeying for some bit of position. But to be a good soldier, one must be a good follower. So, Hatch understood the very delicate balance she needed to strike when saying her piece.

"Go ahead, Hatch. Is this the fresh eyes you were talking to me about before we came?"

"It is," she said. "I listened to you discuss your past raids, the ones with success, and the ones that were less successful. I listened to you talk about the details of the compound that is the base for the warlord's operations. And it sounds like you have a great deal of intelligence on the man, how he operates, and the number of personnel and weapons he has. I won't ask you how you got that information. I can only assume."

The other men around the fire looked at each other and then looked back at Hatch. They seemed interested in what she had to say.

"It seems to me that you look at these problems, these situations as a numbers game. You attack these convoys and outposts because they have less men. It makes sense, but I think you're missing an opportunity," Hatch said.

"How so?" Jabari asked.

"You look for small convoys. Your aim is destructing bits and pieces.

But cut a snake at the tail end, and it continues to move. Cut the head off, and what happens?"

"I get it. I understand, Hatch," Jabari said. "You want to avenge these villagers. These villagers, Miss Hatch, are my people. I've been trying to avenge them, to protect them, to lead us back to a civilized order and not let this warlord set us back twenty years. But you can plainly see we are a small unit. We're not ready to fight Dakarai face-to-face. The villagers are not ready for that fight. We simply do not have the numbers to compete. So, we pick the battles we know we have a higher percentage of winning from time to time. Those are the missions that we take. I do not take my responsibility to my people lightly."

Hatch realized that her opening remarks might have offended the man, and she quickly countered. "Jabari, please don't take me wrong. I think what you and your men have done is honorable and that you have done a great job fighting and protecting the people of the villages around here. And I see what you have done and the challenges you face. But I think there is another way."

Jabari seemed flustered by her comments. He rested his half-eaten plate of food on a rock in front of him, then folded his arms, and sat silently. It was Duke who took up for her. "Jabari, why don't we listen to Hatch and see what she has to say," he asked. His voice was a thick baritone, and very commanding. It went well with the size of the man. "Isn't it what you always say? There's more than one way to skin a cat. That's one of your American phrases. Let me hear how you would skin this cat, Miss Hatch," Duke said with a slight smile, and then he rubbed his throat, still slightly hoarse from the strangulation that had rendered him unconscious a few hours ago. And that was the way of combat. She'd earned his respect on a platform which they both understood, and now there was an invisible bond, a warrior's code.

"Thank you, Duke," Hatch said. "All I'm saying, and it's really simple, is what if we use the numbers we have, coupled with all of the intel you've already gathered? What if we can detour some of those forces away from the compound, create a distraction? Something that brings them away from the stronghold, and then we counter, set a trap, and draw them in. You have the weapons. You have the equipment. It wouldn't be that hard. Divide and conquer. It's a force equalizer. We bring the numbers to a manageable amount. It's not without high risk, but if we can do that, and then have a counter assault at the same time in a different location where there are fewer forces, we have a better chance of entering into their compound. And then hopefully, if your intel proves to be right, and it sounds like your network is solid, we can cut the head off the snake."

Duke laughed. "I don't know where you got this woman from, Jabari. But I like her. And I like the plan," he said, his inflection adding weight to his support.

Jabari loosened his folded arms and seemed to be coming around. "So, what exactly do you have in mind?" he asked.

"I thought you'd never ask," Hatch said.

SIXTEEN

AFTER THEY FINISHED THEIR MEAL, Hatch spent a great deal of time detailing her idea on how to raid Dakarai's compound. It seemed she had won the group's support, including Jabari's.

"When are we making the raid?" Hatch asked.

"Not so fast, Hatch." Jabari said. "You proved yourself to be worthy in the ring with Duke. We were all impressed by that."

Duke nodded his agreement and broke into the wide grin she'd become familiar with in the short time they've spent together.

Jabari continued, "But you must understand something, to truly be tested—to truly earn this group's trust, you must come out with us on a raid. There is no better way to determine a soldier's worth than when you stand side-by-side with them against the enemy."

Hatch understood what he said. She knew it better than most. She knew there was a disparity that occurred between training and the real world. The ability to handle oneself in a controlled training environment, even if it was intense and dangerous, could still be totally different in the way one handled themselves on the battlefield. She'd seen soldiers who could post record setting times on obstacle courses and live fire drills be unable to perform in combat. Hatch had seen some soldiers who'd proven themselves in training fall short in their ability to carry through on the actual battlefield when the bullets started flying and IEDs were exploding around them.

Hatch herself would forever be haunted by the moment of hesitation which cost one of her best friend's life. It was etched in her memory forever and something she punished herself for daily. So, she understood Jabari's need to test her in the field before any major operation. She just didn't know what that field test would be.

"I understand, Jabari. What do you have in mind?" she asked.

"One of my sources has given us intel that there is a cache of medical supplies and food reserves. These items were stolen by Dakarai's men while on the way to support one of the villages in need. I know the location where they are being kept. I would like to get those supplies and bring them back to the village they were intended for, the one your priest friend has been helping. They're in dire need of medical attention and the hospitals can only do so much. The minor wounds can become terribly infected, and those people will need the medication. And plus, with all the damage to their village, the ability to provide for their families and the young children will be limited, and so I'd like to bring them food. But it will be risky, Miss Hatch. Extremely dangerous stuff. Even on smaller missions, we have lost many of our good men. I want you to understand what's at stake. By agreeing to come with us, you are putting your life in great danger. And I will think no less of you if you decide to back out now," he said.

Hatch didn't take offense at Jabari's warning. She understood it was done for the sake of giving her an out, subtly reminding her the fight wasn't hers and that in joining them her risk would be great. Once again reminding her that this was not her country, and these were not her people. But Hatch didn't bite. She didn't take the bait, didn't turn and ask to leave.

Instead, she smiled. "I'll go wherever you guys go. I'll prove myself worthy, and then we can move past this. Actually, I think it's a good idea to handle a small run first, something that can provide aid to the people.

And once they're stabilized, then we can worry about the much bigger problem," she said.

"Then it's agreed." Jabari said. "We'll brief the plans, and I'll show you exactly where we're going and how we plan to implement it. Again, we'll accept your fresh eye perspective, if you have some input for us that you think would benefit the operation. But as of now, we've gotten quite good at these smaller raids."

Jabari and his men stood up from their seats around the campfire. Hatch followed as Jabari led the group to the bunker at the back of the camp.

Inside the concrete room, she saw a large handmade wooden table occupied the center of the room. A desk was set against the back wall and had a pile of stacked papers on it.

Upon further inspection of the table, Hatch noticed there was a mockup of the plans for their upcoming raid. It was a detailed field table. She had used them quite often in briefing and preparation for her operations overseas. Sometimes these battleplans were done on the move with nothing more than a couple of sticks and some rocks piled together in the sand. But when there was time, and an operation dictated extreme precision, as many of hers did, mockups were used. They were then followed by rehearsals.

The layout of the replica in front of her showed that the men in this room were well-trained, well-organized. Even if they were wearing brightly colored Hawaiian shirts and looked better dressed for a luau than a combat operation.

"This is a workup replica of the location where they've stashed the stolen supplies. It's based on some photographs and information I received from one of my sources. I would say it's fairly accurate. I trust the man who gave this to me, so it should be relatively current. If you look here in the corner, there's a small hut."

Hatch looked at the box set in that particular part of the mockup. There was loose string around it.

"This is where they have some razor wire set around it. My source tells me that this is where they are keeping the supplies. It's only a temporary location. The convoy of med supplies was intercepted a few days ago. So, it is possible that we could get there and find it has already been moved. But I think under the current circumstances, with all the injured at the village, it is worth the risk right now," Jabari said.

"How many troops do they leave as a security detail for this?" Hatch asked.

"Dakarai keeps most of his men with him. He has many enemies. Right now, with the current unrest, lots of people will be gunning for him, and some within his own ranks. Because of this, Dakarai keeps a large contingency of soldiers with him. That leaves outposts like this less protected. He leaves maybe four to eight men, depending. If there are more men, we can assume the supplies will still be inside. If he only has a few, sadly to say, it might be a wasted and unnecessarily dangerous operation with little to no yield. If nothing else, we'll add a few new weapons to our arsenal."

Hatch understood. There was probably no government assistance for a rebel like Jabari and his men. Weapons, ammunition, and supplies gathered were done so on the field of combat. Taking the enemy's weapon was smart for several reasons, especially in conditions and circumstances like this. It was a quick resupply. And if the weapons were comparable, then interchangeable parts, such as firing pins, barrels, things that could be traded out when one got damaged, added to Jabari's team's ability to maintain readiness. Ammunition would always be in constant demand, especially when battles raged with increasing frequency. This would not only be a supply run for the village, but also for Jabari's men.

What she liked about Jabari's plan was he had the foresight to know the risks. He weighed them beforehand, and he had no preconceived notions of success. It was a failing of many leaders she'd seen in the past who had a winner-take-all attitude. And typically, in those mindsets, they dismissed the possibility of failure or shortcomings with the operation.

During Hatch's time with Task Force Banshee, they'd always played the contingency game. Murphy's Law was a son of a bitch and seemed to pop up at the worst possible times. Expect the worst and hope for the best. Jabari seemed to be of this same mindset. And she was impressed.

She was further impressed by the man's desire to help the villagers, not only as a warrior and protector, but also in the humanitarian efforts. He was this region's version of Robin Hood. Overseas, she'd worked with numerous militia groups and done extensive counterinsurgency. Many times, the people were fighting for their homeland, sometimes out of anger for what had happened to them personally. And she was sure Jabari had his share of horrors in his life. But what impressed her most was that he seemed genuinely concerned for the benefit and wellbeing of the people.

Jabari's leadership attributes would make a great leader anywhere. Hatch could see why these men would give their lives for him, why they were devoted to him. It was in that moment that she understood why Chris Bennett had given her Jabari's number. Bennett trusted this man completely.

Jabari looked at her. "So, Hatch, what do you think?"

She scanned the model on the table. "I think it's a good plan. It's loose enough that we can adapt to the numbers. You have a rough estimate for how much opposition we may face when we get there. Smart enough to know that it may not yield anything. And we know the point at which we might have to cut our losses. But I think with the men you have here, they have the capability to execute this."

"Okay then, this is our approach pattern. Let's go into the details," Jabari said with eagerness. "We're going to come in from here. It's a little rough going because of the terrain, but it will give us added cover. It's very thick brush, and my source tells me because of the terrain, they don't watch that area as much as the other side where the road goes in. The main entrance is the most heavily guarded side for obvious reasons. So, we're going to approach from this side." Jabari paused and put his hand on his chin. "Hatch, I've been thinking about what you said about the other plan for drawing fire or attention and pulling them in. And looking at this model now, I have an idea maybe you'd like to assist with."

Hatch was all ears. "Sure. Go ahead."

"How about you and I come down the main path here. Obviously, not in plain view, but we will approach by the more direct route. When in place, we'll lay down suppressive fire to the front, better enabling my men to access from the rear. And hopefully, we'll have the element of surprise once inside the compound."

"I like it," Hatch said. She also liked it because in the plan's design she saw that Jabari trusted his men completely. Another winning point in his leadership ability was that he realized capable soldiers did not need to be micromanaged. They could be given a task, and if you trusted them enough and knew their skill sets were strong enough, good leaders allowed them to carry out a mission without oversight. It was the only way specialized groups, or small teams, worked effectively. Sometimes it was one person taking the high ground while others moved around below. Trust was essential. Without it, things just fell apart.

Hatch compared these traits with that of Bennett. And maybe that's what happened after the fallout from the operation that rendered her right arm partially lame. The trust had been fractured. Looking at things in hindsight, maybe Bennett was right to cut her loose at that time. Her head wasn't in it for a while afterward, and it took her a long time to come back. Standing around the table with Jabari and his men, Hatch found it in her heart to forgive Chris Bennett. She was in a different place, on a different battlefield, and fighting a different war. Hatch suddenly realized she was right where she needed to be. The calm in the storm. Strangely, she took some peace in that.

"When do we leave?" Hatch asked.

"We'll get an early sleep tonight. I like to leave well before daybreak. It'll make the going hard in the dark, but if we can get there while they're most tired, we'll have the advantage. They are human, and I'd like to catch them just as dawn begins to break, as their eyes adjust to the light of day. You know that feeling when morning strikes you after being awake all night? It's hard to concentrate," he said.

Hatch nodded in agreement. "BMNT."

"BMNT? What's that?" Jabari asked.

"Before morning nautical twilight. It's something we used to say in the military. It was the best time to do an early morning attack. Right when the light starts to break. And you're right, it's disorienting. The body and mind have to adjust to the transition. And if the guards have been awake and they're pulling shifts, we're going to catch them at their most depleted state. Perfect timing. Well thought out," Hatch said.

"Well, I'm glad you agree with me. It sounds like the mission is a go." Jabari looked at his watch.

"Let's get some shut eye now. A few hours should do us some good. Then we'll set out in the middle of the night. You can sleep in here if you like. I have a roll out cot over there. Sometimes I use this room, but most of the time I stay in my hut. Nobody will bother you in here. You'll have all the privacy you need."

"Thank you, Jabari. The cot should be fine. And I'm not that private a person," Hatch lied. She kept her damaged arm hidden. She thought of Khari, the cafe owner with his burn scars visible for all to see and the fact that he didn't hide them from the world. The fact he didn't may have enabled him to move past that horrific moment in time. Hatch decided to take a lesson from the man's life notebook.

The other men departed. Jabari hung back for a moment and looked at Hatch, "Thank you for deciding to help us, Hatch. It's nice to have an extra hand. The more the merrier, right?"

He seemed to be trying to make light of the circumstances. But she knew the weight of a leader the night before sending his men off to battle, knowing well the possibility not all of them might be coming back. It was a heavy burden, no matter the battlefield. In the short interim since she'd met Jabari, she'd learned the good-natured heart of this man, this warrior, and knew that those decisions must weigh heavily on him. In those quiet hours of the night when he had to think of the fallen, the ones that had saddled up and gone side-by-side into the fight with him. Hatch knew this all too well.

"Thank you for having me, Jabari. It means a lot to me, and I'm glad I'm able to help. Hopefully tomorrow I'll prove my worth to you and maybe we can bring about an end, if not for good at least temporarily, to the devastation your people are facing at the hands of that savage, Dakarai."

As Jabari opened the door to leave, Hatch said, "Have you ever heard of Robin Hood, Jabari?"

He laughed. "Kevin Costner." And followed with a big smile.

"You remind me a lot of him."

His smile got wider, dimpling his dark cheeks. "Get your rest, Miss Hatch. The morning will be here before you know it." He walked out and closed the door behind him.

SEVENTEEN

HATCH DIDN'T SLEEP WELL. Not because the cot was too uncomfortable, as she'd slept in much worse conditions. It was the thought of the morning's events to come. Though she was battle-hardened, the eve of an operation like this always stirred a plethora of emotions.

Some good positive energy flowed from the nerves that came with an operation, enabling soldiers to push themselves beyond normal boundaries. The other part causing her lack of restful sleep was a deep pang of anxiety. Any operator worth his or her salt would tell you there's a level of fear that goes into every operation. To operate without it can be dangerous.

Pre-planned operations always carried an element of fear, sometimes more palpable than others. On this morning, she felt it more than she had in the past, or at least in her recent past. Possibly because it had been well over a year since she'd operated in this type of situation in a true war zone where there would be multiple enemies. For all intents and purposes, this was a military mission, far different from her recent experiences in Hawk's Landing and Luna Vista. Those were different for a multitude of reasons.

This was a true battlefield, and the last time she'd suited up under these conditions, it had nearly cost her her life, as it had for other members of her team. She hoped this morning's operation would yield different results, and in doing so, help her get back to full operational speed. Like riding a bike. Some things never went away.

Hatch sat up and stretched, her body popping in various places, joints loosening from the rigid position she'd laid in for the last few hours. Sleep never really took hold. Her eyes had been closed, but her mind was active and alert. She was replaying the mission, picturing the mockup table in her head, the layout, committing it to memory, knowing that in these early morning hours, her eyes would be adjusting as well.

She stood up and lit an oil lamp on the desk. The dim yellow light was cast across the mock-up, giving it a fire-lit view, throwing shadows amongst the little boxes, twigs, and bits of string used to design the layout of their objective. Hatch stared at it for a few minutes and then heard a tap at the door.

"Miss Hatch." It was Jabari's voice. "Are you decent?"

"Come in, Jabari," Hatch said. "I'm already up."

He entered. His bright Hawaiian shirt had now been traded for an olive drab polo. He would blend into the darkness.

For Hatch, most of her clothes were dull and muted anyway. She wore a short sleeve shirt today, revealing her scarred arm and honoring her new decision to not hide from who she was anymore. If anyone would respect and understand, it would be men like Jabari and his crew.

It would be the first step to making herself whole again. She would no longer hide that piece of herself from the world. Today Hatch wore a tight black dry fit shirt, accentuating her wiry, muscled frame that was typically hidden under loose baggy shirts. She had cargo pants on, a rip-proof material which would serve her well in the jungle terrain. Hatch tied her shoulder length hair back into a tight ponytail and cinched down a black baseball cap.

"Good to see you're ready to go this morning," Jabari said. "Couldn't sleep?"

"I never can before something like this. Mind starts racing, replaying and hashing out alternatives."

"Me neither. I've been up half the night," he said.

She assumed this would be the case. Being the leader of an operation like this, he would be running through the plan a thousand times over in his mind. It was his job to be the first up, to be ready to go, and to get everything situated before the others awoke. Leaders led from the front, and Hatch could plainly see Jabari was one of those men.

"Are the others up?" Hatch asked.

"Everybody but Duke. He's slow to rise. I think slower now because you choked him good yesterday." He laughed at his own joke.

"All in a day's work," Hatch offered, following with a mock bow.

"Are you ready?" Jabari asked.

"I'm as ready as I'll ever be. Not for nothing, but I hope I'm not going there and using my hand-to-hand skills? Do you have a weapon for me?" she asked.

"But of course. I have a small caliber Beretta nine-millimeter and an MP5. Are you comfortable with both weapon systems?"

Hatch knew both guns well, having used them in a variety of capacities, on a variety of operations in her past. "I know them both well, and I'll be good to go. Thank you."

Jabari went over to a wall locker, a large safe-like rectangular box in the corner of the room, and unlatched it. Inside was a small cache of weapons. He removed the guns and took out spare magazines already loaded. Hatch preferred to load her own weapons but didn't argue under the circumstances.

She depressed the top round on each of the magazines to check the spring, and then tapped them against the desk to ensure they were stacked, an old habit. He also handed her a Kydex drop-down holster for the Beretta. The MP5 came with a single point sling. It took her less than a minute to get herself loaded out with both weapons.

Hatch slipped the last magazine into a pouch and looked at Jabari, "Good to go."

She noticed that Jabari had a similar load out, but he also carried several flashbangs on a small bandolier strapped across his shoulder.

"Good idea taking those," Hatch said, nodding toward the distractionary devices.

"It'll definitely wake them up. I should probably use these things for Duke. Maybe he'd get his lazy ass out of his cot." Once again, he chuckled at his own joke. "It'll be our initiation signal that the assault is underway. We'll bang the front guards, which should draw them toward us. And then hopefully the flashbang will give us a moment's advantage so the rest of the team can gain the upper hand."

"Sounds like you've got it all planned out," Hatch said. "I feel like I'm in good hands."

Jabari's face was now serious. She knew the weighty burden resting squarely on his shoulders. With only a few minutes to go before they'd head out for their operation, the weight of leadership, the cost of doing business on the battlefield and the potential fallout, both physical and psychological, were burdensome creatures. But he bore them well.

"I'll be outside, when you're ready. Duke's waking the others. We're leaving in five minutes," he said and then exited.

Five minutes. Five minutes and a new battle would begin for her. Across the world from her last confrontation, in a wholly different environment, but integrally similar in so many regards. The town of Luna Vista had been under the control of a vicious gang. The power and control they had over the good people living there was not unlike here. Hatch had been able to right that wrong and was hoping to be able to repeat the process here.

Worlds apart yet the same. Although the firepower she'd be facing today was far greater, and her likelihood of survival decreased with those odds. But she deemed it a risk worth taking. She deemed these good people were worth saving. And she knew deep down, her father would agree.

Pick your battles, and make sure you win. Something her father had said to her not long before he died. The saying had stuck with her. *Pick your battles.* Here and now she'd picked her fight. Now it was time to make sure she won.

DARKEST BEFORE THE DAWN. They had moved under the cover of night. Jabari and company had taken a gutted Astro Van, similar to the one Hatch's mother drove back in Hawk's Landing. They were tightly packed in it. In spite of the mixture of body odor, Hatch could still smell the lemon scent of Jabari's skin.

Duke was the driver. Apparently, it was the only way the enormous man could comfortably fit in the van. He stopped it about two miles up the road from their intended target.

He pulled their vehicle into the thick brush along the side of the road. The group quickly worked to grab foliage from the neighboring trees and bushes. The branches gave it camouflage. Although, once the fighting started, it wouldn't really matter anymore. The van was their final rally point. After supplies were gathered, they would return here--hopefully, all of them.

They departed the van on foot, the team splitting into the two elements. Hatch and Jabari set out, skirting the road. It was more of a trail than a roadway, the remaining two miles leading down into the gated entrance and heavily guarded checkpoint. Duke and the remaining men went down the deep ravine to the right and were going to work their way back up through the dense foliage toward the weak point in the small compound's defenses.

They moved quickly in the dark. Jabari was obviously accustomed to the area. Hatch stumbled only a couple of times but found her footing and eventually was able to keep stride relatively easily with the native African. They didn't run, but rather moved at a quick shuffle. The two made decent time, pushing a 12-minute mile pace. No land speed records were being broken this morning, but it was quick enough it wouldn't take them all morning to get there. They didn't want to move so fast that it would be a run and leave them depleted when they arrived. Plus, it was imperative to minimize noise. Even quiet clinks of metal from the gear they wore would be foreign sounds in a jungle environment. And so, they adhered to noise discipline as they trekked toward their objective.

Less than half an hour later, they arrived at the point Jabari had deemed most suitable for engaging their enemy. It was dark, a deep darkness, the type of dark that comes just before light breaks.

They settled into position and waited. The silence was now replaced by the chirps and buzz of the jungle as it resumed its balance from the momentary interruption of their arrival.

Hatch could see two men positioned on either side of the road. One was smoking, obviously passing the time. But a poor choice by a sentry, especially one working in the dark. Every time he tugged on the cigarette, the embers brightly lit his face, and in turn, took away his natural night vision. Every toke of the cigarette was an advantage in their favor.

They scanned for any other guards. A few men were set back in the deep recesses of the compound. Hatch counted four at this point. She was slightly disheartened. If the count was true at four, then it would likely mean they had moved the supplies. This mission could be a dangerous gamble with a limited chance of recovering the materials. It looked as though the advantage was now tipped in their favor, based on the number of Dakarai's men currently visible within the compound.

Risk versus reward. It was weighed heavily in those final seconds before the engagement was to commence.

Hatch and Jabari were hunkered down behind a large rock and a line of huge trees acted as a natural fence line, providing them with additional cover for their firing position.

The two guards closest to them, at the front gate, didn't even look in their general direction. They were at the tail end of a long night of standing guard. It's difficult to maintain vigilance for long hours. Time and lack of activity weakened a guard's acuity. This type of duty, the night watch, was often reserved for the low man on the totem pole. Hatch had experienced it firsthand as a military police officer. The midnight shift was primarily filled by the junior personnel. More senior people seized the opportunity rank provided by adhering to a more regular lifestyle. Nobody really wanted to be up all night and sleep during the day. Although, in Africa, maybe it was the opposite. The days were so hot maybe nighttime was sought out.

Regardless, both men appeared weary. A slow night was coming to a close. Idle chit chat had probably dropped off hours ago. Now, they put every ounce of energy into keeping themselves awake, passing time by smoking cigarettes and staring off into the darkness. It was highly probable these guards stayed awake purely out of fear, not of any group of marauders, but more likely because of Dakarai and what he would do if he arrived to find them sleeping. Hatch could only begin to imagine the dire consequence for failing to perform duties for such a man. Fear was a great motivator.

Jabari looked down at his watch. He had a rough calculation of how long it would take for the others to reach their side of the compound. The lemon-scented man looked over at Hatch and gave a thumbs up.

"They should be in position now. Are you ready?" Jabari asked.

Hatch nodded. And without saying a word, brought her MP5 up, pulling the butt of the stock into the pocket of her shoulder. Her cheek pressed flush against the cool, smooth fabricated extension, the tip of her nose brushing against the submachinegun's frame. Hatch sighted down the rear aperture of the factory iron sights of the weapon. The front sight post oscillated at her target's center of mass as she watched the man light another cigarette.

Jabari stirred to her left. From her peripheral vision, she saw him raise up into a low half squat.

Hatch heard the metallic clink as Jabari released one of the flash-bangs from his bandolier followed by a quiet click as he pulled the pin free. Hatch didn't look. She didn't need to. He raised himself just slightly above the rock's top and then she heard a swoosh as the canister went sailing through the air.

Moments later, it dinged on the hardpack ground near the front guards. Through her sights, Hatch watched as her target looked down at it, trying to surmise in that split second what was happening. His cigarette still hung loosely from his lip. Before they could utter a scream, the flashbang erupted with a deafening bang accompanied by a blinding flash of white light.

Hatch was prepared, as was Jabari. Both averted their eyes while maintaining their firing position. Hatch kept her eyes open, but tipped the brim of her hat to block the light.

A split second later, Hatch was back on target. Both guards were temporarily disoriented. Jabari's mark had fallen to the ground. The man with the cigarette staggered back, rubbing his eyes.

Hatch fired twice. The cigarette still hung from the man's mouth as he spiraled to the ground. Jabari came up quickly and fired a succinct shot group of three rounds from his AK47, crumpling the other man. Blood began to taint the dirt around the two fallen guards.

The other two men she'd seen further back in the compound came rushing forward, firing wildly up at the tree line. A few bullets zipped by, striking the tree in front of Hatch, but the barrage quickly moved off to the right of her and away from them. It was obvious these men had no idea where the attack had come from and they were firing blindly. The reinforcements began screaming in Swahili.

Jabari leaned over, "He's calling for more men. There're more men inside. Must've been sleeping."

Two doors to the back of the compound were flung open and more men rushed out. Hatch counted. There was a total of nine, counting the two down in at the front gate. Seven of Dakarai's troops were rushing toward the front of the compound. They joined in on the random, undisciplined gunfire.

Hatch and Jabari waited. There was no need to give away their position just yet. Seconds later, as all the men were now centered toward the front of the compound in a small cluster, an eruption of gunfire came from the far right. Duke and his team had initiated their wave of the plan. Dakarai's soldiers were now caught between by the two-pronged attack.

Jabari's men demonstrated precision in the discharge of their weapons, giving away their veteran experience. Several more of the warlord's men fell victim to the assault. Only three remained standing.

The plan, hatched on the mockup table, was proving to be extremely effective and further proved Jabari's skill as a tactician.

Hatch took aim, firing in the direction of one of the soldiers. The enemy was now scurrying quickly, making the shots more difficult. She saw one of the guards pop out from behind a shack with something in his hand. It took only a moment for Hatch to realize what it was. A grenade.

He pulled the pin and took aim in the direction of Duke and his men.

Hatch raised up and fired twice, the second round striking the man in the head. He dropped the grenade beside him, and seconds later, it exploded.

The fumbled grenade went off with devastating consequence in the proximity of the two remaining enemy combatants, obliterating the remaining men.

In the wake of the blast, there was silence. Firing ceased immediately. Jabari held fast at the ready. Hatch waited, continuing to provide over-watch as she went from target to target, ensuring all nine were no longer moving.

The battle that raged had ended as quickly as it had begun. Based on the speed and surprise of the attack, it was unlikely any of the men had time to radio or call for assistance. But because they had no way to verify that, they had to assume the worst-case scenario in which somebody had managed to send a distress signal. With that in mind, they would have only a few minutes to get in, get what they needed, and then get back out before others might arrive.

Jabari tapped Hatch on her left shoulder. "Ready to move?"

"Moving," she said.

The two stood and began making their way down in tandem. Duke and his men had cut their way in through the fence and met Jabari and Hatch in the middle. They quickly checked each of the downed guards. All were dead. Nine down, no injuries to Jabari's team. A good, successful mission by all accounts.

The grenade blast had damaged several of the weapons, but the ones that were still in good working order were quickly picked up by Duke and his group. Jabari took two men and went to the back structure which contained the medical supplies. They were happy to see a large amount of supplies still inside. They filled the backpacks they had brought with them. When those were full, they stuffed whatever else they could fit inside their pockets.

Jabari's group, plus Hatch, were back out and moving with the supplies, each person carrying a bag full. Hatch carried her load, and Duke and his men carried the remainder of the weapons they had recovered and all the ammunition they could handle.

They used the road for their two-mile return trip. Although the ground was easier to navigate, their pace was impeded by the weight of their newfound gear and supplies. Even with the weight, the group made the jog back to their stashed Astro Van in under eighteen minutes. They moved quickly and made fast work of navigating the roadway.

Hatch was happy to see, as light broke, that their vehicle was there and there were no sounds or signs of an arriving entourage of Dakarai troops. They had effectively neutralized one of his strongholds, quickly and effectively with zero casualties or injuries to any member of their party.

They stole a beat-up old Toyota pickup truck belonging to one of the dead guards. The keys were in the ignition and the supplies were loaded in the bed. Duke drove the van away from the area of their recent assault and headed toward the village in desperate need of the materials and supplies on board.

Hatch felt good. The success of the operation was exhilarating. It provided a psychological counterbalance to her last mission with Taskforce Banshee. For the first time in a long time, she felt a sense of connection to the person she used to be. She didn't realize how much she needed that feeling of success on the battlefield in order to minimize, if not erase, her memory of the moment when she didn't pull the trigger.

Success is measured in a wide variety of ways. And the taking of a human life is never a true success. But in this particular circumstance, the needs, risks, and associated mental fallout from such decisions outweighed everything else.

She wondered what the former operator-turned-Catholic priest would say when she rolled into the village with the lemon-scented Robin Hood and his merry men.

EIGHTEEN

HATCH and her new team rumbled their way into the village. Hatch peeked out from the gap between the driver and front passenger seat. She saw the faces turn at the sound of the arriving van and the fear in their eyes. The trauma of the recent attacks had left them wary of any new arrivals, and it took them a moment before they recognized the convoy wasn't a threat.

McCarthy was standing among a group of villagers, his dark clothing of the priesthood standing out among the brightly colored ensembles of the people surrounding him. His eyes brightened at the sight of Hatch. He looked genuinely happy to see her.

Duke brought the vehicle to a stop. Hatch exited and was greeted with an uncharacteristically warm embrace from the priest.

"Rachel, I'm so glad to see you're okay. I was terribly worried. I know you were in good hands, but these are dangerous times. I see that you've linked up with my friend, Jabari."

Hatch cocked her head and looked over at Jabari, who had overheard the conversation. He shrugged and offered a conciliatory smile.

"As big as Africa is, Miss Hatch, the connections make us feel small. People like Father McCarthy have been helping me and my people for a very long time. And I him. Our goal to revitalize and hopefully bring prosperity to the villages is the same. Only our methods may differ," Jabari said.

" I hope I will be able to assist in furthering that cause," she said.

"Indeed, you will, Miss Hatch. Indeed, you will," Jabari said as he walked away toward the back of the van to begin unloading the supplies they had gathered.

"Father, we have much to give you to help the villagers recover from the recent attacks, both medical and food rations. Hopefully, it will keep you in good stead until you get yourself and these people back on their feet," Duke said, giving the priest a hearty slap on the back.

If Jabari is Robin Hood, then Duke must be Friar Tuck. Hatch laughed to herself.

McCarthy's smile broadened, and he gave a grateful handshake to each of the men who had risked their lives for the benefit of the village, graciously thanking them in Swahili. Jabari's men encircled McCarthy, and they bowed their heads. The priest then gave what Hatch could only assume was a blessing.

Strange how the hand of God is so close to the hand of vengeance. These men had just spilt the blood of nine others in the thick jungle wood line, and here a priest was shaking their hand and thanking them for the great deed performed. A contradiction in Hatch's mind, but one somehow made right by the fact that she believed what they were doing was of greater benefit to the people of the village. She liked to believe if there was a God, he sided with those who sought justice and good, blessing acts of violence done to benefit others. St. Michael was known for his ability to take on evil, the iconic image of the sword-bearing angel stepping down on the devil's neck. War and religion went hand-in-hand, and at times, overlapped, blurring the lines as the perpetual ebb and flow of power, control, either spiritual or political, continually raged on. It had been like this in the world since time began, and Hatch doubted much would ever change.

The blessing complete, Hatch assisted in offloading some of the supplies. Several of the small children circled around as she opened a box containing chocolate bars. She handed them out, and the children squealed with glee as they danced away like fireflies in the evening sky.

Laughter filled the air. Something she hadn't heard in the village in the days since the attacks. It's funny how a simple thing like a chocolate bar could temporarily alleviate the anguish these children faced. Hatch hoped to permanently relieve it at some point, although she knew the scars of war would last a lifetime. No amount of chocolate and good will would heal that.

What if she was wrong? What if there was a way to bring about an end to the nightmares? Hatch thought of Khari, the wounded child turned gregarious café owner, and how he had literally turned the other cheek on tragedy.

Jabari stacked up the medical supplies as several of the able-bodied women came and began carting them off toward the shack where Father McCarthy resided. Hatch knew he would need to go through those supplies later to determine what was needed.

Hatch had a new respect for McCarthy, who had been serving this tribal area for several years. He was not only a spiritual advisor, but beyond his duties as a priest, McCarthy had to be a jack-of-all-trades, a medic, a tradesman, and also able to build houses and provide medical care for the sick. She was sure his time in the Army and in the years after had well-prepared him for such tasks. Hatch wondered what other of his skills he kept razor-sharp.

McCarthy caught Hatch eyeing him. "Hatch, can I talk to you privately for a moment?"

"Sure."

"Over here." McCarthy walked away from the group.

Jabari and his men were still offloading. The women were setting the medical supplies aside, and they stepped out of earshot of any of the other members. The kids played gleefully, mouths and teeth now covered in melted chocolate. A storm brewed in the sky above, a downpour about to break free of the dark clouds masking the clear blue. Even with the cloud cover, the heat continued to swelter, with humidity reaching a breaking point. She was damp, every piece of her clothing was wet with sweat. She looked forward to whatever rain would soon fall, washing away the grime of the morning's assault. A cleansing.

"Hatch," McCarthy started, pausing as a small cluster of children ran by. "I know you came to Africa for one purpose. And now you've been sucked in, partly my fault, to helping these villagers. As you can see, they're in desperate need of it. Men like Jabari do the best that they can. I'm grateful for what you did. Jabari briefly told me how brave you were and that your assistance was greatly needed."

"I didn't really do anything they couldn't have done themselves," she said.

"Don't be so dismissive or humble, Hatch. You're much like your father. I keep saying that, I know. But the more I'm around you and the more I hear you talk and see the things you do, the more I see him in you. And please take that as a compliment. I know you did not know your father in your adult life and I'm sorry for that. But I will tell you, he was a great man. Honorable, kind, and one hell of a shot. All the makings of a great soldier. And more importantly a great person. And I was a better man for knowing him."

Hatch listened and something about the tone and look in the priest's eyes told her there was more to what he wanted to say.

"I owe him a great debt. I'm going to tell you something now, Rachel. Something I should have told you earlier, when you first arrived here. I want to give you the closure you deserve. I feel wholly responsible for involving you in this fight with Dakarai. It was never your fight to take on. You came here for one reason--closure. And I owe you that. I want you to be burden-free in your decision whether or not to stay, I don't want to hold you here anymore, by teasing out the knowledge of your father's death. It's too dangerous. And I'm hoping that maybe if I tell you who was responsible, you'll head back to safety."

Hatch stopped herself from laughing out loud. *Safety?* The last two places she visited, her home and New Mexico, turned out to be anything but safe. Hatch felt as safe here in the jungles of Africa as she did back stateside. Trouble had a way of finding her, she figured. And it would find her wherever she went. Or maybe she would find it.

"Rachel, years ago, two decades now, your father was tasked with an operation. I know you know the back story. It was designed to take a shot, to kill a child, in the hopes that the threat would be seen as a message sent, redirect the political course, and get people in line. The politician who the shot was aimed at guiding was considered to be in need of a wake-up call. His child was initially threatened, but when he didn't bend to the demands, a more definitive message was deemed necessary. Empty threats are weakness. And it was your father who was assigned to take the shot. But he didn't."

Hatch interrupted. "I know this story. I've heard it before. Please tell me this isn't all you have. I didn't come halfway across the world to hear what I already knew before getting on that damn plane."

"There is more. A lot more. After your father didn't take the shot, a kill order went out. He was deemed a threat, a high priority target."

"Gibson Consortium," Hatch stated.

"Yes," McCarthy said. "Talon Executive Services now, but yes, one and the same. They gave the kill order."

"Like I said. I've heard this before."

McCarthy continued, "But what you don't know is I was assigned to kill your father."

Hatch felt herself stop breathing momentarily, enough that it caught her off guard. She stopped herself from gasping. The words had a dizzying effect. Fat Tony hadn't lied. *Was the priest standing before her the man that had pulled the trigger? Was this his confession? If so, what would she do? Would she kill this man who was doing kind works and had been doing so for nearly two decades now? Was this his way of atoning for what he'd done?*

Hatch's mind raced, trying to process this potential revelation. She'd always thought the moment she faced the killer of her father, she would put a bullet in the man's head. Her left hand drifted to the drop-down holster containing the Berretta. The onslaught of internal debate continued. *Could she put a bullet in this priest's head for killing her father over 20 years ago? Was she capable of such a thing? What would it do? More damage, she thought. Whatever peace and safety he provided for these families, these villagers who needed him more now than ever, could she pull the trigger?*

Time seemed to stand still as she looked at the silver-haired priest, contemplating the meaning of his words. He must have seen the sense of confusion and despondency in her face.

"Rachel, please," McCarthy said, "I need you to understand it wasn't me who killed your father."

Hatch was immediately grateful, but her left hand continued to dangle near the pistol's grip.

"Don't get me wrong. I was assigned the task. I just couldn't bring myself to do it. I knew the moment I heard your father hadn't pulled the trigger that he had made the right decision. Regardless of the political fallout, a child of any person, good or bad, doesn't deserve to take a bullet for the decisions of their parent." McCarthy looked away.

Hatch continued to evaluate every aspect of McCarthy, from his voice inflection to his body mannerism.

"I'm going to be honest with you, had the shoe been on the other foot and I had been at the ready with the rifle, I don't think I would have had the strength, the intestinal fortitude, that your father showed. I think I would have taken the shot," McCarthy said, more to himself than Hatch. "Like I said, you are him and he is you. You see the right in the world and the wrong, and when it's wrong, you do something about it. He was brave like you, strong like you. And he made the right decision."

Hatch then cut him off. "So, you're telling me you didn't take the shot? You were given the order but didn't follow through?"

"Initially, the order came to me. I was one of our unit's designated marksmen. When your father went underground, any member of Talon Executive, Gibson Consortium at the time, was authorized to kill on sight. The multiple attempts made to locate your father all ended up dead end leads. He legitimately went off the grid--disappeared. And after he did, so did I. Not completely, if you will, but I left and agreed not to talk about it any further, not to disclose anything about the operations. And I agreed that, where applicable, I would provide intelligence in my new line of work. But as the years passed, I became less valuable as an intelligence operative and became more priest than I ever was covert killer. And in time, the calls for my service stopped and the secret meets ceased happening."

"Then who took the shot?" Hatch asked.

"Anthony Amaletto."

Hatch had an entirely new sensation of sickness at hearing the name. A week ago, she was sitting in Fat Tony's Tattoo Shop, talking to the man who had killed her father. He'd had a gun to her head and then lowered it. And now, she was halfway across the world, facing off against a warlord in the jungle of Africa. She could have already been back home in Hawk's Landing. She could have closed out the chapter of her life, brought closure to herself, to her family.

Everything about the disclosure read true. Although Amaletto had seemed truthful too, there was a distinct difference. There was no reason for the priest to lie. In fact, McCarthy could have let her roll the dice with Dakarai in the hopes she would end up dead. He didn't. And that simple piece in the puzzle made clear the truthfulness of his story.

"So, why come clean now?" Hatch asked.

McCarthy looked at her, his eyes serious but with an element of concern. "I don't want to see you die out here, Rachel. Things happen. It's a dangerous place. I realized holding out this information, and the longer I did so, meant the longer you would probably stay. And I was being selfish at first. I needed the help. I needed somebody here in the village with me, and I used it to my advantage. You joined up with Jabari, and I'm truly concerned for your safety."

There was that word again—*safety*. No such thing. Just those who are prepared and those who aren't. It's the truest measure of keeping oneself safe.

"It goes beyond you. As I've had time to think on it, I needed to bring closure to that chapter in my life as well. I needed to get it off my chest. And you needed to know. So, there you have it. The information is yours to do what you will. If you decide to stay and continue to help, now it's completely on you, your decision. If you decide to go back to the United

States and right whatever wrong, that's also yours. And I wouldn't judge you either way."

Amaletto knew she was looking for him. *Would he even be there when she went back?* She didn't know the answer to that question. One thing was for certain, upon their next encounter, he would definitely be better prepared. But so would she. Any element of surprise, any conversations left would probably not occur. She kicked herself. How could she have known, though? Sitting across from the man, he was good. Hatch had given him fair warning that she'd be back if she'd found out he lied. And now, hearing he had been the triggerman, she would definitely be back.

But here she was in Africa, and she had made a commitment to Jabari and to these villagers. She had to see it through, and she now had more reason than ever to get it done—and quickly. Besides, going back to her family, to Daphne, to Jake, and maybe possibly to Dalton Savage, she could finally go back and face the man who had changed the course of her life and her family's.

Hatch softened her expression as she stared at McCarthy. "Thank you. I know that must've been hard for you."

"What now?" he asked.

"I'm going to stay," she said. "These people need me, at least in the interim. Jabari and his team are tough, but they need me. Plus, I've got a code I live by, and I wouldn't be able to leave now even if I wanted."

"I've got to say, Rachel," McCarthy said, "telling you lifted a weight off my shoulders that I have been carrying around with me for over two decades. I'm not sure what the fallout will be. I don't care on my end what happens to me at this point. I care for the sake of the people, and the villagers that I serve. But as far as for me as a person, I no longer care and haven't for quite some time. I guess a piece of me died the day your father did. When I heard the news, it rocked me. Learning he had a family made it all the more devastating. I should have done more for you early on. And hopefully, whatever peace I've given you now gives you that closure you and your family deserve. I hope you live long enough to reap the benefits of it."

"I don't plan on dying any time soon," Hatch said. "Let's get back to the task at hand. There's a lot of people who need you right now."

The two walked back, making their way over to his makeshift medical center. The villagers were lining up to receive whatever treatments they needed. There was an order to the line based on the neediest first to those requiring only minor medical aid to the rear. Some that didn't need anything had already resumed their work.

Hatch linked up with Jabari.

"So, Hatch," he said, "will you be staying on with us for a bit or heading out, heading back home?"

Hatch shot a glance over at McCarthy and realized the priest had given him fair warning that she might not be sticking around.

"I told you I'm here to help and I want to make right what happened to these villagers. So, I'm here as long as you need or want me."

Jabari gave the same wide smile he'd given when she'd bested Duke, his dimples prominently on display. "This makes me very happy to hear. After we get these villagers settled, let's head back to our compound. We have much to discuss and plan in preparation for our next mission."

NINETEEN

BACK AT THE compound where Jabari's men lived, the rain subsided, giving way to steam rising from the ground. A couple of men grabbed dry wood that was aged and underneath the protective shelter of a thatched roof as Duke slowly turned the roasting pig on the spit above the flame. Hatch smelled the meat as it cooked. It was a small pig and would not take too long for it to cook. The surrounding muggy air carried notes of the sweetness of the spices and the saltiness of the meat, like maple bacon cooking in a pan.

"It's how we celebrate our victories, Miss Hatch. I hope you'll partake."

"Of course," she said.

"We roast a pig every time. Sometimes they are bigger. Today's pig is a little bit smaller, but nonetheless it will be delicious. Have you ever had pig before?"

"I've never had it like this. Bacon is quite common back home, but I've never been to a pig roast. Although the smells make me feel like I've been missing something my whole life."

They both chuckled softly.

"Hold on one second." Jabari retreated to the room where Hatch had slept, the one with the cot and the training table, the mock-up. And he came back out with a bottle and held it up. Cheers resounded from Jabari's men as they saw the bottle. It had an amber hue to it. There were no markings or identifiers of what it was. "This too is tradition, Hatch. Will you drink with us?"

"I don't see why not. What is it?"

"You'll have to try it first. It's our homemade recipe."

"Moonshine?" she asked.

"I don't know what moonshine is," Jabari said. "But it's like wine and vodka mixed. Have you had vodka before?"

"Of course," Hatch said. "And I don't mind wine either."

"Then think of it like a sweetened vodka. It's the best way that I can describe it. Duke makes it himself," Jabari boasted.

Hatch raised an eyebrow. "He's kind of a jack-of-all-trades, isn't he?" she said. "I mean, he's the size of a house, he's basically your cook, looks like he's a trained killer, and now you're telling me he makes homemade wine," she said sarcastically.

"Moonshine," Jabari said, laughing. "I like the way that sounds. You Americans have funny names for things."

"I guess we do."

Jabari popped the cork and handed it to Hatch first. She accepted the offering and took a swig. It was strong, almost like gasoline. The sting of it tingled in her nose and caused her eyes to water. The aftertaste was sweet like honey. It settled on her empty stomach and she felt her cheeks warm. She hoped the pig would be done soon because the strength of the booze after the long day and the early morning combat was sure to go straight to her head. Whatever the proof, it was definitely high.

Hatch then passed the bottle back to Jabari, who took a swig. He winced, too. She was glad to see he was just as affected by it as she was. Acquired taste or not, it looked like the first pull of the jug for everyone was difficult.

The last to drink was Duke, who was tending the fire and turning the spit to evenly cook the pig. He was the only one not to wince at his home-made beverage. "It is good, yes?" he said to everyone.

Everybody gave a thumbs up or smiled. Hatch laughed at the African Friar Tuck holding the bottle with a big thumbs up and a big smile etched across his face.

They took seats on tree stumps that had been set up around the fire pit, close enough to the actual flames to dry them from the rain. But not so close that the heat warmed them uncomfortably. Although, Hatch was becoming quite accustomed to the heat of Africa. It's funny what you could get used to. She reminded herself of the cold mountains of Afghanistan and how the acclimation process took time. But once it took hold, it was barely noticeable, or at least not as noticeable as it should have been. That was beginning to happen here in Africa. Her body was starting to condition itself to the heat and humidity. Partly it was psychological. Hatch had sweated so much in the past week, she'd lost the ability to tell if the dampness of her clothes was from sweat or rain, or a combination of the two. At some point, the brain just accepts circumstance and pushes forward.

"Miss Hatch," Jabari said, leaning in, lowering his voice to speak only to her. "Did Father McCarthy tell you what you came here to hear? Did you find whatever it is you were looking for?"

Hatch nodded and took another swig as the bottle came around for its second pass. She tightened her lips to keep from letting too much of the liquid go down. She was still in foreign territory. They had just run an assault on Dakarai's camp, and she was still on guard. Hatch was also careful not to offend the hospitality of her new teammates.

"He did," she said, the liquid burning the back of her throat as she swallowed.

"And did he give you the closure you were looking for? It is why you came to Africa in the first place, no?"

"It's funny, I'm not sure how I feel about it," she answered honestly. "I know what I have to do now, but I'm not sure that it's going to give me the end I seek."

"Whatever it is, Miss Hatch," Jabari said, "I hope it gives you the peace that you look for."

"Me too," she said.

Duke looked out at the group as he tore off a piece of the pig's hind quarters and put it in his mouth. He chewed hungrily and gave a satisfied smile.

"The pig is done. We shall serve our guest first," he announced.

Duke cut a piece of the hind quarter. He used an oversized fig leaf as a plate. And as he began to plate it, Hatch heard a familiar crack in the distance.

One of the men sitting closest to Jabari launched forward and fell into the fire. He didn't scream. He was already dead. It took only a split second as the blood pooled out of the back of the man in the fire for Hatch to realize what was happening. She dove to the ground. The other men also quickly responded, running toward their shelters, and grabbing their weapons as they did. Several more gunshots rang out, rounds skipping across the ground. Several struck the meat of the pig, knocking it off the spit, causing the fire to hiss wildly as the fat from the animal sizzled on the hot embers.

Hatch clamored to her feet, and just as she did so, noticed Duke was slow to react. Maybe it was the extra indulgence in the moonshine, but he was standing in the open. Duke was a big target.

Hatch launched herself, tackling him to the ground as several rounds burst overhead.

He looked wide-eyed at his rescuer. "Thank you," he said, as both scrambled back to their feet and they began running toward the concrete bunker, the only place that would have the potential of stopping a round.

Hatch, as she moved, tried to pinpoint the locations of the gunfire in the darkness. As her eyes began to settle, she picked out three distinct locations, two from the right, one from the left.

"At least three shooters," she yelled to Jabari.

Jabari was already relaying the information to his soldiers in their native tongue. Gunfire erupted from the men as they began to return fire, suppressing the attackers' relentless wave.

Hatch stopped by the concrete as a round skipped off the wall near her. *Find the shot. Look for the muzzle blast. Spot the shooter.*

Hatch brought her weapon up. A quick flash in the distance. Maybe seventy-five yards away. She aimed. She fired three shots. Then moved herself to the right and fired three shots from her MP5, for a total of six. She waited. No more fire came from the left-hand side of the tree line.

"I think the shooter's down on the left. Still two more on the right," she called out.

Jabari's men began leveling their weapons and unloading heavy fire into that direction. Hatch watched for return fire. Sporadically, they continued to press until a loud explosion lit the wooded area on the right side.

Hatch looked back to see the empty rocket-propelled grenade canister on the shoulder of Duke. He was smiling again.

The area where the gunfire came from was burning. The dampness of the most recent rain helped to keep the fire from raging out of control.

Two of Jabari's men ran into the wood line. They called back something in their native language.

Jabari acknowledged them and then turned to Hatch. "They're down. It appears the threat's neutralized. They're going to scan the perimeter, and then they'll come back. The rest of us should go inside the bunker. It's not perfect, but it should stop some of the rounds. If nothing else, we won't give them a target."

Duke, Jabari, Hatch, and one of the other men entered the briefing room where Hatch had slept the night before. "What the hell was that?" Hatch said.

"I guess it's safe to say Dakarai knows where our compound is now. Intelligence is a fickle thing," Jabari said.

Hatch understood his meaning. It was likely whoever had fed them the intelligence earlier had probably seen an opportunity to work out a sizable payout once the attack on the compound holding the medical supplies occurred. Spies were often men and women of profit, and whoever this source was most likely saw a window of opportunity to make some cash from the warlord by giving up Jabari's location.

"Why only three? I mean, if that's all there is out there. Why would you attack seven men?" Jabari asked aloud, but seemed to be asking himself as much as anyone in the room.

"And a woman," Duke added, giving Hatch a nudge in the shoulder.

"Right," Hatch said. "Eight of us. Why would you attack eight with just three men?"

"Maybe he got cocky," Jabari said. "Maybe he didn't think we were a formidable enemy."

"Do you really think so? Do you really think that's it?" Hatch asked, feeling as though something was amiss.

Jabari shrugged. "The fact that you don't, Hatch, makes me want to ask why."

"Why is a good question to be asking right now. We hit a supply stronghold. He had a security contingent, nine in total. And then you're telling me after we kill nine men, he sends three here. It doesn't make sense."

They were silent for a moment. And then, as all of them came to the conclusion at the exact same moment, Hatch mouthed the words, "The village."

The room fell eerily silent. Hatch continued. "This was a distraction. They're keeping us occupied."

Jabari's mouth went slack as he picked up his weapon, grabbed some extra magazines, and rushed out the door.

TWENTY

THEY TOOK TWO VEHICLES, the Astro Van and an armored Jeep. Duke drove the van with the surviving members of the team. Jabari was leading the pack in the Jeep with Hatch in the front passenger seat. The two-vehicle caravan rolled toward the village. Jabari slammed the brakes, bringing it to a jolted stop.

In the distance through a clearing in the dense jungle foliage, Hatch could see black smoke rising high above the canopy. Her eyes traced upward as her mind tried to anticipate what lay in wait, preparing herself for the worst.

Hatch looked over at Jabari, whose gaze was locked on something. She followed his line of sight and realized what had caused the veteran soldier to come to such an abrupt stop.

Hanging from the same branch of the Fever Tree as the young boy had only a week ago was Father McCarthy. His body swayed in the breeze. His feet dangled freely above the ground, one of his shoes had come off. It was a horrible sight to behold.

Hatch jumped out of the vehicle just as Jabari began to drive forward. She ran in a dead sprint toward McCarthy.

There was no sign of the warlord's men. Just the aftermath and destruction left in their wake.

As Hatch approached, she could tell just by looking at him that he was undoubtedly dead. But something broke inside her. A visceral response caused her to grab him at the knees and try to hoist him, alleviate the strain and pressure of the rope across his throat. It was a foolhardy attempt and there was no way to release him from the noose that way.

Masika, the mother who'd lost her twelve-year-old son, was at the feet of the priest and wailed uncontrollably as tears streamed down her plump cheeks. Even over the roar of Jabari's engine, Hatch could hear the tribal woman's cries of anguish. The sight, and the accompanying sound, sickened Hatch.

Masika's anguished cries continued as she knelt on the ground, unable to assist. Hatch could hear the doors opening and closing. Jabari and his men rushed to assist.

Hatch, not waiting, quickly climbed the tree. The divided, rooted base of the Fever Tree's knotted trunk gave her a foothold from which to launch herself up and onto the thick branch where McCarthy dangled.

Pulling a large knife sheathed along her left leg, Hatch sawed at the rope, fraying the ends until it snapped, releasing the silver-haired priest into a crumpled mass on the dirt ground below.

Hatch lowered herself and swung down to the ground, landing beside McCarthy's twisted body. Holding out the last iota of hope, she knelt beside him and pressed two fingers hard against his carotid artery, silently praying for a pulse, faint or otherwise.

Finding none, she sat back on the dirt ground momentarily lost in both contemplation and despondency.

Jabari came up beside her and rested a hand on her shoulder. She didn't even look up. She could smell the familiar lemon of the man's scent. Under circumstances as dire as this, the smell seemed out of place.

Hatch gave herself a short spell to put her emotions in check before snapping her mind back from the brink. She made a mental checklist of the things she needed to do. Busying her mind and focusing on the task.

First and most importantly was to remove the noose from around Father McCarthy's neck. It took a lot of effort to free the binding. His weight had cinched the rope down tightly against the back of his neck. She tried not to think of the distorted shape of the bones which had been crushed where the noose had tightened. Hatch worked it lose with the help of Jabari, and they slipped it over his head. Deep markings denoting where the rope wrenched against the holy man's flesh spoke volumes to the tragic way his life ended.

Hatch, out of an attempt at decency, pulled up McCarthy's collar in an effort to mask the visible trauma.

With the help of Jabari and Duke, she picked up McCarthy. The three carried the fallen priest into the village. Masika continued her shrill screams at the base of the tree but it was nothing compared to the sounds inside the village center. A horrific scene played out before them.

The burned bodies of villagers were scattered throughout. All of the huts were destroyed. It was an indiscriminate mass killing the likes of which Hatch had never witnessed. If her rough estimate calculations were correct, Dakarai's assault had slashed their numbers by half.

She also knew the reason for survivors. This is how word would be spread of the devastation at the hand of Dakarai and serve as a warning not to cross him in the future.

A fire continued to burn where McCarthy used to stay. It was the same location where several hours earlier they had delivered the medical supplies and food. Hatch and Jabari rushed to save what they could. Through the shattered door, they could see all of the supplies were gone.

"My God," Hatch said under her breath.

"God has no hand in this," Jabari said seriously. "What you are witnessing is the work of the devil himself."

Hatch stood with Jabari's men. All of them stunned into silence. A feeling of complete and total helplessness was apparent on their faces. Even Hatch could feel it. McCarthy was dead, the village lay in ashes, and all the supplies were now gone. Whatever small trace of hope they had given the villagers earlier had just been demolished.

With the priest dead, their supplies destroyed, and half of the village burned, Hatch wondered if it was humanly possible to rise above such tragedy. She ground her teeth. A rage bubbled up from deep inside, quickly replacing the grief of moments before. She looked over at Jabari and could see that he and his men were reaching a similar mental state.

"This ends now," Hatch said.

"Agreed," Jabari said.

"You know where he is, you know where Dakarai's compound is located, correct?" Hatch asked.

Jabari gave an uneasy nod. "It's not going to be that easy. Trust me, we've looked at this from all angles."

"Every fortress compound has a weakness. There's got to be an entry point. You just haven't seen it yet," Hatch said.

Jabari threw his hands up in defeat. "So, help us find it!"

"We need good intel, somebody who isn't selling us out to the highest bidder. We need somebody close to Dakarai who is capable of giving us what we need. We need to know the number of personnel, access points, levels of security, and his compound's contingency plans. Do you have anybody who can get us those things?" Hatch asked.

Jabari remained silent for a moment as he pondered this proposal. "I think I know exactly who we need to talk to."

"Then what are we waiting for?" Hatch retorted.

"Getting to the man will not be easy. But if we can snatch him up, he'll have everything you listed and then some."

"Point me in the right direction," Hatch said.

"If we are able to get to this person – and that is a big if – there will be the tricky part of getting him to talk."

Hatch gave a knowing smile. "If there's somebody out there with the information we need to gain access and eliminate Dakarai, then let's come up with a plan and pick him up. Give me time with him, and I guarantee you he'll talk."

TWENTY-ONE

AFTER RELOCATING the surviving villagers to another camp, Hatch and company spent the majority of the night planning. The last few hours were spent in the back of the Astro Van as the team prepared to embark on their snatch and grab mission.

Jabari left two of his men back with the villagers to provide security. It was all he could spare. And even in sparing those two, it left them shorthanded for the task at hand. But it was a necessity under the circumstances. The villagers needed somebody not only to guide and assist them but also able to prevent another attack.

Hatch and Jabari were in agreement, it was unlikely at this point that the villagers would be targeted again so soon by Dakarai. His message had been sent loud and clear. If he had wanted the entire village to be decimated and left for dead, he would have done so unquestionably. Hatch knew he left those survivors for a purpose. Even so, the people needed leadership and guidance during this tumult. With McCarthy dead and many of the people incapable of carrying that torch, Jabari's men were a good temporary bandage for the short-term solution.

Today's plan was simple. The best ones were. But even with its simplicity, the mission was overly wrought with potential complications. Especially if Murphy's Law were to kick in.

Jabari had briefed Hatch on a target of opportunity. A man by the name of Baako, one of Dakarai's top lieutenants, if not his very top lieutenant. Jabari had information on the lieutenant's daily routine, and one of his daily stops left him vulnerable. Baako had a proclivity for the local women at a particular brothel located in Mombasa town center. Prostitution wasn't something openly favorable in the region, but as in any country, in any community in the world, where there was a need, there were those who were ready and willing to supply it.

And the brothel that Baako attended on a regular basis was not too far from where Khari and his wife ran their cafe. They were right. As big and vast as Africa was, the longer Hatch stayed, the smaller it felt. Things were interconnected here in ways she couldn't fathom.

They sat in the van parked across the street from the brothel and waited. Jabari had had one of his trusted sources guarantee Baako would be at the brothel today. The source also stated the lieutenant came about the same time every day; it was his routine. Apparently, he'd gotten comfortable. His routine had set him up for failure. As with any criminal activity, like a burglary, all they needed was to know what the pattern was. Routine created opportunity. And they planned to capitalize on Baako's routine this morning.

The source intel said the lieutenant traveled with no less than five men. Four, he posted around the exterior of the brothel, and one he kept in close proximity to him while he engaged with the women inside. From what the intel said, his personal bodyguard did not enter the room. He stayed outside and secured the door.

Five men. The odds were even. The plan would be simple. Eliminate the externals before they had an opportunity to transmit a warning to the bodyguard inside.

From what Jabari had learned, the bodyguard had extensive military background and, of the five, he'd likely be the most formidable adversary the team faced. The other consideration was the civilians. The women working the brothel were not targets, and so it was agreed by all members of Jabari's team, the goal was zero civilian casualties. And that's why Hatch wasn't outside with Jabari's men.

According to the plan, Hatch entered the brothel thirty minutes before the lieutenant's predicted arrival. She went in with a large sum of money, enough to keep the worker's mouths shut until their mission was completed. Jabari had put together enough money to cover wages for any lost revenue.

Hatch handed the brothel owner the money. She spoke good enough English that Hatch was able to convey the importance of her silence and that she should run business as usual. That it was essential. The brothel owner had a bruise under her left eye that was beginning to change from purple to yellow. Hatch noticed she touched the bruise under her eye at the mention of the lieutenant.

When she asked the brothel owner where the bruise came from, the plump woman confirmed Hatch's suspicion. Baako was not only a man who liked prostitutes but was the type of man who took pleasure in hurting them. If his affiliation with Dakarai wasn't enough, this additional bit of information made the lieutenant a bad person. Hatch didn't like people who took pleasure in hurting others.

The brothel owner quickly explained to Hatch the way it worked when the lieutenant, Baako, came in. He picked one, two, or up to three girls, and then he would go into his room and get ready. The girls would then enter, only after being frisked by his personal bodyguard. Although the man came there quite frequently, he trusted no one. She also revealed the bodyguard enjoyed his frisk a little too much before sending the women inside.

Hatch explained to the brothel owner that the bodyguard would not be a problem because she was already going to be inside. The woman nodded again, her understanding clear.

She showed Hatch to the room used by Baako. He always used the same room. *Routine creates opportunity.*

The room was simple in design. A half-wall divider split the small room in half. Behind the partition was an area for placing one's clothes. On the other side, closest to the door, was a twin bed with a sheet and pillow. It was meager furnishings, but in reality, the room was designed for only one purpose.

Hatch slipped inside the room as the brothel owner let herself out, locking the door behind her. Hatch then took up a position behind the half wall and waited, stilling her mind as she prepared for the next phase of the operation. Mental rehearsal was a critical component to mission success.

The plan was simple, but her part in it had to be executed with absolute perfection. Control the lieutenant within the room and keep him contained so the rest of the team could move in and handle the bodyguards while minimizing any potential civilian casualty.

Hatch waited patiently. She was grateful for the ceiling fan, even though it only worked to circulate the muggy air. Just shy of a half hour later, she heard the voice of a male speaking in his native tongue. Hatch could hear the plump brothel owner's voice respond. Although Hatch didn't know the dialect, she didn't pick up any tone that would indicate the owner whispered a warning to Dakarai's top lieutenant.

Everything seemed to be going according to plan.

A few giggles from some of the other girls as the man spoke. No doubt, Baako was naming his prize picks for the day.

Then Hatch heard the man's voice lower as he said something barely audible. A different male voice returned in a similar hushed tone. *The bodyguard.* The two men were close, just outside the door.

Hatch felt a prickle of adrenaline course through her veins as she waited the final few seconds.

The door opened and closed quickly. Hatch peered through a slit in the partition and watched as the lieutenant entered and stood by the bed facing the door. He seemed to be eager to get started. She heard his zipper go down and the clang of a belt as it hit the floor.

Hatch slowed her breathing. And continued to wait. Her original plan was to snatch him when he went behind the partition to undress. His decision to drop his clothes on the end table next to the bed caused her to change plans on the fly. Now, Hatch decided to wait until the bodyguard outside the door was preoccupied with his frisking before she made her move.

The lieutenant, Baako, called out in a short burst of Swahili followed by a clap of his hands. Hatch guessed it to be his signal to send in the girls, or something to that effect. The bodyguard gave his response from the other side of the closed door.

The giggles of girls could be heard followed by the bodyguard's voice. As the brothel owner had indicated would happen, the frisking had begun.

Hatch took this opportunity using the background noise created by the conversation and frisking outside the door to slip from around the half wall. Her Beretta was at the low ready. She was prepared to take the shot if needed but hoped it wouldn't come to that. The lieutenant was their best chance at finding a way into Dakarai's compound. Killing this man would be an unwanted hindrance.

Baako's back was to her, and he now sat at the edge of the bed. He was naked minus a thick braided chain he wore around his neck and a gold watch, which looked to be a Rolex, most likely real. Hatch saw a pistol on the end table, where his clothes were piled alongside it.

Take him alive. Control the room. Handle the bodyguard, Hatch repeated to herself. Adrenaline always kicked in at times like this. Controlling it was a skill learned on the battlefield. Breathing helped, but planning helped more. Experience had taught Hatch to recount the steps in her mind, slowing herself down so she didn't allow her physiological reaction to dictate her actions.

Always have an alternative. Her Plan B, should the need arise, was to wound the lieutenant before taking control, then take out the bodyguard. Both scenarios required the bodyguard to die. Jabari had given her a silencer for the pistol she carried. Hatch was familiar with silencers, having used them many times in her past life. The weight of it changed the feel of the gun in her hand. And she knew, any suppressor at such close range where she could hear talking on the other side of the door would do little to mask the gunshot if she was to fire inside at the lieutenant. The benefit of a suppressed shot would come into play when taking out the bodyguard. The security detail outside the building would unlikely hear anything wrong.

Hatch had asked the brothel owner to stand nearby when the girls were being frisked. To act as though she was helping guide them into the room. Hatch asked her if that would be out of place, and she said no. Sometimes she did things like that. Sometimes she tried to offer different girls at that point. More expensive girls.

Hatch explained that she needed the door to open wide, wide enough that when the first girl came in, Hatch would be able to see the bodyguard on the other side. The owner said she would brief all of the girls, that if they were picked, when they entered the room, the first thing they were to do was drop to the floor once the door was open. Hatch didn't like involving so many moving parts in an operation, but her goal was to minimize casualties. There was to be zero civilian fallout from this operation. There had been enough dead innocents since Hatch's arrival in Africa, and she didn't want to see any more, especially at the hand of something she'd planned.

Timing was everything. Hatch knew this and prepared for it. She was close to the man, who was at arm's reach on the other side of the bed. He still hadn't noticed her. Her silenced muzzle was aimed squarely at the back of his head. Should he move, she would fire. Hopefully having time to take lower aim and not killing him. She was determined to interrogate this man, and alive was the only way that would work. But if it came down to him or her, she'd choose her.

Hatch watched as the knob turned and the door began to open. As requested, the brothel owner was standing nearby, and she pushed the door wider. The bodyguard was facing the next girl in line, and his hands were busy groping the young girl. His submachine gun was slung down by his side. His hands were free of a weapon.

The first girl entered. Upon seeing Hatch with the gun, and even though she'd been briefed on what was going to happen, her eyes widened for a split second. It was a natural reaction to the situation, but one Hatch had not factored in.

Baako must have noticed the young prostitute's facial cue. He began to spin to face Hatch.

Hatch's initial concern wasn't for the naked man without a weapon, it was for the bodyguard who was still busy fondling the second girl in line. Even with the moment's hesitation and her wide-eyed reaction to Hatch, the first girl still remembered to drop to the floor. Although it was a few seconds later than she would have liked, it was enough time for Hatch to get a clear shot at the bodyguard.

As the lieutenant moved and called out a warning to his most trusted employee, Hatch fired twice. The blood and brain matter from the man who was groping the second girl in line painted her dark skin a thick, dark red. The prostitute screamed.

Baako dove to the right, reaching for the dresser and the weapon that lay on it. Hatch was quick and predicted this move. She jumped up onto the bed and then launched herself at the man, knocking him against the wall. He was big, but not muscly like Duke. This man had softened over the years through whatever lavish lifestyle afforded him a gold Rolex.

But he was still strong, heavy. And at one point in his life, Hatch guessed he had been a physically impressive man. She thought of the brothel owner's bruised eye. The additional mental armor enabled her own strength reservoir.

He was slippery from sweat, and butt naked. Not an ideal dress for a fight. Baako's slick skin made it extremely hard to get a grip on him. Hatch at first had tried to grab him by the neck and lock in a choke hold, but he slipped out. So, she struck him at the base of his neck with the butt of the heavy pistol. The blow caused him to let out a whimper as his arm went limp. His reach for the gun resting on the table was temporarily diverted.

Hatch was now on top of the sweaty naked man, but he wasn't completely out.

She hesitated to strike him again with the gun for fear that another heavy blow to the base of a skull with the hard butt of the Beretta could crack his head. The last thing she needed was a dead man and no one to interrogate. Instead, Hatch drove her elbow into the side of the man's exposed temple. She struck hard, and with the man's face lying flat against the floor and offering no area of recoil, the impact was devastating.

She felt whatever residual tension and fight in the man dissipate immediately as his body went limp.

Though the gunshots taking out the bodyguard had been relatively silent, the screams of the young prostitutes were not. Hatch prepared herself for the coming wave.

She used zip ties given to her by Jabari to cinch up the naked man. Both hands and feet were secured, with a bit of rope connecting them in a hogtie. If Baako tried to move, it would only serve to tighten the restraints further.

Hatch took up a crouched position behind the unconscious lieutenant and aimed out toward the entrance. The girls had scattered. Seconds later, Hatch heard footsteps noisily approaching the door. The exterior security detail was advancing on her location. Using Baako as a human shield, Hatch lowered herself further behind the naked man's torso.

The footsteps grew louder, and she knew it was only a moment now before they would breach the main entrance to the lobby area of the brothel, putting her in direct contact with the next threat. Her weapon was aimed at the door.

As the knob began to turn, she heard the suppressed fire of a semi-automatic machine gun. Several quick bursts followed by silence. No return volley of shots. Without a doubt, Hatch knew Jabari and his men were leading an assault on the security team.

Hatch remained in position. No reason for her to rush the door. It could easily turn into a friendly fire situation. *Trust your teammates.* She knew their role, as they had rehearsed it several times while in the van. Jabari had told her, "Once you're inside and you have him secured and the bodyguard eliminated, we'll take care of the rest. If they come for you, we will come for them." Hatch had come to trust the man in the short time they'd worked together. She'd seen firsthand the efficiency with which his team operated. And she put her faith in them now.

Hatch watched as the doorknob turned. Several bullets had passed through the door, splintering the wood. She took up a point of aim just above the doorknob. If it happened to be the lieutenant's security team, then she would be prepared. Her point of aim gave her predictive options. If they were crouched low and it was the enemy, it would be a head shot. If they came in high and ready, it'd be center mass.

A split second before the door opened, she then heard the familiar voice of Jabari. "Enemy down. Hatch, it's Jabari, I'm coming through. Do you hear me? It's Jabari," he said, clearly enunciating his words.

"Bodyguard's down. I have the package."

And with that, the door opened. Jabari and his men, including Duke, entered. Hatch was happy to do a quick head count and see all were alive and unscathed.

Duke and the other men picked up the unconscious lieutenant. Jabari looked at Hatch, then down at the dead bodyguard. "Good work," he said. "Now our next goal will be to get him to talk."

Hatch nodded. "I'm looking forward to that."

TWENTY-TWO

"HE'S BEEN in there for two hours, Hatch. We must move on whatever information we can gather at this point. It will only be a matter of time before they come for him, and I would imagine they will assume it is us. There's only so many places that Dakarai will look," Jabari said. "And it won't be long until he finds us or takes out his anger on the remaining villagers."

"I understand," Hatch said. "I know what's at stake here, but to do this right, to get the information and to do it in a way where we know that he's telling us the truth, we have to apply certain constraints."

"I will admit, for all the people who we've dealt with on the information highway, I've never seen this tactic before."

Hatch shrugged. "Different strokes for different folks, I guess. But when you deprive somebody of their senses, when you disorient them long enough, their reality becomes skewed. Time becomes a formidable enemy. And although he's only been in there for two hours, the heavy tape that we put over his ears and his eyes will be very difficult for him to account for how long he has been inside. It's a long time for somebody to sit in absolute silence and darkness. I've seen this cause strong men to break."

"I understand the logic, Hatch. My worry is we are running out of time."

"I'll go in now," she said. "Let me make first contact. Let me do this my way. Give me time and I will get the results we need."

"Fair enough."

Brutality was not always the way to do it. Hatch knew this. Some of the high value targets she'd encountered during her time with Taskforce Banshee could resist pain, tolerate it better than most. In some ways, it would seal their decision not to open up, not to divulge their secrets. She'd learned subtle ways of twisting the psychological knife, bending the will of those she interrogated.

It was a multipronged mental assault. First, she would isolate, separate them psychologically from the circumstances of their capture and give them a sense of unease. Some interrogators that she'd worked with in the past tried to predict a person's fear, capitalize on it, and build from there. Hatch had taken a different approach. She'd learned under the very best in the business. One thing she found was that people, when left alone to their own devices and left trapped and cut off from the outside world, filled in the gaps. Worry and fear gave way. Their mind, subconscious or conscious, would begin to play tricks on them. Sometimes this would give rise to their deepest, darkest fears, and then those raw nerves could be capitalized on and used to an advantage.

Hatch knew men like the Lieutenant. But each responded differently to interrogation. Baako was in captivity right now, being deprived of his sensory awareness. Some people were capable of holding out for long durations. She was banking on this not being the case. The Lieutenant witnessed his top bodyguard murdered. He was rendered unconscious by a woman, hogtied, and dragged out to an unknown location naked and alone. Baako would be terrified. His soft physique showed that he'd grown accustomed to a much nicer lifestyle than most. He was weak.

Hatch opened the door and studied the man. The husky lieutenant sat naked on a metal chair. The only bit of clothing he'd been given was a rag to cover his groin area. Duct tape shrouded his face. His eyes and ears were completely covered, blocking out all light and sound.

She knew that he could not hear her enter, but she still made every effort to quietly close the door behind her. She stood in the man's presence. He could smell but could not speak. There was a gag in his mouth secured by a thick piece of silver duct tape. Sweat poured profusely from his brow and body, and there was a funk, an odor permeating the air around this man who had been sweating in this room for over two hours.

Hatch needed to further disorient him. She got close to him. She knew he would eventually smell her but did something to quickly remedy that. Just beneath his nose, she lit a match. He couldn't obviously hear the strike against the box, but he could smell the flame and the phosphate and potassium chlorate as it burned.

He began to murmur and writhe against his restraints, obviously concerned that somehow in his darkness, the room was on fire. He couldn't see. All he could do was feel the heat of the flame near his face and smell the smoke as it rose off the end of the wooden matchstick in her hand. Disorienting. Hatch shook it out.

The flame doused, heavy black smoke filtered up and into the man's nostrils, again further disorienting, adding to the discomfort. Without his ability to breathe through his mouth, he was inhaling the smoke. It wouldn't choke him to the point where he would pass out, but it would make him extremely uncomfortable, restricting quality air. The one way in, one way out between his nostrils now was inhaling the acrid smoke, and Baako swung his head from side-to-side to avoid it.

Hatch removed the match from the man's face. The writhing slowed. His breathing was deep and ragged. His inability to talk, hear, and see were designed to disorient. But the added insertion of fire and smoke was panic exemplified. *What games was his mind playing on him now? What fears dominated the forefront of his brain?* It was probably far worse than whatever Hatch or Jabari could do using an element of physical torture. Psychological warfare was a devastating weapon, and when used effectively, was more impactful.

Hatch decided to give him one of his senses back. She took the knife, the same knife she had used to cut down Father McCarthy from the Fever Tree. Hatch slid it across the tape along the man's face near the left side of his temple where a large lump swelled from the elbow strike she had delivered. She cut a slit, releasing the tape and cloth around his ear. She only did it to one ear. He didn't need two to hear. And she could simply secure him again if she needed, if he did not cooperate with what she was going to ask.

She then leaned in and whispered in the man's ear. Sometimes a quiet, calm voice was more alarming than a loud threatening one. And that of a female would have additional impact, especially for a man who seemed to take such pride in hurting women.

"Remember me?" Hatch whispered. She knew he could feel her breath on his ear. He would know she was close.

The man leaned away.

Hatch leaned in further. "Are you ready to talk?"

The man didn't move. No gesture, no bob of the head up or down. For a moment, she wondered if he could hear or understand her. She assumed Baako, as Jabari and Duke and the other men she'd met since being in Africa, would have at least a basic command of English, especially being a commanding lieutenant in Dakarai's army.

Her questions were simple. She decided to wait for the man to respond and prepared to tape back up the ear. Maybe he needed more time to think about it in her homemade deprivation chamber.

"Need more time to think? Six hours wasn't enough?" she said. The number intentionally given to disorient the man further. He would wonder why no one had come to rescue him. In such a long time, he would begin to doubt his leader's ability to save him. The more time that passed in his mind, the more at risk he was. The longer people were in captivity, the more they sided with their captors. Hatch played with the lieutenant's mental clock, trying to speed up the desired response to the stimulus.

"That's fine. I have nothing but time to give you. You're going to get hungry soon, but you won't be able to eat. You're going to get tired, but you won't be able to sleep. And then there are other things that'll happen. But I'm sure you can figure out what those might be." Hatch paused to let the man's mind wander, feeding into his darkest fears. "So, I'll ask you one more time before I close you off to the silence again. Are you ready to talk?"

The man gave the slightest of nods. One that if Hatch had not been staring directly at him only inches away from his face, she might not have noticed.

"Good," she said. "Then let's begin. And please remember, everything I ask you has a consequence. If you lie to me, the blindfold and tape go back on. And if you force me to leave again, you'll be left alone for a much longer time. Nobody knows where you are. Except for me and the people I work with. So, if something happens to me, nobody else will come for you. Nobody will be able to find you. And here in this room, blindfolded in the dark, you'll die alone. But it will be a slow and painful death. Starvation is a not a pleasant way to go." Hatch poked the man's soft stomach with the butt end of the knife for added effect. "And mark my words, I do not lie."

And Hatch wasn't lying, although she had hoped there'd be no reason to lock him away for a longer period of time. Time was of the essence, but this man didn't know it. According to her, he'd been in there for six hours. She could leave him for another hour and tell him it was three. She could leave him until night and tell him it was day. He would be totally disoriented. She hoped it wouldn't come to that. But she was committed to getting the information she needed, the answers they required to effectively handle the threat of the warlord.

Hatch took the knife to the man's bindings, relieving his tape around the other ear, and then removing the gag from his mouth, and finally the duct tape wrapped around his head coating and covering his eyes. She peeled it back with little care for the pain that it caused. His sweat loosened the tape's adhesive quality, making it less painful than it might have been otherwise. It was still definitely not without its discomfort, and the man winced. Some of the hair from his brow came off with the tape.

He looked at Hatch and then down at the restraints tying him to the metal chair in the center of the room. He said nothing. He took several deep inhales, and then she realized he was looking around for something.

The fire. He was trying to figure out what had caused the fire, the flame, the smoke.

Hatch said nothing to enlighten his confusion. The more he doubted what he smelled, heard, and thought, the deeper his fear would take hold and the more easily he could be manipulated.

"Let me explain something very carefully. You need to understand this before we talk. I'm going to ask you for certain things and you're going to answer me. It's simple, really. You don't know me. You won't know me. You'll never see me again after today. But I'm going to tell you this, I'm extremely good at what I do, one of the best. If you lie, I'll know it. If you lie, there's a consequence. If you lie, you'll go back to the dark. And the next time may be the last."

Hatch said these words for a couple reasons. First off, she needed to establish primacy. She needed him to understand that she was extremely good at what she did. On that count, she wasn't lying. It was the truth. But part of getting people to talk in an interrogation was they had to believe wholeheartedly that the person asking the questions was so good at their job that there was no point in lying. She needed him to understand that she was a human lie detector. Somebody able to read any type of miscues. In a perfect world, Hatch would have done background research and had a set series of baseline questions she could have asked him, where she knew what the true answer was. And the moment the person deviated from the truth, she would follow through by taping him up and walking away.

But she was on a time constraint and didn't have an intel packet on this target. In fact, she knew little about him to be able to check to see if he was bluffing. So, in turn, she used primacy to make him understand, believe that there was no point, that it was futile to lie to her, in the hopes that she could convince him to tell her the truth. She would have to trust her gut instincts, her skills in reading deception, and hope it would be good enough. "Do you understand?" she asked.

The man nodded, a little more pronounced than his initial acceptance and agreement to speak.

"I need to hear you say it."

"Yes," he hissed. His voice was one that tried to show resistance, but underneath it all, Hatch heard nothing but a raspy desperation.

She was right about her initial assessment of him. He was not a man accustomed to such treatment and maybe years ago he would have been able to withstand this simple bit of torture. But under his current circumstance, he was weakened.

"Good," she said. "Then we have an understanding. There are people outside that door right now that want to come in here and put a bullet in your head for the crimes you've committed against their people. I stopped them from doing that." Hatch said this to build fast rapport with the man, to give him the idea that she was his only lifeline. He needed again not only to believe that she was capable of interpreting and reading any lies and mistruths, but that she was the only one capable of saving his life.

He nodded his understanding. "What do you want from me?" he asked weakly.

Hatch was quiet for a moment and eyed the man cautiously. "We'll get to that in a minute, Baako. I understand that you must be afraid. If I were in your shoes and I knew what was on the other side of that door, I'd be terrified too. So, you have to understand that I want to help you." It was a lie, of course. But Hatch delivered the message with a sincerity worthy of an Oscar.

Inside, she despised everything about the man. She knew many like him. She'd seen their kind, the damage and devastation of the things they did and what little care they had for the fallout from their actions. People were beneath them. They were bugs on the bottom of their shoe and barely paid mind to the bodies left in their wake.

Hatch tucked down her personal repulsion for the man and put on a face of compassion. She didn't want to seem kind, just caring enough that he felt she was keeping his best interests in mind. Maybe he'd believe she was some type of humanitarian aid worker, there to help him, saving him from whoever it was. More likely, the lieutenant would probably think she was CIA. He'd seen her put two bullets in her bodyguard's head.

"I know you're probably wondering who I am. It's not worth your time to try to figure that out," Hatch said. "I'm not going to tell you. You're never going to know and you're never going to see me again. The minute that door closes behind me is the last time you'll ever see me. You're a pawn in a much bigger game, and I need to know some things."

"Whatever I tell you won't matter. You're going to kill me anyway. It doesn't matter," the man said and looked away.

"I have no intention of killing you. What you tell me decides what will happen to you. Simply put." Hatch knew exactly what was going to happen to him. She knew Jabari's plan for the man, and it would not be good. But lying was an integral part of an interrogation and was a much-needed platform of negotiation.

"Listen, you're really not in a place to argue your point. I need to know the best way to get into Dakarai's compound."

"Impossible," he said. He gave a dismissive laugh, but there was a little hint of nervousness also. She knew there was something more to it.

"Why is it impossible?" Hatch asked.

"It just is. He is one of the most powerful men in this region, and he is protected. Many people want to see him rise or rise with him. There is no getting to him."

"I got to you," Hatch said. "And it wasn't that difficult. I will get to him. I promise you. I just figured I didn't want to kill all of your people. But if that doesn't matter to you, then we can end this conversation now and you can go back to the darkness."

There was a flicker in the man's deep brown eyes as they widened. She could see from his subtle reaction that the portly lieutenant had no interest in having the blindfolds put back on, to go back into the induced deprivation. A deep-rooted fear had surfaced. Hatch didn't know what, didn't have time to dig it out. But whatever she had accessed through those hours in the dark and silence had triggered something in the man, something usable.

"I can see that doesn't please you," she said, showing him she was able to read his body language, however slight. Another demonstration of her primacy, of her ability to interrogate. "Let me ask you again. And this time, remember, there is an answer I'm looking for. And if I don't get it, I walk out that door."

The man swallowed hard.

"What is the best way to get into the compound unseen?" she asked. She had a metered cadence to her voice, leveled, calm, controlled, and quiet. These were things she deployed now, disorienting him further. Her calm was juxtaposed to Baako's anxiety. It also showed that she was the one in control, a small but important power play.

Hatch moved a step back from the bound man and looked toward the door but said nothing, a nonverbal gesture that her follow-through, her warning, was about to be carried out. Then she looked to the table where the roll of duct tape sat next to the pack of matches. She began a slow count in her head and began to turn away.

"Wait," he said, desperation at the forefront of his voice. "I sometimes bring girls in. He doesn't like it. He doesn't want me to have them in the compound. Thinks it causes problems. Sometimes I go to town center where you found me, but I send for them and they come to me."

"How do you bring these girls in if Dakarai doesn't allow it?" Hatch asked.

"There's a gate that's not heavily guarded. There are usually only one or two soldiers at most. It leads down to a small riverbed. It's where we get our fresh water from. And the terrain is a little bit rocky, so people don't use it. It's not the main entrance. And there's a little path cut down there where I bring my girls through."

"And the guards?" Hatch said. "How do they get past the guards?"

He smiled weakly. "Money. Well, cigarettes mostly, but I give them a little something to look the other way. I am their lieutenant, although everybody has ears and everybody is making moves to take someone else's position, so I have to be careful not to offend them."

"Is it always guarded?" she asked.

"Yes, but at night, only one guard watches the back gate. It's not even really a gate. It's a gap in the fence only wide enough to let maybe one person in at a time. No vehicle could come up through there."

"Don't worry about how we're going to approach. I just need to know the particulars. When do the guards change?"

"At dark. And again in the morning."

"The night guard, there's two at night you said?" Hatch intentionally asked the wrong number to see if she could catch him slip in his answer.

The man shook his head. "No. At night, there's only one. No need for more than that. Day time, they put two out there. But at night, the extra guard mans the front."

"Are there any booby traps?"

"Booby traps?" he asked.

"You know, bombs, trip wires, alarms, something that would alert the guard to somebody approaching."

The man shook his head. "No, nothing like that. The front, they have something set up there. A couple claymores. And the guard tower overlooks the road in. The men are well-armed and equipped to handle it if somebody was to make a frontal attack. But the back, like I said, is relatively easy in comparison."

Hatch studied him, evaluated his answers, and listened carefully to his voice inflection. Nothing she could sense hinted at deception. From what she gathered, he was telling the truth, or at the very least, his version of it. With time running out, Hatch decided to move on the information she had just acquired. She stood and walked toward the door.

"Wait," he said. "What are you going to do to me? I told you what I know."

Hatch didn't look back. "I know. I told you you'd never see me again."

Duke and two men entered as Hatch came out.

"But I told you what you wanted to hear!" Baako screamed out.

"This is for Masika," Hatch said coldly.

"Who?" Baako's face contorted in confusion.

Hatch watched as Duke unsheathed a large machete. "You signed your death warrant when you strung her little boy from that Fever Tree."

The door closed as Duke raised the blade high overhead.

Jabari seemed unfazed by the things taking place in the other room and raised his eyebrows as if to ask, "And?"

"There's a weak point. It's the back. Small break in the fence line and only guarded by one soldier at night. He says there are no traps set for that location, that it's used to grab water from the river. Small path, no access by vehicle." Hatch gave a quick rundown of the interrogation. No need to go into the details as far as how she gathered it.

"Do you think he's lying?" Jabari said.

"No," Hatch offered. "Although we don't really have the time to press any further. It's enough to go on. He said the front is extremely well-guarded, with overlook watchtowers, claymore mines, and a heavier contingent of soldiers."

"I think I have an idea," Jabari said, "of how we can draw some attention."

"I'm all ears," Hatch said. "But we better move quick."

Night began to fall and as Hatch and Jabari walked out into the waning light of day, they waited for Duke and the others to finish with the lieutenant.

TWENTY-THREE

DARKNESS WAS a tricky thing in Africa, Hatch found. The moon seemed brighter here than she'd ever seen before. When the clouds were not in the sky, it cast the shadows into strange patterns from the trees' canopies above. It was brighter than she would have liked, but on the flip side, it made navigating the narrow and winding trail toward the back of the compound easier than if it had been pitch dark. They staged themselves in a low point down by the river. The path Baako had described led up a hill. And in the distance, using binoculars provided by Jabari, she was able to see the top post of the fence line. Beyond that, she couldn't see much else.

Jabari, Duke and Hatch silently approached and waited for their distraction to arrive. They crept up the hill slowly. They didn't want to get too close before it was time to move, but they wanted to be close enough so when it began, they were ready to take action quickly and make their entrance into the compound.

"It should be only moments now. Be ready," Jabari said.

Duke gave a big thumbs up.

Hatch nodded.

Their weapons were already at the ready, and they maintained a low crouch. The trio were packed into a tight stacked formation with Jabari in the lead, Hatch in the middle, and Duke bringing up the rear.

Then they heard it. Yelling from inside the compound, warning cries as an alarm sounded. Although Hatch couldn't understand the words, the tone was obvious. Their distraction was approaching. The initiation of the frontal assault was about to begin. They could hear the roar of the truck now over the voices of the men.

Hatch knew the plan by heart. Jabari had come up with it and the team had agreed to it.

They needed to draw fire from Dakarai's men in the compound so they could make an easy entrance in the rear.

The truck was being navigated with the dead lieutenant duct taped to the steering wheel. The gas pedal was rigged and sent barreling down toward the main gates.

If the intel she had gathered held true, they would hear gunfire from the towers and the explosion of the claymores Baako claimed lay in wait for anyone who would try a frontal assault. If nothing else, the vehicular distraction would empty some ammunition from the men who they would undoubtedly have to battle. If things went as they had originally planned, the only shots fired would be when they found Dakarai. After he was eliminated, it would be a quick exit with their rally point several miles away from the compound.

It was never the intention to take on the entire compound. That was deemed a suicide mission. Plus, many of the soldiers had been forced into servitude. The goal was to cut the head off the snake in the hopes it would dismantle Dakarai's command and control.

If the distraction worked to their advantage, then they'd be able to make quick work of entering undetected. Jabari's intel source confirmed the compound's defense protocol would dictate Dakarai would be relocated to a building at the far end of the compound and secured by a small contingent of guards.

Dakarai's bunker was their objective. Any additional resources would be allocated toward the front and would minimize the number of guns they would have to face once they entered.

The truth of the dead Lieutenant Baako's interrogation was confirmed as dual explosions sounded from the compound's front gate area. Hatch immediately recognized the distinct sound of the detonated claymores.

Sporadic gunfire from the towers above erupted. The distraction vehicle with the dead man at the helm was continuing its relentless progression as the pedal was spiked to the floor. The steering was tied into position so the vehicle would not change direction.

A loud crash of metal on metal sounded as the front end of the truck collided with the gate. Heavily damaged and on fire, the rolling fireball assisted in drawing more of the men away from the back area where they would be entering.

They were already on the move, Hatch following Jabari as he quickly ascended the last several feet of the hill leading to the gate. The guard was not looking, although he was still standing there. He seemed torn, wanting to go toward the action but apparently disciplined enough to stay at his post. Jabari fired once, dropping the man immediately. Baako had not been completely truthful. There was a gate at the back entrance. Jabari then fired a second time at the lock. The clink of the lead against the metal lock would have been louder had there not been the cacophony of noise coming from the front of the compound. The distraction served its secondary purpose to mask any noise from their gunfire.

They pushed the gate open, and it dragged noisily across the dirt.

Following the information provided by Jabari's intelligence source, the trio made their way to Dakarai's hideaway. Hatch had a strange thought, stranger under the current circumstances. *If Jabari was Robin Hood and Duke was Friar Tuck, did that make Hatch Maid Marian?*

They could see one building in the back stood out from the rest. Several guards were posted out front who were directing their attention toward the front, their weapons up at the ready. Hatch could see they were nervous.

Jabari, Hatch and Duke swooped around, trying to flank the men using the variety of obstacles to conceal their movement. A wood pile and a small shack served that purpose.

To her dismay, the bright moonlight spotlighted them as they made their final dash, approximately thirty feet away from the building. They were going to have to break into the open. There was only one way to get there, and there was no more cover.

The trio paused behind the last semblance of cover and waited for their secondary distraction to start. Two of Jabari's men were in the tree line outside the front gate.

The second wave of the assault began, initiated by the delivery of two rocket-propelled grenades. Their targets would be the overwatch towers.

A loud explosion and bright flash lit up the night sky as one of the towers collapsed with the impact of the first rocket. The second rocket missed its intended target and whistled off into the distance, crashing loudly and exploding into a web of trees beyond the compound in a dazzling display of battlefield fireworks. Several trees caught fire, back-lighting Dakarai's bunker. The shadows of the four guards protecting their leader danced wildly in the fire's light.

Using this as their opportunity, Hatch's team rushed forward, engaging the men outside the warlord's stronghold. Firing quickly, in tight controlled bursts, they directed their attack on the enemy.

Rounds were fired in return. Hatch heard the zip and pop as a round went by her ear. She crouched low, moving quickly, keeping her eye on the target, and continued firing while doing so. One of the guards went down.

The three pressed forward as shots continued to ring out from both sides.

She heard Duke yell out in pain. Hatch looked back to see the large man holding his upper leg. He continued to lay down suppressive fire from his AK47 in the direction the shot had come from. His rounds found their mark, neutralizing the threat.

Hatch scooped him up, taking the large man's weight on her shoulder as they hobbled toward the wall of the bunker like a pair of three-legged racers at a Fourth of July picnic.

Hunkered down on the nearest wall, the three took a moment to catch their breath. Two of the four soldiers tasked with providing security for Dakarai were down. That left two more.

Hatch tried to evaluate the damage to Duke's leg when the window above their head shattered as shots emptied out of the bunker. Hatch shot back, firing blindly. The gunfire from within the bunker subsided, at least for the moment. One thing was certain, the element of surprise was gone.

Jabari pulled a flash-bang from his bandolier and threw it through the shattered window. It exploded, knocking the rest of the glass out in a blinding flash. Using the tight window provided by the distraction, the trio seized the opportunity and rushed the door. Duke was losing a lot of blood and righted himself as best he could, but there was no time to deal with the wound in his leg. Although it looked bad, the blood saturating his khakis into a rust-colored brown, the man seemed to find strength in the moment of chaos and stood upright.

Hatch fired twice into the center of the doorframe and kicked hard at the door, splintering the frame. Jabari was tight on her heels. The three made their way into the hornets' nest. Duke lagged a fraction of a second behind.

The bunker was small, not unlike the one Jabari and his men had used for their mockup at their own compound. The flashbang's effects had temporarily stunned the two guards who'd entered to take cover.

Hatch quickly found her target and fired her MP5 striking one of the guards with three tight shots, two in the body and one in the head. Hours of range training coming to bear on the man. Jabari fired from a staggered position to her left, eliminating the other threat. Neither guard got a shot off.

At the back of the room was an overturned mahogany desk. Behind it a door. Based on the external size of the one-leveled structure, this was the only likely place Dakarai could be. Hatch began firing into the wood, ensuring the warlord wasn't hiding.

Silence followed.

Hatch took this opportunity to do a combat reload, exchanging the magazines, putting the half-used magazine in her cargo pocket.

Still no gunfire returned, except from outside. Inside the room, there was no sound of movement.

The three stared at the closed door. Hatch looked at Jabari and Duke and nudged with her chin in the direction of the door.

"Ready to move?" Jabari asked.

"Moving," Hatch replied.

They came from two different worlds, but the language of combat was universal; the communication was clear, crisp and succinct. Both here in Africa among Jabari and his men and where Hatch had come from, warriors were warriors, regardless of country or community.

They both moved quickly. Duke stayed back, covering the door they'd breached. Hatch and Jabari cleared the overturned table, coming at it from opposite ends. She saw that the other man lay dead in a pool of blood near the door.

Jabari shook his head and whispered, "It's not Dakarai. Must be his personal bodyguard."

"Last door. How many do you think are in there?" Hatch asked.

"No telling. We took the few outside. We had three in here. Maybe it's just him. How many flash-bangs do you have?"

"One more."

"Ready?"

They walked up. Hatch kept her body beside the wall near the door and slowly checked the doorknob. Duke kept watch on their six as they prepared to enter.

A deafening blast from a machine gun ripped through the door, making a curved frown line across the wood, splintering it, sending rounds into the opposite wall.

Both Hatch and Jabari ducked low. Hatch crawled over before the next volley erupted, grabbing the knob.

"It's locked. Hit it."

Jabari pelted the lock with his AK47. The powerful rounds tore a hole in the frame near the doorknob as Hatch peeled back and shielded her face.

The door flopped open just a crack, the lock effectively disabled.

"Now," Hatch said.

Jabari tossed the last flash-bang into the room through the separation between the door and its chewed-up frame. The metal canister clanged on the wood plank floorboards for a few seconds before releasing the blinding flashing and high decibel bang. Light blasted through the cracks in the door as the concussive force slammed the door closed.

Jabari kicked the door open. Hatch brought her weapon to bear, maintaining her low crouch.

Dakarai was on his knees, teetering from side-to-side, rubbing his eyes. He then began blindly feeling his way across the floor. Hatch saw what he was doing. He was looking for the weapon that had come loose when the flashbang went off, and he found it.

His hand touched the grip of his AK as Hatch brought her front sight on target.

Hatch fired one time. The round landed smack dab in the middle of the man's forehead, slamming him back against the wall, dead on impact.

Strangely, in the heat of combat, there is no satisfaction in those moments. Leading up to them, the mind plays tricks, telling you that it will bring about closure. It'll feel good to right the wrong. But all her mind had time to contemplate was the next threat.

They had to get out now. The warlord was dead. She'd pulled the trigger. She'd completed her objective, but there was still an army of men outside. And once they realized that the threat was no longer from the front, they'd come to check on their leader.

"We got to move," Duke hollered from the front. "They're coming."

They stacked up on Duke's massive frame.

In the short time the African Friar Tuck had stood guard, a thick pool of dark blood had leaked out around his foot. The wound to his leg was bad. Hatch could see that more clearly now. He'd need a tourniquet. The bullet hole needed to be tied off, and pressure was needed to slow the bleeding. Right now, there was no way to address it. There'd be more enemies coming within seconds.

"Can you move?" Hatch asked. "Can you run?"

Duke looked at her and gave his best attempt at a smile with a blood-covered thumbs up. It was a shadow of the one he had given after her first day with the group when the two had tussled. She had a profound respect for the man, more so now after witnessing his grace under the dire circumstances of his wounds. "You lead, I'll follow. Don't worry about me, little lady."

Hatch led, with Jabari in the middle, and Duke took up the rear.

The trio made it as far as the wood pile before gunfire erupted again. This time the assault wave came from the center of the compound moving toward their location. Chunks of the chipped wood showered them as they came under the heavy fire.

All three began to return their volley, conserving ammo for the onslaught.

The approaching soldiers suddenly diverted their gunfire back toward the front of the camp. The two men from Jabari's unit who had initiated the assault and fired the RPGs at the watchtower continued to engage the enemy from their position as well.

"They're covering our movements," Hatch yelled. "We're going to have a window. It's going to be short. We should be able to make it. Duke, you're going to have to run!"

Hatch could see the gunfire in the wood line from Jabari's men as they rained down a barrage of bullets into the compound. A focused return attack from Dakarai's men quickly ended Jabari's men's suppressive fire.

Hatch knew sadly that their attempt to cover their movement had most likely cost them their lives. Using the split second of time their sacrifice gave, Hatch made a dash for the opening fence line, the same gate where they had entered.

She crossed through the gate and tumbled down the hilly path, rolling to a painful stop against a thick bush. Jabari stayed sure footed as he came through the gate.

Duke lagged behind, unable to run as quickly with the damage to his leg. The gunfire picked up again. Duke stopped near the fence and began firing back.

"I'll hold them off! Go!" he shouted down to Hatch and Jabari.

Hatch started to ascend the path toward the big man as the enemies' bullets crashed into the Duke's massive upper body.

Jabari grabbed Hatch's arm. "We must go now, Hatch, if we plan on living past today."

Hatch was frozen for a moment, looking up at Duke as he provided a human shield for them to escape. A loud roar erupted from Duke as he was struck by several more rounds.

He continued firing as they made their way down the path. Hatch looked back just as Duke crumpled into the opening gate, firing his weapon until it ran dry. The big man slumped and fell forward.

Hatch ran hard, pushing herself by the rage swirling inside as she fled deeper into the dense jungle and away from the compound. The sound of gunfire gave way. The only thing she heard was the ragged breath of her exertion.

TWENTY-FOUR

HATCH AND JABARI waited at the rally point a few minutes past the time they'd said they would wait. Hoping beyond reason that the other team members would return. The two men who'd led the frontal assault on the compound and deflected the attention, giving them a window from which to make their escape, were nowhere to be found. It felt wrong not to wait longer, knowing that without their efforts, they would have surely been dead.

Hatch thought of Duke, and the ultimate sacrifice that he gave so they could escape. He did it with no regard for himself, knowing the cost and what would undoubtedly be his end. And he did it for his leader Jabari, but also Hatch, a woman he'd only known for a matter of days.

In the world of combat, Hatch knew friendships and the bonds forged were different than the common place relationships that occurred through mundane circumstances. The battlefield has a unifying effect, and people who have served together understand this. Hatch felt a closeness to the large man she'd bested in the hand-to-hand match earlier in the week. She felt a deep sense of loss at his death.

"I think we need to move," Jabari said, interrupting her thoughts.

Hatch agreed with him but felt better upon hearing him say it.

"You're right. If they're coming, they'll be coming soon. Daylight's going to break, and we'll be sitting ducks."

"Plus," Jabari added, "got to get back to our compound, to the villagers. We're going to be their only source of protection now. And the fallout from this could be cataclysmic."

She understood exactly what he meant. If they beat Jabari and her to the village, the people would have no defense except for the two men he'd left behind. And the people they set out to protect would be cut down. Hatch could not envision another scene of the innocent, another burning village, another crying mother, so she prayed it would not happen.

Closing her eyes for a brief second to clear her head, she said, "Let's move."

Jabari took off moving through the shrubs, breaking from the trail they had taken when approaching the compound, he was surefooted and moved quickly. His endurance was impressive. Hatch was rarely challenged by another's fitness, especially when it came to running. But she found herself having a bit of difficulty keeping up with him. Made sense that he could navigate the terrain well. He'd been doing it his whole life.

They moved through the darkness, trying to minimize the noise. If there were any outlying foot patrols or people searching for them, they didn't hear anything, but it didn't mean they weren't there.

A short while later, they came upon their Jeep. The rugged beast of a machine was capable of handling the rough terrain. They uncovered the foliage, which had masked its location, similar to when they hit the supply raid.

Hatch got in the passenger seat, and Jabari the driver's side, and then he sped away down the road. Less than a mile later, they saw headlights in the rear.

Hatch looked at Jabari, and they simultaneously gave the same knowing glance. There was no such thing as coincidence at this point. It wasn't a wayward traveler in the early morning hours. It was most likely some of the warlord's men. They'd probably been driving the one main thoroughfare looking for any sign of them. Jabari cut the lights, but he knew at that point it was counterproductive and most likely unnecessary if they'd already been spotted.

Hatch assumed they had already seen their vehicle, but maybe the blackout would help to elude them. The headlights were beginning to approach fast, and any doubt about whether they might have been a wayward traveler was quickly dashed as an eruption of gunfire from a turret mounted on the back of their truck burst around them.

Even though it was a mounted weapon, center point in the vehicle, the winding and uneven roads made aiming difficult, not as easy as one might think. It wasn't a video game. Jabari accelerated.

A couple of rounds smacked the back end of the Jeep, but nothing hit Hatch or Jabari. It was still too close for comfort though. It wouldn't be long until they were close enough to take aim and have a more effective shot group. Hatch didn't want that to happen. Jabari continued to accelerate, flooring the pedal and pushing the vehicle's limits as it rattled and banged along the rough surface of the road.

Hatch looked at him. Jabari was bouncing his eyes between the road ahead and the rearview mirror.

"Keep it as steady as you can, I'm going to try to end this," she said.

Jabari nodded, keeping his eyes straight ahead. He kept his head lights off. Hatch knew why. Without the lights, the shooter wouldn't have a reference point for a better target. Jabari intentionally swerved, kicking up dust and dirt to act as a makeshift smoke screen. This technique had been effective thus far, minus the few strafing rounds.

Unlike what many see in movies, Hatch had no intention of rolling the window down and leaning out the side of the car. It would be an ineffective platform for firing a weapon, especially to the rear. She would also have to lean out extremely far. There would be no way to truly get a good balance point for steadying her shots, and she'd be as haphazard in her grouping as the men racing behind her. So, she did something different. Hatch turned her body completely to the rear, straddling the front passenger seat, and pulling her chest flush with the backrest of the chair.

She then brought up the MP5 and wrapped her arm tightly around the head rest, creating a balanced shooting platform, supported by the chair's back and then further supported by taking the shoulder strap and looping it one time around the head rest. It was worth taking the time to secure her shooting platform so her aim would be true. Two well-placed shots were better than thirty blind ones. Hatch knew this. It was a principle she'd used before in order to survive multiple deadly encounters.

Hatch tightened herself and steadied her aim, looking down the iron sights of the weapon. It was dark and the headlights blurred out any clear distinguishing features of the operator, or the shooter in the back of the vehicle. She had two targets in her mind that she was going to eliminate.

Target number one was the man standing at the weapon at the back of the Jeep. She couldn't clearly see him, but the latest volume of gun fire identified the location of the muzzle. She knew from experience that his torso and head would be at, or slightly up above that reference point. And that's where she took aim. The rear of the Jeep she was riding in had dark tinted windows in the back, and it was a closed cab. The tints didn't help her sight picture, but it did mask the fact that she was taking aim at them.

Hatch needed to end the primary threat first, and then she could focus on the occupants within the vehicle.

Hatch breathed in slowly and then exhaled. As she completed her exhale, her finger slowly squeezed the trigger. In cyclic loop between inhale and exhale, the natural respiratory pause, Hatch fired three times.

After releasing the rounds, she kept her point of aim.

She couldn't see if her target was down. Seconds ticked by. No return gunfire. The mounted weapon ceased.

Hatch took this as a win. Either the shooter was wounded, dead or momentarily ducking for cover, which would give her time to focus on her next target. Although she couldn't see into the cab of the vehicle that was chasing them, she knew by basic design of any car that the driver's column would be, as she looked at it, slightly to the left of the driver's side headlight.

She aimed and fired five shots. The first two rounds skipped off the hood, giving her a reference point to raise her point of aim for the next three. The windshield of the pursuing vehicle spiderwebbed.

This time, the answer to the effectiveness of her shots was immediate.

The car jerked violently to the right, and Hatch watched as it careened off the roadway and then slammed into a dense network of trees. The front-end crashed loudly, the impact so hard that it lifted the backend up into the air. The truck teetered momentarily on its frontend, sending the turret gunman's limp body sailing through the air. The back of the vehicle hung in the air for a few seconds before crashing back down.

Smoke and steam erupted from the engine compartment under the crumpled hood. Hatch assumed the men, at least the driver and most likely the shooter in the back, were dead. It didn't matter anyway. The vehicle was completely totaled. There'd be no further pursuit from this contingent of Dakarai's men.

Hatch scanned the rear, remaining in her shooting position.

Jabari continued to drive, looking forward, and then said, "Nice shooting."

Neither looked at each other, each focused on their specific task. Trust in combat was critical. Jabari's task was effectively navigating the roadways with no headlights in the dark at high speeds. Hatch, meanwhile, provided rear security to any potential threat.

Minutes passed; no additional threat came. Jabari maintained his current speed. Their worry was if there were no further threat coming for them directly, it might be heading toward the village...if it wasn't already there.

They didn't have far to go now. And without any further sign of trouble from the rear, Hatch removed the weapon's strap from the headrest and turned her body to face forward. She kept the gun between her legs at a modified vehicular low ready.

"I'm not sure what we're going to find there, Hatch, but we must be prepared for the worst," Jabari said.

"I always am," Hatch said softly.

TWENTY-FIVE

JABARI PULLED around the last bend leading into the village. Hatch's subconscious ran wild, preparing for the possible devastation she might see, holding her breath momentarily. But as the sun began to rise, giving way to morning, she saw there was no smoke filtering up from the huts. Nothing was on fire. She heard no screams of anguish, as she had the other day when entering the village.

The two men assigned with protecting the villagers rushed to them with their weapons at the ready. They lowered them upon seeing Jabari and Hatch. The men came alongside the driver's window as Jabari slowed to a stop. They looked into the backseat and realized what it meant when they saw the vacant seats. Jabari said something softly in their native tongue. Hatch didn't need a translator to understand the exchange. The eyes of the security detail were a mixture of sadness and anger.

"No time to mourn," Jabari said. "It's just us now, and you have to get ready. They'll be coming."

The men nodded and set out to corral the villagers.

Hatch looked at Jabari as he pulled her into the center of the compound. A few villagers were lingering about, and there was an old man and a heavyset woman preparing to make a fire.

Jabari shut the engine off. The two sat in silence for a moment, quietly processing the events of the night and preparing for an equally difficult morning.

"I don't think we have the numbers to hold them off," Jabari said quietly. "And most of these people have never fired a gun. They'd be useless, probably more likely to shoot us or themselves if things broke in a bad way."

Hatch nodded in agreement. Just giving someone a gun didn't mean they would increase any chance of survival. A lot of people stateside carried one for self-defense purposes, but few trained properly with those weapons, and if push came to shove and stress dictated, those weapons could easily be turned against them when confronted by a committed adversary.

"So, what's your plan?" Hatch asked.

"Move them to the back. Tuck them away out of sight so we can focus on the fighting. Unlike the other compound, there is no secret passage, no backdoor entrance. If they want to come for us here, they have to come through the front."

"Then that's where we'll meet them," Hatch said.

"This was never your fight, Hatch," Jabari said, "but I'm glad you made it yours. If not for you, I'd most likely already be dead. And however this breaks out today, at least Dakarai is no longer in power. That's not to say that someone else won't rise up in his stead, but we proved to these people and to the other villages who've come under attack recently that people can take a stand, that a few can make a difference against the many. And maybe, if this is our last stand, someone else will take up the charge," Jabari said, and then exited the vehicle.

Jabari began going from hut to hut and speaking to the people inside, explaining the situation.

Hatch began reloading her magazines, preparing for the battle to come. Having been awake for over twenty-four hours, sleep was the furthest thing from her mind.

Hatch watched as the two men who had guarded the villagers grabbed an RPG and set it nearby. The villagers began making their way to the back. The guards stood side-by-side near the main entrance to the village with their AK-47s slung center mass. They exchanged a brief embrace and took up a firing position behind trees on either side of the dirt road.

"They're brothers." Jabari's eyes were sad. "I saved them years back. Now, I'm sending them to their death."

Hatch didn't have words.

"There's only four of us left, Hatch. And if they attack with the remaining soldiers, we're doomed. Regardless of how good we are, it's unlikely we'll be able to handle those numbers, if you understand what I'm saying?"

Hatch nodded. "I do. If we're going to die here and now, I want them to see our face and see it coming. Let them know that if this is our last stand, we're going to give them a hell of a fight. Those bastards are going to earn every step they take in this village. And whatever they do, it's going to cost them." Then she offered a weak attempt at a smile. "And who knows? Maybe a little luck will be on our side."

Hatch looked down at the scar on her right arm. She had survived hell and come out on top. Maybe she could do it again.

"For what it's worth, Miss Hatch," Jabari said. "You're one hell of a warrior. And I for one am proud for this short time to have shared the battlefield with you. I'm grateful to our mutual friend, Chris Bennett, for connecting us here in my Africa."

Hatch put the MP5 single point sling over her neck.

"We have a saying. And if we live past this day, maybe it will mean something to you," Jabari offered.

"I'm all ears."

"When there is no enemy within, the enemies outside cannot hurt you." Jabari then rested a gentle hand on her damaged shoulder. "Maybe someday you can find the peace you are looking for."

DAYLIGHT BROKE and the heat began to rise. It was the routine of the morning here. The dew and moisture of the night rose up and created waves of steam. The sun beat down quickly, raising temperatures dramatically. The sweat from her run and their encounter had started to dry, but was now starting to pool again, saturating her clothes. She and Jabari, with their weapons at the ready, had reloaded in the interim. There was no more conversation now, but rather total focus, mental preparation, and the silence that came before the battle. The calm before the impending storm was upon them. They both could feel it. The intangible point in which battle was about to break wide open.

She did her best to control the nerves and adrenaline filling her body. Breathing slowly helped. A steady hand was needed in these types of situations. Every shot would count if the numbers they were expecting arrived.

Then in the distance they heard a rumbling, the loud sound of a diesel engine. Something big was coming. A truck, maybe more than one truck. It sounded more like a convoy.

"Here it comes," she said, as much to herself as to the man standing beside her.

Jabari grunted and said something in Swahili to the two brothers nearest the road.

Hatch and Jabari stood approximately ten feet back from the entrance point to the village. They were effectively standing between whatever was coming and the innocent civilians behind them. They were the first and last line of defense.

Whatever was coming was big, too. They heard it crashing into the brush and trees that protruded out along the winding path leading to the village.

Hatch brought the weapon up to her shoulder. No point of aim, but she kept it at a slight downward angle, and she was just looking over its frame. It would be a simple adjustment to bring it up on target, whatever the target may be.

"I see it now, I can see it," said one of the brothers, from behind his post at the tree. He was speaking in English, for Hatch's benefit.

"Hold your fire, I'll tell you when." Jabari's plan was to let the first or lead vehicle get inside and then hit the middle with the RPG, bogging down the others and splitting the enemy as best they could. Standing in plain sight was part of their calculated misdirection. It was a tricky plan at best, but it could work.

"Hold," Jabari said again.

All weapons were up.

Hatch looked down the iron sights of her MP5, trying to find a target as the front end of a large personnel carrier came into view. "Shit," she said.

It was dark when they attacked the warlord's compound, but she hadn't seen a vehicle like this within its boundaries. This was bad. A heavy personnel carrier could carry numerous troops. It was armored and well-fortified. It would be difficult to effectively engage this threat.

As she scanned for a target, she saw something else. One of the brothers saw it too and yelled something in Swahili.

Hatch couldn't hear or understand what he said. As she looked down through her sight, it became more clearly visible.

Painted on the front end of the vehicle was the UN flag.

And then as she scanned the driver compartment, she saw the telltale blue helmets of the UN peacekeepers. She brought her weapon to the low ready, so as not to be perceived a threat.

Jabari said something to his men, and they stepped out from behind the trees and lowered their weapons.

A smile spread across Jabari's face as several UN trucks rolled into the village. Hatch never thought she'd see the kind-hearted leader's dimples again and was glad to be proven wrong. A cheer erupted from the two brothers as they welcomed the new arrival.

Jabari turned to Hatch and said, "Looks like the cavalry's arrived finally."

Hatch raised an eyebrow. "I guess better late than never,"

"Good to see my message was finally received. I think we have our mutual friend to thank for this."

Khari, Hatch thought. The scarred cafe owner with a rich history, one Hatch now realized was much deeper and more complex than she had originally thought.

Maybe the United Nations Peacekeepers were waiting for Dakarai to fall to decide which side they would favor. The politics of war was something Hatch never got into. For her it was always about the men or women standing beside her. Those were the people who mattered, and the people they were trying to protect.

"We're not out of the woods yet," Jabari said. "But this is a good sign of things to come."

With that, Hatch felt a sudden longing, a longing to leave, to finish what she had come here for, to close out a chapter in her life that was long overdue and then hopefully start a new one back in Hawk's Landing, with the people who mattered to her most.

TWENTY-SIX

THE PEACEKEEPERS HAD COME in and immediately assisted in the recovery of the villagers. They told Jabari there was a plan to construct a new village not too far away. Jabari knew a few of the senior members of the UN peace keeping crew. Although it was an international organization, this local conglomerate contained several people Jabari had grown up with. These were people he knew personally and trusted. They had assured him that everything would be done to redistribute Dakarai's caches of supplies and to restore order to the area.

Jabari relayed this to Hatch, who was not wholly convinced it would be as smooth a transition as described, but it was definitely beginning to look up for this area. It seemed as though whatever political upheaval was taking place, the control mechanisms at work were momentarily putting that in check.

This gave Hatch some sense of peace in her decision to leave. Jabari did not offer any resistance, but said he was sad to see her go. He offered to drive her to the airport, but Hatch had another stop she needed to make first.

Outside the cafe in Mombasa town center, Jabari pulled to a stop.

Hatch grabbed her duffle and left the Jeep. Jabari came around to her side and uncharacteristically gave her a warm embrace.

"You are a very special person to us here now, Miss Hatch. What you did, the sacrifices you made, and the risks you took have given my people a better chance at life, and I thank you."

Hatch, uncomfortable with compliments, offered a gentle shrug. "He was doing bad things to good people, and I just can't let that ride. It was never my intention to get so involved, but after seeing the devastation those villagers faced, I felt compelled, and I'm glad I was able to do something to help. Hopefully, you'll keep in touch with me in the years to come and let me know how things go."

Jabari smiled broadly. "I would very much like that, Miss Hatch, and I hope someday you come back to Africa. It seems a good fit for you."

Hatch smiled. Shouldering her bag, she turned and walked into the cafe.

Behind the counter was Khari, who was embroiled in a deep conversation with Josefina. Khari rushed around the counter and ran to her, as if seeing a long-lost friend for the first time in ages. Life is more precious when in a combat environment. What she'd been through in the last week could fill some people's entire lives as far as adventure went.

Instead of shaking hands as he had done in previous engagements, he took her up in a warm embrace. Hatch accepted the greeting and returned it with a gentle hug and pat of his back. She thought she would never see the man again.

If Hatch were to be truly honest with herself, she had thought she was going to die here in Africa.

The thought now haunted her. So many things undone. Her father's death never righted, but more important now to her were the relationships with her niece and nephew. The things unsaid to her mother and Dalton Savage.

"We're cooking up something wonderful this morning, Hatch. Do you have time to eat?" Hatch looked at her watch. She had a few hours until her flight, but it was international travel and she wanted to make sure she got there early. But thinking about leaving before one last meal seemed plain wrong.

"On one condition, Khari," Hatch said. "That when I'm done, you drive me to the airport."

"Only if you shower first," Khari boomed with laughter, making an exaggerated wafting of his nose.

Hatch laughed. Nearly a week in the jungle, and she was ripe. "That bad?"

"The towels are in the bathroom."

Hatch decided to take him up on the offer. She had planned to ask, but Khari beat her to the punch. She grabbed her duffle and headed upstairs. Khari watched her go, smiling broadly. A little ripple formed along the discolored flesh of his scarred face. And then he walked back toward the kitchen to begin preparing her last meal in Africa.

Ten minutes later, Hatch was seated at her table, clean and feeling refreshed. Khari returned a short while later and laid the plate in front of her. Hatch was already on her second cup of the tea that she'd become addicted to during her short stay.

Khari took a seat across from her. The same place Jabari had sat when they first met. His large frame filled her vision, blocking the view of the post office where she first linked up with the now deceased Father McCarthy. The wooden chair creaked under the man's girth.

"I'm so glad you survived. I was very worried about you."

"Thank you. To be honest, I was worried too. I was worried I'd never get this cup of tea again," she said jokingly.

He laughed.

"But seriously, Khari, thank you for doing whatever it was you did to bring those troops to our aid. I don't know what would've happened if–"

He waved a dismissive hand, not letting her finish the sentence. "It was nothing. Trust me. It was long overdue. Sometimes things here are delicate. Alliances are formed, and they can be reshaped when certain events take place. What you did to..." He got his voice lower to make sure whatever he said next was not picked up by the ears of the other patrons in the cafe. "What you did to remove Dakarai was a very brave thing. And in doing so, it enabled me to do some things I otherwise would not have been able to do. He was feared by many."

"Rightfully so," Hatch said. "I can see why."

"Yes," Khari said. "But you did not fear him. You stood up to him. You took the fight to him. You, Jabari, and his men showed an uncommon valor I have rarely seen. I hope now, Miss Hatch, that you see Africa in a different light. I hope you come back to see the beauty you helped rebuild. You're going to see the strength of the African people, and it is a wonderful sight to behold." He fanned his hands out to his cafe, and then he touched his face. "From burning ashes to my wonderful cafe. Life is a series of choices, Miss Hatch. You can let the scars never heal or you can choose to see them for what they are. Reminders of a past, sometimes dark. But only in experiencing a cold night can you appreciate the warmth of day. And only in tragedy can you appreciate true bliss. As you finish your meal and I get ready to take you back to the airport, I hope you leave this place, the tragedy you experienced behind and you can go to wherever it is you need to find peace. You deserve it," he said.

I do deserve it, Hatch thought to herself. It was something she never truly believed until now. *I deserve to be happy. I've earned the right to be okay. I've paid my dues. I can go home. With a minor detour, of course.*

Hatch had finished her meal and a third cup of the tea before leaving the cafe. When Khari dropped her at the airport, he had taken her mother's address in Hawk's Landing and promised to send her a care package containing Josefina's tea so she could make some when she was back home. Hatch was delighted at the prospect and promised to keep in touch with the man, but she was also a realist and knew that sometimes that didn't happen.

She boarded her plane. There were a few days of travel ahead, and Hatch was extremely exhausted. She doubted she would have any difficulty falling asleep on this return trip.

Hatch was excited to be heading home to Hawk's Landing by way of North Carolina.

TWENTY-SEVEN

HATCH WALKED INTO THE BAR. Ernie Wenk was wiping down the counter in the back and clearing out some empty mugs as a few patrons left, paying her no mind as they passed by. The odor of alcohol and the scent of the spices used to make his legendary wings filled the air. Even though an overhead fan was working overtime above, the room had a stagnant quality to it. Nothing compared to the swelter of Africa and the last week or so she'd spent in the invariably hot climate however.

He looked up at her, his eyes, his body language not as welcoming as when she had first seen him before making her trip across the world. That first reconnection with the man had a genuine nostalgic quality. At the time, there were no barriers, psychological or otherwise that existed. Now it was a wholly different connection the two would soon share. Hatch knew things now. Not all of it, but enough to hold Wenk in a different light. The fact that she'd returned from Africa after going on a fact-finding mission seemed to raise alarm in him.

She wondered if it was just her mind being overactive after the experience of the last week. The revelation that the man responsible for her father's death was the former operator turned tattoo artist made her pause. She had sat only a few feet away from him inside his office after being guided there by Wenk.

During the long trip back stateside, she began to seriously wonder how much more Wenk knew. And she decided before making the next visit to see Fat Tony, she would have a conversation with the bar owner, a man who for many years had been held in the highest regard by Hatch.

Hatch walked over to the area of the bar set aside for those in the special operations community. She cast a glance at the glass set at the back with a couple fingers of whatever bourbon or whiskey had been set aside for the fallen who would never be able to take the drink. Hatch sat at the table nearest the glass with her back against the wall, eyeing the front door as she waited for Wenk to make his way over to her.

He seemed hesitant to do so, but a few minutes later, he was standing beside her table.

His apron was covered in a variety of sauces splattered and mixed to create some kind of Rorschach painting. If things weren't so complicated, she would have made a comment, maybe stared at it long enough to figure out what she could make of it. But she was not here for jokes, and she was not here for comradery. She was here for answers. Answers that he could give her, or should have given her, before she travelled halfway around the world and faced deadly odds.

Maybe that was his point all along. Maybe he knew sending her out there or her going there would bring about her end. And then they could wash their hands of whatever secrets they held.

The fact that she didn't know bothered her.

"Rachel Hatch, back in my bar again so soon," he said. Although he sounded his usual self, there was a hesitancy, a quietness in his voice. The same energy wasn't there. Something was definitely off.

"I think you and I need to talk."

He dismissed the comment and continued. "How was your trip? Did you find everything you were looking for?" He rubbed his hands nervously, wiping some of the grease and sauce onto a wet towel that hung from the waist strap of his apron.

It looked as though he had wiped more sauce onto his hands from the dirty towel than he removed.

"Seriously, Ernie, have a seat. We need to talk."

The big man looked around to see if any of the patrons had heard her subtle command. He was obviously not a man to be ordered around, especially in his own establishment. But Hatch had experience with that. As a military police officer in the early days of her career working bases around the country and the world, she went on many a domestic call. And going inside somebody's house, their domicile, their castle, she had to take charge. Take ownership. Give commands, control the scene. Many did not like being told what to do in their own house. Especially from a cop. Even more so from a female one. Hatch had no problems controlling a scene. And she had no problem now reminding Wenk again to take the seat.

"Ernie, I'm not here on a social visit. I need some answers, and I need you to give them to me."

He took his seat with a huff and folded his arms across his big chest. "I don't think I like the way you're talking to me, Rachel," he said gruffly.

"I don't think I like what I've learned. And if what I know is true, then the way I'm talking to you now is going to seem extremely civil to how I'll deal with you after."

"What are you getting at?" he asked.

"I learned some things. And trust me when I say this, the information I have now is as good and clear as it can get. And don't worry, nobody from Talon Executive Services or Gibson Consortium will be able to threaten or intimidate the information holder anymore because that source is dead and gone."

Wenk looked down and played with his apron, adjusting it unnecessarily as a distraction. He must've known who she was referring to.

Nobody knew Hatch was back. She didn't call Bennett or anyone else. She did plan to reach out to Bennett and thank him for putting her in touch with Jabari. Without it, she would have undoubtedly been killed. She felt she owed him that.

That could wait. The person she was most interested in talking to right now was sitting in a huff across from her with arms folded and a coldness in his eyes.

"So, you think you know some things? What is it you think you know?" Wenk asked.

"Ernie, that is not how this is going to go, and you know it. It's not a give and take tonight. You're going to tell me everything you know revolving around my father's death. And when you finish telling me, I'll decide what I'm going to do next. But trust me, at this point, you don't want to hold anything back."

"Are you threatening me, Rachel? Are you out of your mind? Did you come into my bar, my restaurant, and threaten me?" He leaned forward, unfolding his arms and pressing his thick gut against the edge of the table, his forearms reaching halfway across.

Hatch remained unmoved. The effort at intimidation was an utter failure.

"I'm not threatening you at all, Ernie. I'm making you a clear-cut, unequivocal promise. I'd better not find out you had anything to do with my father's death. And you're now going to tell me what you know about that day and who is responsible."

He pushed back just slightly. He relented in his attempt at intimidation. His shoulders dipped slightly. Something she said had resonated. The invisible tug of war between body language was over, and Hatch was the victor. He sighed quietly, and then he looked back toward the patrons at the bar and at some of the scattered tables around the restaurant area.

Hatch followed his eyes. She assumed he was looking to see if anyone could hear what he was about to say next. As she scanned the restaurant, she saw the ginger-haired soldier from her last visit who had tried to intimidate her and cast her out of the reserved section. He was sitting with his cronies again. They looked to be several pitchers deep into a night of drunken frivolity. They didn't pay her any mind this time around.

Wenk turned his gaze back to Hatch, barely making eye contact. And whatever reserve of strength he had used to puff his chest and make his claim seemed to be all but gone.

"Look, Rachel, that was a long time ago. And I told you, your father meant a lot to me. Times were different then. The Vietnam War was a tumultuous time at best, and those of us coming back from it were really trying hard to find our way."

Hatch held up her hand, stopping him. "Ernie, don't waste any energy trying to explain or reason why my father's dead. No amount of justification for time, setting, place or people is going to make it right. There's only one way to fix what was done. To bring justice to an unjust act. And I need to know who pulled the trigger." She spoke softly, knowing that Wenk was concerned about eavesdroppers. But forcefully enough that he could hear the intensity in her tone.

There was no question that she would not be leaving without an answer. And how that answer came about would depend wholly on Wenk's cooperation.

He seemed to shrink down in his chair ever so slightly. "Tony. Anthony Amaletto was the trigger man."

"And you're sure?" Hatch knew this was the right answer but wanted to see if he tried to back out or cast any doubt.

He nodded slowly. Made no effort to the contrary. "Yes."

"And how do you know this with one hundred percent certainty?" she asked.

"Because I was his spotter. I was there. The unit, like any type of special operation, always sent teams in to handle a target. Especially one as difficult as your father."

His cheeks blotched with a red pattern similar to the color of the stained apron he wore. The recall or open admission of his involvement in her father's death caused internal conflict with the large man. Hatch hadn't quite expected him to say this. She hadn't expected the confession to come about, but maybe the burden of it, the years in which he'd held this secret, and the unburdening of it now, gave him motivation to get it off his chest once and for all.

Maybe some of the things he said about her father, about their relationship, about the connection they shared was true. She hoped it was. She hoped everything she'd been told by this man wasn't a lie. She wanted to take away some of this and hold onto the memories of her dad carried by friends, coworkers and fellow operators.

"What are you going to do now, now that you know?"

"I'm going to clean the slate. I'm going to fix it all. And I'm going to put an end to this chapter in my family's history book."

A flash of anger came across his eyes. He balled his fists. "I told you my responsibility in this. I didn't pull the trigger. You know who did. And maybe you're going to find out you shouldn't be digging too deep into these people."

The threat was back. Whatever Wenk had conceded in his confession, and his airing of guilt, was now tucked back into the place where he kept it. The guard was up. Threats of the fallout from exposing his involvement, the defensive measures were back in place.

"You know what, Hatch, just let it go. It was dirty business what we did back then. And you keep digging around, and they won't just come for you or me. They'll come for anyone that they think may know. Anyone that can expose them. Do you understand me? That means your family, your friends, anyone you care about." He stood up, pushing his weight down on the table, shifting it on the uneven leg.

"You're scared. I can smell it on you," she said.

This comment only seemed to infuriate him further. "Get out. We're done here, Hatch. It's over. And I don't ever want to see you in this bar, my restaurant, or near me again. Do you understand me?"

This time he made no effort to hide his conversation with her. In fact, he said it in such a way that the other patrons in the bar took notice. In particular, the ginger-haired soldier and his tablemates. The ginger nudged one of his buddies, and they both turned their attention to the bear of a man and the woman seated at the table.

Hatch didn't bother to get up yet. She wasn't ready to give back the control of Ernie Wenk's restaurant. She still owned it. And her subtle, unmoved stance showed that. And it seemed to infuriate the big man even further.

"Did you hear what I said? Get out. I don't ever want to see you here again. And the only reason right now I'm not casting you out by the back of your head is the respect I had for your father."

Now Hatch stood. She felt a well of rage rise up in her. She wanted to smash her knuckles into the side of the man's cheekbone. But she knew she had other things to tend to first.

"You don't get to talk about my father anymore."

Wenk looked around. "Get out, Hatch. Now."

"You know where I'm going from here. And he better not know that I'm coming, or when I'm done, I'm coming back for you," she said. Even enraged, her voice was calm and controlled. She was saving the burning rage inside her for somebody else. Something two decades in the works.

Like a long slow burning fever, she felt the heat of it take hold.

"Get out!" the big man boomed as he stepped aside and pointed toward the door.

She walked past him, offering nothing further. The restaurant grew quieter. The man at the table, the young soldier who had tried to intimidate her had leaned down and whispered something to one of his friends close by. There were four of them. Young, fit, agile soldiers. And drunk. She could hear their thoughts.

Then, as Hatch opened the door, she heard Wenk say not to her, but to the four men, "Make sure she doesn't come back in, ever."

She heard the words as the door closed behind her.

Hatch stood on the sidewalk in front of Wenk's bar. The night air of North Carolina was thick and heavy. And when she had first come here a week ago, it had felt wholly oppressive. But now after spending time in Africa acclimatizing herself to what real heat was, what real humidity felt like, the night air felt refreshing in comparison.

Hatch waited because she knew what was coming.

Moments later, the door behind her opened.

Hatch slowly turned. The four men who were several pitchers deep into their night staggered out in a loose semicircle around her. One of the men looked slightly younger than the rest and definitely showed obvious signs of nervousness at this confrontation. But the others seemed happy to carry out Wenk's bidding. They were obviously looking to stay in the good graces of the bar owner and Special Forces legend.

The ginger who had confronted her previously seemed to be running the show, and there was an eagerness in his eyes.

"Listen, guys, I get it. You want to prove your worth to the old man in there. You want to show him that you'll do his bidding. Trust me, this isn't a fight you want," Hatch said calmly, bordering on nonchalant.

She had squared herself to the ginger-haired soldier whose fair complexion was dotted with light brown freckles. He looked like a fit version of Opie Taylor.

Hatch was fit and strong as well, and she had something he didn't. A depth of experience. She really didn't want to waste time with these men, with this foolish attempt at intimidation and macho bravado. She had other places to be, more important things to do. And any time wasted here now, any injuries sustained now, would slow her primary objective.

"Is she for real?" The ginger asked for his friends' benefit. "Are you crazy, lady?"

He seemed genuinely confused by the fact that she was the one giving the warnings. Hatch secretly liked this.

"Listen, go back inside. This isn't your fight. You don't know what this is about."

The ginger interrupted. "I don't care what this is about. Wenk says you need to go—you go. Wenk says there's a message to be sent—we're going to send it. That's the way this is going to work. Do you know who he is? Do you know what he did?"

Hatch knew the answers to this question. Knew the idolization of these men had of him. And the reasons why. And under other circumstances, they would be valid reasons to respect Wenk, but she had peeled back the layers of that onion. And she knew the stench that lay beneath.

"Like I said, you don't know everything. And let me make this even more clear to you four. Should you choose to make this mistake, not one of you is walking back in that bar tonight."

"What?" Opie asked, throwing his arms out to the side, like a peacock posturing in front of his friends.

Hatch didn't repeat herself. She tried never to repeat herself. She knew the message was received.

"What do you mean we're not walking back in there?" Opie pressed further.

"Because," She offered one last comment before making her decision to act, "None of you will be able to."

His eyes widened. Hatch knew that when dealing with multiple threats, the best way was to put one in front of the other to control the movement of one so that the others were rendered useless. But in the strange semicircle they'd formed around her, there was another alternative. Devastation. Hurt the first one so badly that the shock and awe aspect of it freezes the others. Take the one most committed, the leader— in this case Opie—and then hurt them in a way that makes the others hesitate to act. Then capitalize on their momentary lapse.

And that's exactly what she did. She had trained with some of the best in the world. And in circumstances like this, there were no rules. Except one—do whatever it takes to survive. They had made the decision, and Hatch was the answer to their poor choice. During her conversation with him, she had bladed herself slightly to him, shifting her weight into a south paw stance. Very subtle, barely noticeable. When the man had bowed his arms out, she edged forward ever so slightly. Hatch was now within range, not for her hands, but with her long legs.

She raised her knee and drove out hard, striking downward at a forty-five-degree angle to Opie, who was standing square to her and was still trying to formulate his next witty comment to intimidate her before he launched his attack. A poor decision to chat when the fight was already on.

The knife edge of her foot, the outside blade of her boot, smashed down into the center of the man's knee, buckling it backwards. She heard the crack and felt the shockwave as it went up her leg. Hard to break a bone with that technique. A baseball bat would do justice in circumstances like this. But a boot across the front of the knee striking downward did a different level of damage.

It buckled his knee backwards, reversing the way in which the body was supposed to move. And the effect was devastating and immediate.

Opie howled like a wounded animal, grabbing at his legs. He fell backward to the ground. She could see that her objective had been achieved. The strike had been extremely effective, and the blow greatly damaged the man's right leg. He fell to the ground and was holding it. Hatch deemed him zero threat at this point.

Her eyes immediately scanned the faces and body language of the other three men. They looked down at their leader. And then back toward Hatch. That moment in which they tried to surmise the situation, to come to grips with what was happening, was enough for Hatch to reposition herself. She had shot to the left, now putting one of the men in front of the rest of the others. Keeping one in front of the others, she'd be able to fight one at a time.

They were still psychologically dazed, but anger was now filling their eyes. All but one seemed committed.

Hatch attacked the soldier closest to her, striking the man in the throat with her elbow. The man gasped for air and clutched his neck where the hard impact of her forearm and elbow crossed the soft tissue protecting his larynx. It was equally devastating.

He staggered back, clutching his throat. The injured man didn't fall immediately but bent forward. Hatch drove a knee upward, cracking him across the bridge of his nose as an arc of blood sprayed out, following his head backward.

Hatch shoved the bleeding soldier's forehead back while hooking her leg behind his. She swept his foot and shoved hard in a downward motion, guiding his body to the concrete. The side of his head smacked against the hard sidewalk; he lay unmoving.

Two down, two to go.

She turned her attention to the next man. He was already in motion, coming at her with fists up in a fighter's stance. His movement was controlled and tight. He was obviously trained, whether it was through the military, life before or some combination of the two.

He feigned a punch. Hatch went to block, and he shot low, gripping her down by the waist and hoisting her into the air. In a few seconds, she would be slammed to the ground. He drove her down. Hatch's goal as she fell was to break the fall and lessen the impact.

When he had wrapped her up, he had left her hands free. As he descended to the ground, Hatch tucked her chin tight to prevent it from snapping back into the concrete and slammed outward at an angle to disperse the devastation of the impact with the ground. In martial arts this was called a break fall.

She was not in a controlled environment of a martial arts studio, and the man's weight against her diaphragm temporarily knocked the wind out of her. But as she hit the ground, Hatch had the presence of mind to hook her legs tightly around the man's waist and reverse the position. She stomped into his hip pocket with her right leg, and with the left, she under-hooked the back of the man's opposite leg.

She did a counter-push, sweeping her bottom leg toward her and kicking hard out against the man's hip line with her right. The movement twisted his body, throwing his weight to the side and sweeping him off his feet. In doing so, Hatch took the mounted position.

From the bottom, the soldier made a critical mistake by extending his arm and reaching out for her neck.

Although the soldier showed some decent skills, his groundwork needed some help. And Hatch was about to give him a very unforgettable lesson. With the man's left hand outstretched, reaching for her throat, Hatch shot up only partially and spun her body so the man's arm was trapped between her thighs. She rocked back to the ground with his arm pinned. As she did so, she tucked her foot under the man's ribcage, and her right foot slammed across his throat. Once her buttocks hit the ground, she arced back. There would be no slow application and waiting for a tap out.

His elbow was across her thigh. In the world of mixed martial arts, in a training environment, she would hold that position until the person realized they were in a compromised state and could no longer get out. They would then tap and be released to continue training. But this wasn't training. This was the real world. And she still had one more opponent to deal with. Being on the ground for any amount of time was a disadvantage when fighting multiple enemies.

Hatch arced hard, yanking the arm as she did so. The elbow went in the opposite direction with a sickening crunch.

The man screamed and rolled to his side. He came up to his knees and held his damaged elbow with his good arm. The ligaments were definitely torn. His arm hung loosely, flopping about.

Hatch launched up at the last man standing. The one, who in her initial summation of the four, seemed the most reluctant participant.

He looked down at his three wounded battle buddies and then back at Hatch. He threw his hands up in surrender as she stepped toward him.

"They're stupid. I'm sorry. I got no beef with you." He slurred the words, spitting them in a pitchy, frightened voice. And then he did something Hatch didn't expect. He ran. The young soldier ran down the sidewalk and disappeared around the corner.

She looked at the three injured men and walked away without saying a word.

TWENTY-EIGHT

HATCH SAT in the rental car, parked a block away from the tattoo shop, where only a little more than a week ago, she had sat face-to-face with her father's killer, though unbeknownst to her at the time. Returning now, she assumed the man had to know she was coming for him. Wenk had turned on her at the bar and then sent those men after her as she left. It wouldn't have been uncharacteristic of him to call ahead and warn his former teammate of her impending arrival. She was surprised that Wenk himself hadn't shown up to tell him. She had half thought he might.

It was getting late and nearing closing time. Hatch had done a drive by an hour earlier, and she caught a glimpse of the thin, long-haired tattooist walking between one of the tattoo rooms and the office where they'd last talked. The receptionist, the same man she had spoken with, had been seated at the front, and there were no customers she could see. Nobody had come in and nobody had left since Hatch had been parked down the street.

Hatch waited with the car's engine off. Her plan was similar to that of the last time she'd encountered the man. She wanted to catch him as he exited. And she needed to wait until the receptionist had vacated the building. It would be a telling sign that the owner and proprietor of the ink shop would soon be taking his leave as well. At least that was the limited pattern she understood from the last time she had been there.

Armed with only a knife, Hatch knew Amaletto had at least one gun at his disposal. And he was quick on the draw. Something she'd learned firsthand during their last experience. She assumed not much would be different except for the fact that she was now a threat to him.

Knife to a gunfight, she thought. Hatch was a walking contradiction to everything she knew, but she couldn't allow the man to escape. And after her meeting with Wenk, she knew it was only a matter of time before he either came for her or disappeared altogether. Both of which would be unsatisfactory in achieving the closure Hatch sought.

A weapon was only as good as the person who wielded it, and Hatch was as deadly with a knife as she was a firearm. The only challenge was proximity. If tonight went as planned, it would not be the first time she would have used a knife to take a life.

The glowing neon yellow of the fluorescent open sign went dark, as did the shop's interior lights. Hatch knew it was now only a matter of time before the receptionist left.

Taking the same path she had during her last visit, she skirted the alley adjacent to the billiards room. She moved quickly, now having a better sense of the layout, and where she would have the best advantage if he exited the rear of the store as he did before.

Peeking out from the alley, she saw his Prius was parked in the same spot as it had been when she had last encountered him.

Unlike last time, Hatch was here for a different purpose. She peered up at the walls, looking to see if there were any external cameras on the rear of the surrounding buildings. Seeing none, she made her way to a dumpster nearest the rear exit to the tattoo parlor. There was enough space between the concrete wall and the side of the metal dumpster to squeeze herself between the two.

She moved into position. Hatch had already removed the knife from the sheath. The blade was just shy of four and a half inches. She rested it cutting-edge-out along her left forearm. She gripped it tightly, keeping her thumb on top of the handle.

When wielding a knife, one typically carried the blade upside down. This enabled the user to strike in a punching motion for maximum speed and damage. It also enabled easier transition for different strike patterns.

Timing was everything on a mission. Hatch knew that and was prepared for it, keeping her plan of attack simple. As Fat Tony left, she was going to move in while he locked the back door, take him when his guard was down and while his hands were occupied with the keys. She counted on being able to exit the small cramped space behind the dumpster and close the distance quickly enough before the ponytailed ex-Special Forces operator could react. It was going to be close, and it was going to be extremely dangerous.

If Wenk had warned him, it would be a wholly different situation.

It wasn't long before she heard a rustle from the back door. A second later, Hatch saw Anthony Amaletto exit. He scanned the parking lot. Maybe Wenk had, in fact, called him and given him advance warning of their most recent conversation.

Her father's murderer stepped cautiously out into the heavy night air. He then closed the door behind him and pulled the keyring from his jean pocket. There were several keys on it, and they jingled noisily as he searched for the key to lock the door.

Commit to the action, then act.

Hatch seized her opportunity and sprung forward. She moved swiftly, closing the distance. The knife held tight against her forearm, her body was poised to strike. The man responsible for her father's murder was only inches away. The man who had, with the pull of a trigger, shattered her family and re-directed the course of her life. This man had made her what she was. Good, bad, or indifferent, the fork in the road created on that day in mountain terrain behind her childhood home was now coming full circle.

As she began punching out with the blade, Amaletto turned. For an older man, he moved quick, quicker than she anticipated him being able to.

Dropping the keys Amaletto side stepped and slammed down with his bony forearm against her knife hand. The impact struck a nerve, causing Hatch to drop the blade.

The steel of the blade banged loudly on the concrete step.

Adjusting on the fly, Hatch resorted to hand-to-hand. It was better than nothing. She regained her initial falter and struck out at the man with a closed fist, her scarred hand coming down in an arc.

Amaletto dipped back as the two fore knuckles of her index and middle fingers snapped at his chin with the grazing blow. He did not receive the full-force of the swing. He remained standing, not even staggered.

Because of the miss, she was off balance. Murphy's law had taken hold. She had brought a knife to a gunfight and now had no weapon at all. Hatch was now unbalanced and careening forward. The former Special Forces operator-turned-tattooist used this to his advantage.

He snatched Hatch by the hair, spinning her in one move and tightly wrapping his other arm around her throat, sinking in a vicious choke hold. She struck back with an elbow, hitting the man in the midsection, but he had already cinched in tight around her throat and was now using his other hand to tighten it further.

Hatch saw stars glimmer across her vision as the pressure increased.

She was fighting for oxygen, stomping on the top of his foot with her boot heel. The effect was minimal at best. Her ability to fight was slipping as she began to blackout. Then she felt the grip loosen ever so slightly.

Hatch writhed to escape the chokehold, but the shorter man had her off balance. She now understood why Amaletto had released his other hand. She felt the cool metal of his pistol's muzzle as it was pressed firmly against her right temple.

This is it, she thought, *the man who had killed my father is now going to end my life. It was a dark, poetic moment for her, a Greek tragedy. Twenty years in the making.*

Her mind reeled. She struck out again. The man seemed impervious to the blows. They were having little effect. Her right arm was up, working its way between his forearm and her throat, fighting to create a gap just enough so that blood and oxygen could flow to her brain. Hatch's motor function slipped with each passing second.

"Did you think you could come here and kill me? You think I would be that easy? I should have killed you last time I saw you. I guess I get a do-over now."

"I told you I'd be back," Hatch said between ragged breaths, her larynx being crushed by his forearm.

Her fingers were wiggling in between, just enough to keep her from passing out, but not enough to stop the relentless pressure. She stomped down hard, back where his toe should have been. Her vision was beginning to blur. She didn't know if she was going to be strangled to death or shot.

"If you move again, I pull the trigger now," he said in a hiss.

Why was he hesitating? Why hadn't he pulled the trigger? Hatch wondered. The tunneling aspect of her fading vision made it difficult to search for the reason why. Maybe he was waiting to make sure they were alone. It wouldn't take long for him to realize that was the truth. He'd probably wait a few more seconds, verify there would be no witnesses, and then pull the trigger. Or maybe he was going to render her unconscious and take her somewhere else. She fought for breath, each one harder than the last.

Consciousness was slipping. She was on the edge. She felt it. If he rendered her unconscious, it was over, and he would have won. *Stay awake, breathe.* She continued to fight. *No way I'm giving in. I will fight until my last breath.* She willed herself forward, fought for air, forced her fingernails to dig into the man, hoping that at least a little bit of pain would cause him to loosen his grip. But a man whose body was penetrated by needles on a regular basis had undoubtedly thick skin, and a high tolerance for such things. She clawed at him anyway.

"I told you to stop moving," he said through gritted fake teeth.

The gunshot was deafening in the small alley, the sound reverberating off the walls around them.

Hatch crumbled to the ground.

It took her a second to regain her composure. The man's arm was now loosely draped across her throat, and she lay on him like he was an uncomfortable mattress. The gun that he had pressed to her head was now sprawled out beside them. Hatch rolled to her side and stood.

She looked down at the man who was just moments before intent on killing her. A bullet hole was now centered in his forehead. It took a moment for her to register it as oxygen flooded her system.

Wenk was standing near Amaletto's car, the gun still pointed in Hatch's direction.

"This ends here tonight, Rachel. You understand me? It's over! Something I should've done a long time ago, and I'm sorry I didn't." Hatch eyed the gun down by Amaletto's lifeless hand.

"Don't even think about it."

Hatch rubbed at her throat, thinking hard to figure a way out of this current predicament. "You're just going to let me walk away after I watched you murder a man?"

"Can't live with it anymore," he said, softer. The gun lowered a little further.

"You seemed pretty hard-set on sending me to my death, writing me off back at your bar, little less than an hour ago. Here you are, saving my life. I don't get it," she said.

The man's weapon lowered further again. "I don't know what to say. What happened to your father was awful, and I'm sorry."

Hatch bent down and picked up the knife she'd dropped, sheathing it behind her back. "Sorry doesn't fix it. Sorry doesn't make what he did right. Sorry doesn't change the fact that you knew, all this time. Twenty years went by. Twenty years of suffering. So, forgive me if I don't accept your apology."

Hatch walked past the man and back toward the alley that connected her to the rental car she had parked on the other street.

She heard sirens in the distance. There was no doubt one of the patrons of the billiards club or one of the neighboring apartments had heard the gunshot and called it in. Wouldn't be long before the cavalry would arrive, and Hatch wanted to be nowhere close to this scene when they did.

Wenk began to whimper. It was strange to hear a man so distraught when he had been so confident earlier, so resolute in his decision that Hatch was in the wrong for digging this up.

Hatch gave the man no satisfaction, no accolades for saving her life. She deemed him as responsible for her father's death as the man who had actually pulled the trigger.

As she turned to make her way up the alley, she heard another gunshot. Looking back, Hatch saw Wenk lying flat on the asphalt as blood seeped out of his head onto the asphalt beneath him.

HATCH, drove away into the night, leaving North Carolina behind. And finally bringing closure to her father's death.

Hatch was still riding high after hearing Daphne's squeal at learning she was coming home.

She dialed the next number on her list.

"Rachel?" he asked.

"Dalton, I'm coming home." It felt good to say those words. "Do you still have a job opening?"

"I'm looking at your badge right now."

When there is no enemy within, the enemies outside cannot hurt you. Maybe Jabari was right.

Read on for a sneak peak at Smoke Signal (Rachel Hatch book 4), or order your copy now:

https://www.amazon.com/Smoke-Signal-Rachel-Hatch-Book-ebook/dp/B089KT6VCV/

Join the LT Ryan reader family & receive a free copy of the Rachel Hatch story, *Fractured*. Click the link below to get started:

https://ltryan.com/rachel-hatch-newsletter-signup-1

GET your very own Rachel Hatch merchandise today! Click the link below to find coffee mugs, t-shirts, and even signed copies of your favorite L.T. Ryan thrillers! https://ltryan.ink/EvG_

THE RACHEL HATCH SERIES

Drift

Downburst

Fever Burn

Smoke Signal

Firewalk

Whitewater

Aftershock

Whirlwind

Tsunami

Fastrope

Sidewinder (Coming Soon)

RACHEL HATCH SHORT STORIES

Fractured

Proving Ground

The Gauntlet

Join the LT Ryan reader family & receive a free copy of the Rachel Hatch story, Fractured. Click the link below to get started:

https://ltryan.com/rachel-hatch-newsletter-signup-1

Love Hatch? Noble? Maddie? Cassie? Get your very own Rachel Hatch merchandise today! Click the link below to find coffee mugs, t-shirts, and even signed copies of your favorite L.T. Ryan thrillers! https://ltryan.ink/EvG_

SMOKE SIGNAL (SAMPLE)
RACHEL HATCH BOOK FOUR

by L.T. Ryan & Brian Shea

SMOKE SIGNAL CHAPTER 1

Waiting was the hardest part. *Patience is what separated average from greatness*, Billy Nighthawk's grandfather's wisdom came to mind as it always did during times like this. In his youth, the lessons had been hard fought. *Little Hawk, you're as thick as the fog*, he'd say. It had taken him until adulthood for it to make sense. But the fog of understanding had lifted. And those lessons learned had served him well.

He'd been lying under the spiny branches of a gray horsebrush for several hours. The shrub looked like dried coral turned gray. The ground was damp, as morning thawed from the past night's dip in temperature. He had remained unmoving for the last several hours, even as the dampness soaked into his legs, through his thick, winter-lined jeans. His surroundings came into focus as the sky slowly brightened. Billy looked through the eyepiece of the binoculars, scanning the horizon for a sign of the two men.

In the distance, about three hundred meters away, he saw movement. The rubber eyecups pressed lightly against his leathery skin as he gently toggled the Bushnell's center focusing lever, bringing the enhanced image into clarity.

He blinked his eyes, trying to clear his vision. Maybe it was the cold start to the morning or the two days of tracking and his mind was beginning to play tricks on him. Billy did a double take of a cluster of tightly woven chokecherry shrubs jutting out from behind a boulder. The animal dipped its head low, skulking beneath a low hanging branch. Cheetah-like black spots dotted the fur lining the sleek muscular body of the big cat. At first glance, he thought it was a bobcat. With a flick of its tail, he realized, to his surprise, he was wrong. The end of the animal's short tail was completely black, as if it had been dipped in tar. The lynx's subtle physical differences made it unique. Feathered tufts of hair protruding from the top of its ears and the Fu Manchu beard gave the majestic beast an air of wisdom.

In Billy's culture, the lynx was believed to be the seer of secrets. And on the night of his passage into manhood, it had been his spirit animal.

Billy hadn't thought about that day in a long time. The return of the memory seemed fitting. It had been a day similar to this where the sky was gray and the ground was still cold from a late spring thaw. As was tradition, he'd spent the previous twenty-four hours in a fasted, detoxified state. He remembered the solemn look on his father's face when he was brought to the sweat lodge.

The lodge itself was not much to look at. It was set away from houses just beyond a slight rise in the land. A small hill blocked it from view of the other homes on the reservation, giving it a sense of isolation. Each family approached the use of the lodge in slightly different ways. In Billy's family, the tradition had been clearly laid out by prior generations. Only for the men. And the first time was when a Nighthawk turned sixteen.

The lodge was a place of transcendence and transformation. A connection of Mother Earth. Although at the time, Billy hadn't taken the spiritual journey seriously, at least in the beginning.

He remembered the stone lined pathway leading up to the lodge. The opening to the domed-shaped structure faced East, a purposeful connection to the rise of the sun, to new beginnings. Three paces from the opening was a wood post with the cleaned skull of a bear affixed to the top, a marker set to warn of the danger.

Billy had entered the sweat lodge led by his grandfather and father. The withes of aspen were lashed together by rawhide to shape the deer-skin dome. The opening was only a few feet high and each entrant needed to dip to a crawl when entering, forcing each to supplicate themselves in a gesture of humility.

The cramped space, only fifteen feet in diameter, was quickly filled by the three men. Billy's grandfather presided, beginning the ceremony with the passing of the chanupa, or peace pipe. The stones were heated and each man's cheeks were then smudged with smoldering sage. The fire heated stones glowed red as the flap dropped closed, shrouding them in relative darkness. The heat was intense, and Billy remembered sweating before the stones were set in place.

Billy's grandfather, one of the reservation's esteemed elders, set the four large red-hot stones in a tight circle in the center of the lodge. He placed the first stone toward the west and worked in clockwork fashion until all four were in place.

Then came the water. As Billy's grandfather ladled the cool water onto the stones, an intense steam filled the confines of the space, swallowing the oxygen. Billy remembered the initial sense of panic. He never admitted it to anyone, but he was claustrophobic, and the experience tested his resolve. Billy remembered fighting the urge to push his way out of the lodge. And then he remembered the moment when he relented and gave in to the power of the sweat. He breathed in the steam as his mind drifted.

The ceremony consisted of four rounds, or endurances. At the conclusion of each, Billy was given the opportunity to leave the sweat lodge and cool himself. He didn't. His grandfather and father didn't and so neither did he.

At the onset of the third endurance, Billy remembered his frustration. He'd heard the stories from friends and relatives about the spirit walk. The connection made along the Red Road, the spiritual connection to the East, to wisdom. But Billy felt no sense of enlightenment. He'd found no spirit guide. And his sixteen years of buildup to this moment seemed a fanciful dream.

Then, as the fourth and final round began, something happened. Billy's grandfather's face shifted before his eyes. At first, the change was a flicker. Billy blinked his eyes to clear it. As the steam rose, his grandfather's salt and pepper long hair was now that of a lynx. His eyes glowed, penetrating deep into his soul. Billy stared into the shimmering gold and in that moment came a clarity unlike any other.

As the flap to the lodge opened and cool air washed over his bare chest, Billy Nighthawk knew his purpose in life, and he'd been following it ever since. It was what brought him here. In the thick cloud of the lodge, he had committed his life to protecting the people of his tribe. And that meant the animals of their land. Seeing the lynx, here and now, felt like a connection to his beginning.

Besides the flickering image of this majestic wildcat, Billy had only seen one other one in his entire lifetime. It was a rare find, even rarer now in these parts. In the late 90s, due to the potential extinction and endangerment of the species, several of the rare cats were released into the San Juan Mountains Range, extending from southwestern Colorado into New Mexico. They'd been hunted and killed for sport previously, but since the humanitarian efforts, their population had been protected. Even with all of the efforts made to protect them, they were still rare, still endangered. There were believed to be less than two hundred fifty left in the area. Seeing one now was like finding a diamond in the rough. He took a moment to absorb the majestic beauty of this rare beast.

Its head suddenly canted slightly and looked, not at him, but off to the left of him. The cat lowered itself slightly, as if ducking from view. Billy took one last look through the scoped lenses of the binoculars and silently said goodbye to the creature, knowing that it might not be there when he returned his gaze.

After making his silent goodbye, he slowly guided the binoculars over the rough and rugged terrain, looking for what spooked the lynx.

It took more time than he liked before he was able to pinpoint the target of the lynx's focused gaze. Off to the left, equidistant to him from the animal, was a heavyset man in a thick camouflaged jacket. A strange triangle of man and beast formed. Each in a different role, one as a protector, the other endangered, and the worst, the man who was preparing to break laws of both man and nature.

The large hunter was tucked neatly alongside a tree, his camouflage was atypical for a hunter. Bright orange disregarded in lieu of military fatigues. He paid Billy no mind, focusing down the scope of his long-barreled rifle.

Before he could shout, the deafening crack of the rifle interrupted the silent peace, causing him to flinch. Gunshots rarely had that effect on him, having spent years around them and being an avid hunter himself. But this was different. This was something he had come to prevent. This was something he was supposed to stop from happening.

The world spun as his binoculars traced the direction of the shot back toward the lynx. He made a silent prayer that the cat had reacted to some noise prior to the pull of the trigger, that he had heard it, anticipated it, and in doing so escaped the impact of the high velocity round.

Billy scanned the area where the cat had once been, where he had locked eyes once again with his sprit guide, memorizing the detail and uniqueness of its face, but it wasn't there. A wave of relief crashed over him and he exhaled loudly, suddenly aware he'd been holding his breath.

He'd finally caught up to the hunter he'd been tracking for over a day, and although he had gotten the shot off, it looked as though he had thankfully missed.

Billy began to rise up from his position when he heard the strangest sound. A wailing, pitchy, like a broken siren, echoed out of the distance ahead. Whatever calm he'd experienced in the split seconds following the shot after not seeing the animal was dashed completely.

He repositioned himself. The wail rose up again. The noise of it caused him to jump as much as the rifle shot had, maybe more so. Each pitched wail was like a knife in his heart. And then he saw it.

The lynx hobbled out from the other side of the rock. It took a few staggered steps and collapsed to the ground. Its hind legs kicked as if trying to run, like a dog in sleep, dreaming of a big open field. It kicked three times before all movement stopped. No more sounds, no more cries filled the air.

He set the binoculars down as the shock and fear and sadness gave way to anger, both at himself for not reacting quick enough, but more, at the man responsible.

Billy shifted again, this time scanning back across the uneven terrain to the camouflaged figure moving forward. The solitary hunter stalked closer, his weapon at the ready. He watched as he crossed the distance from where he'd taken the shot to the animal. *Where's his partner?* There had been two of them. That he was sure of.

Billy slowly rose up from his hiding position and unholstered the revolver at his side. He stepped forward slowly, using the trees as cover and knowing that two men who had apparently broken the hunting laws might not be reasonable when confronted by law enforcement.

He moved carefully. Billy knew this land well. These men had desecrated the ground which he walked on.

About twenty feet away, he could hear the hunter clear his throat.

"Would you look at that?" The hunter said to himself.

Ten feet away now, he was close. He could smell him; a combination of day-old liquor circulated in the air around him. Not only did he just hunt and kill a protected animal, he did it drunk. Rage, a blinding red, the kind of anger that defies reason took hold. The kind of anger that throws a person into action without thoughts of recourse.

Billy stepped out into view and leveled his gun at the thick chested hunter.

"Drop your weapon," he said. His voice steady, he fought to control his nerves. It had been a long time since he'd pointed his gun at somebody, longer since he'd pulled the trigger. Although the thought of it now, seeing the dead animal down near their feet, the thought of it seemed more reasonable, more appropriate and more just.

"Whoa now there, Sheriff," the large framed hunter said. He raised his rifle up, but in a way that looked like he was yielding. Both hands up around his chest area, and he took a few steps back.

"I said, 'drop your weapon. Do it now!"

The hunter lowered it but didn't drop it.

Billy looked down at the animal. Its patterned fur was matted with dark blood. He felt the tingle of adrenaline coursing through his veins, and even with all the willpower he mustered, the end of his gun trembled slightly.

"Why don't we just go on about our business here, chief, and we'll call it a day? You go your way and we'll go ours."

"Not going to happen." His voice choked up a bit, his steely nerves beginning to disintegrate. The hunter still hadn't dropped his rifle. He was refusing to drop his weapon and was now bartering with him, as if he had some kind of leverage. "Don't make this any worse than it is."

"Like I said, boss, let's go our separate ways." The baritone, larger man who reeked of whiskey seemed calm. "We were out here just hunting, minding our own business."

"You don't have permission to be here. Plus, you just shot an endangered species," Billy spat the words.

He threw his hands up again, this time the rifle coming up a little higher. "Well, I don't right reckon I knew that when I pulled the trigger. Thought I was killing me a bobcat."

"You thought wrong. And you're hunting on reservation land." He eyed him carefully and took in the pasty white complexion of the barrel-chested hunter. "And from the looks of it, you two don't seem much like you belong on the reservation to begin with."

"Is that some type of racist comment?"

"Just an observation. Why don't you throw me your hunting permits?"

The hunter nodded and lowered the weapon to his side. He smiled.

It took Billy a second to realize what the hunter was smiling at him. He was looking just past him.

Billy spun as the wooden buttstock crashed down on the base of his skull. The blow sent ice down his spine and his legs buckled. Everything flickered dark as his face struck the cold dirt of the ground. He fought to remain conscious as his mind swirled. He felt a tugging of his arms, but he was incapable of mounting any resistance. "Make sure it's tight," came the muffled voice of the big hunter.

Billy's vision cleared but the searing pain pulsing from the back of his head increased. His arms were bound behind his back at the wrists. He looked up to see the skinny, shorter hunter standing above him. Billy felt sick when he saw his duty revolver in the hand of the man who'd just incapacitated him.

The skinnier man then walked the few feet over to the dead animal and knelt. "That's the strangest damn mountain lion I ever did see." His voice was like a bunch of rusty screws rattling around in a tin can, screechy and intolerable.

The larger hunter looked down at the dead animal, and then in a deep, baritone voice said, "That's because that ain't no mountain lion. That there is a lynx."

"You don't say?" the scratchy rattle echoed.

"It looks like we might've just made ourselves some extra money today."

"What do you think it will fetch?"

"Enough."

The answer seemed to satisfy the skinnier, screechy-voiced man. The smaller man's beady eyes seemed disproportionately larger than his face. It was almost cartoonish, as if he were a life size version of Gollum from The Lord of the Rings. He then turned his attention from the animal back to Billy, tapping the end of Billy's revolver on the rocky ground. "What do we do about him?"

"He's a problem," the bigger hunter said, rubbing his chin thoughtfully. "He's seen our faces. Not sure we have much choice."

Billy tried to speak out in his defense.

The Gollum stood and cocked back the revolver, putting it into single action. The sound caused Billy to lose his train of thought.

The bigger of the two then stepped in front, blocking him. "No. Not like that. I've got a better idea." He disappeared from view.

Billy tried to twist his head to follow the larger hunter, but any movement of his head was met with a searing pain. There was a strange tingle over his extremities. Panic filled him. He worried the blow to his head might've done some damage to his spin. Hard to tell from his bound position.

The big man returned, filling Billy's field of vision.

"What's that?" Gollum squeaked.

"My momma used to make the most delicious jam from these berries."

A split second later a thin branch with dark berries wafted in front of Billy's face. The big hunter teasingly tickled the end of his nose with one of the leaves.

"I don't get it," screeched the thinner hunter.

"The berries of the chokecherry are edible. The seeds are not. The seeds contain cyanide."

Gollum's eyes grew wider, which seemed an impossibility. And Billy did not like what he saw in them.

A moment later, berry after berry were forcibly being shoved into his mouth. Billy fought to keep his jaw locked but found he could offer little in the way of resistance to the large hunter's enormous hands. He was either going to suffocate or swallow the berries. Survival instinct overrode resistance and he swallowed the berries, seeds and all. He lost count. Not that it would matter anyway. He had no idea how many he'd eaten or how many it would take to reach a lethal dose.

The force feeding stopped as abruptly as it began. Billy spat the tart remnants into the dirt. The two hunters left him and returned to their kill.

His gut twisted into a knot. A pain resonated from his stomach to his chest cavity. Each beat of his heart pounded like a war drum, the cadence increasing exponentially. A sudden disorienting punch of pain knocked the wind out of him. His vision clouded as if he were back in the sweat lodge.

He couldn't breathe, the pain of it now, surging, radiating outward from the center of his chest. He reached for the blade in his boot, trying to pull it free in a last-ditch effort. The end of the bone handle just out of reach when the big man stepped in, pressing his dirty boot against the side of his face, pushing hard, turning his head to the right. The claustrophobia welled up inside him as he lay gasping.

Billy locked eyes with the dead lynx, as he slipped into darkness.

SMOKE SIGNAL CHAPTER 2

This time, the bump and skip landing of the small aircraft as it touched down on the concrete tarmac of the Durango-La Plata Airport didn't come with the same sense of anxiety as it had the last time when returning after a fifteen-year absence. Although, that's not to say she was completely comfortable either.

Hatch was now nervous on a different front. It was initially hard connecting with her niece and nephew after having spent their entire childhood apart. Now, with their newfound relationship established, a different pressure mounted. Living up to their expectations unnerved her.

Up until this point in her life, Hatch only had to look out for herself or her teammates. She'd emotionally disconnected from others, and in particular her family. All that had changed. And with change comes adaptation. Adapt and overcome. A mantra repeated throughout her time in the service. Resetting to an acceptable normal may prove to be the biggest obstacle for Hatch to overcome. That was saying a lot.

She'd taken Jabari's advice to heart, the African soldier who had proved himself every bit as worthy as any of her American counterparts. The saying he wished upon her, "When there is no enemy within, the enemies outside cannot hurt you." There was beauty in its simplicity. Hatch gave serious thought to the idea that in closing the chapter on her father's death, she would be capable of finding peace. A lifetime of war weighed heavily against her odds of achieving this, but it was worth a shot.

She set her sights on her family, on building a new sense of normal in the hometown she'd long since abandoned. Landing in Durango, she was again entering into uncharted territory. Her new role as an aunt would require her to take on a motherly figure for the children who had lost both mother and father within a few years of each other, both to tragedy. Motherhood frightened Hatch more than staring down the barrel of a loaded gun.

Beyond the children, Hatch was going to need to resume her role as a daughter herself. Mending the long-severed bond with her mother would be a daunting task. So many years stretched between them. Even though Hatch uncovered the truth about her father's death, the distance forged in its wake left their relationship in tattered shreds. Hatch wasn't totally certain she would be able to put to rest all of those feelings. The distance she'd put between her mother over the years since leaving home and joining the Army was unfillable. It would be a true test of Hatch's strength, will power, and ultimately her humility. *Can I let go of the past in the hopes of a better future?* Hatch thought to herself, though she did not know the answer.

The pilot made the announcement of their arrival, updating gate and baggage claim information in a delivery akin to a weekend anchorman. Hatch listened on autopilot as she absentmindedly rubbed her fingers across the raised web of scars extending from beneath her short-sleeved shirt and down to her wrist. An acceptance of self was the other wisdom she took with her from her experience in Africa.

She'd learned it from the gregarious cafe owner, Khari, who'd been burned on half of his face, and yet seemed unfazed by it. His courage had given Hatch the strength to not hide her damaged right arm anymore. The looks she got and the questions that were asked no longer forced her into hiding. She exposed herself wholly and completely to the judging eyes of those around her.

In unveiling herself, and no longer hiding behind long-sleeve shirts, Hatch felt the burden lift. It was as if exposing the scar to the light of day helped burn away some of the memory which caused it, the firefight that had left her maimed. The same battle had taken the lives of some of her dearest and closest friends. A moment in time that forever changed the course and direction of Hatch's life.

As she waited for the plane to taxi to a halt, she realized that all the roads of her life led here. Every step taken had been a long journey back home.

The passengers deplaned. Hatch headed down the metal stairwell that extended out of the fuselage to the white concrete below. She picked up her duffle bag from a line of carryon suitcases and shouldered it. Hatch then proceeded with the shuffle of people into the airport's main space. It was small and didn't take her long to navigate her way past the baggage claim to the arrival area.

Up ahead, maybe forty feet in front of her, Hatch saw the ponytail flop in the air as Daphne leapt up and down, bobbing her head from side to side.

Catching sight of Hatch, Daphne squealed with delight. The excited fervor of the little girl drew the attention of a few nearby travelers. Daphne broke into a sprint, dashing toward Hatch at full speed.

Hatch, upon seeing this, began picking up her pace as well, taking up a slow jog. She accidently bumped shoulders with a thin man of almost equal height, nearly knocking him over. She caught him by the arm and kept him upright as she offered an apology. The man's stern face softened slightly at seeing the approaching child.

Her heart raced as she caught another glimmer of the girl zigzagging her way toward Hatch. It hadn't been that long since the two had last seen each other, but much had changed, at least for Hatch.

And yet, even though the passage of time had been minimal, Daphne seemed to have aged. The trauma of her mother's death and then the chaos that followed undoubtedly left a mark no amount of time could completely heal. Nothing seemed to be able to diminish the light in the girl's eyes however, the infectious nature continued to shine brightly.

Hatch slowed to a walk as Daphne increased her speed, closing the distance rapidly. Only a few feet away, Hatch dropped to her knees, throwing aside the duffle to her left and outstretching her arms wide. Daphne filled the void. Hatch absorbed her niece's delicate frame into hers with a swoop of her arms. Daphne's ponytail whipped wildly about as she peppered the cheek and neck of Hatch with a barrage of kisses. She giggled wildly, squealing in excitement.

"Auntie Rachel, Auntie Rachel, I cannot believe you're home," she said, loud enough for anyone inside the airport to hear.

"I missed you too," Hatch said.

Daphne ratcheted down her hug even tighter around Hatch's neck.

"Where's Jacob?" Hatch asked.

"He's over there," Daphne said, releasing her death grip on Hatch's neck.

Hatch stood, taking the girl by the hand, almost forgetting her duffle in the excitement. The two nearly skipped back to where Hatch's mother and nephew stood side by side. This time, Jake didn't duck behind and hide. He was different now.

Jake had shown a rare kind of bravery several months back, a bravery that enabled Hatch to get the upper hand in a dire situation. That act had christened the ten-year-old into early manhood. Although he was still just a boy, certain things in life cause you to grow up faster. He too seemed to have grown from the experience during her absence and actually looked a bit taller than she remembered.

He broke free from his grandmother's gentle hand resting on his shoulders and ran to Hatch. A boy not accustomed to overt gestures of happiness and kindness, Hatch was caught off guard, but in a good way. The surprise was an amazing gift. She didn't have to bend as low to take his hug but did so anyway. Taking a knee, brought her eye to eye with the boy. "You look good, Jake."

"Thanks. I've been practicing again too."

He held up his arm in front of Hatch. The cast was off and he proudly displayed his arm, the one broken in the car accident. He turned it as if displaying a new toy.

Hatch grabbed his arm and ran her finger across the bone. She could feel the slight bump where the bone had snapped. She then gave a playful squeeze of the boy's bicep. "You're getting strong," she added. Hatch stood, kissed him on the forehead and bent down to grab her bag.

She walked over to her mother who seemed overwhelmingly happy to see Hatch. It was such a difference from the last time they had met in this airport. That awkward arrival seemed like a lifetime ago. Those versions of Hatch and her mother, Jasmine, no longer existed. What this was, what their relationship had evolved to was still in its infancy.

Hatch stood still for a moment. A new awkwardness presented, as they entered this unfamiliar territory, a relationship still budding. *Do they hug? Shake hands? Just wave hello? What was the protocol to somebody trying to reconnect?*

She didn't know, nor did she care. Hatch dismissed her insecurity and put her arm around her mother, pulling her close. She felt her mom release a gasp. This impromptu hug dissolved whatever angst lay hidden, and she felt the tension in her mother's body ease with the droop of her shoulders.

"We're so glad you're home," Jasmine Hatch whispered. "We can talk later, but I hope you'll be staying for a while."

"I don't plan on going anywhere anytime soon," Hatch said.

SMOKE SIGNAL CHAPTER 3

Hatch had spent the last several hours reacclimating herself to her family. Each came with their own unique share time. Daphne got first dibs, taking Hatch by the hand and guiding her up to her room as soon as they arrived home. The chrysalis nestled inside a small terrarium on her bedroom dresser was the most important thing in the soon-to-be seven year-old's life. On the wall behind the glass encasement were dozens of handmade drawings. The anticipation of the butterfly's pending transformation was captured in vibrant colors and designs.

Jake couldn't wait to show her some of the new moves he'd learned at his karate school during her absence. He had learned the way to swivel his hips to deliver a more devastating impact with his kicks. Hatch could tell he'd been practicing extra hard. The boy's movements were clean and precise. He demonstrated how a variety of different kicks were performed. Jake was able to chamber his knee and thrust out with surprising force for a boy his age. Hatch held her palm open as a target. She was confident the boy would develop into quite a fighter. The life and death incident that forced Jake to play the role of hero had forever changed him.

The last blow she absorbed with the palm of her hand struck with such ferocity that it still tingled minutes after his demonstration ended. It tingled now as she held onto the porcelain mug her mother had handed her. Even though it was midday, the piping hot coffee was refreshing.

Her mom's special brew. The one that Dalton Savage had become addicted to during her short stint as a member of the Hawk's Landing Sheriff's Office. Thinking about Savage, she had told him she wouldn't be arriving until the following day. She didn't feel good about the lie, but she had needed some time to settle in before meeting up. In reality, she wasn't sure what she would say to the man. She wasn't sure about the status of their relationship. If there even was such a thing. *Were they more than friends?* Some things had been hinted at but never spoken aloud Savage had pleaded with her to return to Hawk's Landing telling her it might be her chance at a normal life. Did normal mean something more? Maybe the old adage was true, and her absence had made her heart grow fonder.

She had the answers to none of these questions, but after setting foot back in Hawks Landing, Hatch couldn't imagine going a full day without seeing him. She thought she would need time to settle in and collect herself before seeing the lawman's face again. After only a few hours, she'd given up any resistance to the idea. The thought of seeing him called to her like a lighthouse beacon.

She wasn't ready yet to speak to her mother about what she had been through in her absence. The things Hatch uncovered regarding the murder of her father and the closure she gained for her family was a conversation best left for when the children weren't around. Hatch wasn't completely sure how much she would share with her mother, but she planned to tell her enough to provide her closure. Hatch owed her that much.

After finishing her cup of coffee and some small talk with her mother, Hatch decided she would go and spend a little time visiting with Savage.

"Auntie Rachel, you just got here," Daphne whimpered as Hatch made her way to the door.

"I know sweet Daphne, but I'll be right back. I've just got to stop over and see an old friend."

"You're going to see Dalton," she said in a sing-song way.

Hatch blushed slightly at the child's ability to read her so easily. Dismissing the tease, Hatch bent low and kissed her niece on the forehead. "I'll be back before you know it."

Hatch walked from the house out into the crisp clean Colorado air.

She surveyed her transportation options. There was only one. Hatch was forced to drive the raggedy old Chevy Astro van. She missed the beat-up F-150 but it had been totaled in the car crash that left Jake's arm broken. The insurance claim had been quick and painless, but Hatch hadn't used the check for the total loss to purchase a replacement vehicle. At the time she didn't have any plans for sticking around on a long-term basis, but now things were different, and she put finding a new car on her mental list of things to do.

The van's engine whirred to a start. She pulled down the winding dirt driveway to the main road. Hatch stopped at the bottom and stared for a moment at the boulder. The two identical handprints, faded with time, of her and Olivia. Like a phantom limb, Hatch still felt her sister as she drove away and headed into town.

Once on the main road, it wasn't long before Hatch was pulling to a stop in front of the sheriff's department. She sat in the van for a moment. Her heart rate increased. Hatch took two quick breaths and loosened her death grip on the steering wheel, alleviating the white of her knuckles. *Why am I so nervous?* Hatch was angry at herself. Deep down she knew the answer but didn't allow herself to hear it.

She stepped out of the car and made her way into the main lobby where she saw a familiar face seated behind the bullet-resistant plexiglass. Receptionist, administrative assistant, and heart of the Hawks Landing Sheriff's Office, Barbara Wright sat tending to her duties.

Wright looked up from a stack of paperwork. Seeing Hatch approach, a smile brightened her face as she set aside the papers. "Well, looky here, Rachel Hatch alive and in person!" Barbara's voice was sweet. Everything about the woman was kindness personified. Her eyes, her smile, the gentle way in which she spoke to every person who entered or left the building.

Hatch felt at home seeing her. This place, this town, it all felt right again. Like her world had been spun on its axle, righting itself.

"You look great Barbara."

She swatted at the compliment with her hand as if shooing a fly. "Oh, don't flatter me, sweetheart. I'm closer to the end than I am the start."

"Lies," Hatch said.

"And I know you're not here to see me."

"Sure, I am," Hatch said, a little more defensively than she intended.

"He's back in the briefing room. Everybody is. Well—except for me. I'm guarding the fort," she said with a smile. Then she reached over and picked something up off her desk. Hatch laughed out loud at seeing the bronzed three-hole punch. At the base of it was a plaque that read, "The Cramer Club."

Barbara set it back on her desk as an enormous paperweight. Patted it gently, and then smiled. "Best gift I've ever gotten in my forty years of working here."

The Cramer Club, the three-hole punch used to save the life of both Hatch and Savage when Donald Cramer, former deputy and now prison inmate, had held them at bay in an armed standoff. It had been Barbara who had rushed to their aid, wielding the three-hole punch had rendered the man unconscious, saving their lives. Savage, or one of the others, had bronzed it and gifted it to her. A wonderful memento for a courageous act and a courageous woman.

The door to her left buzzed followed by a metallic click, announcing its unlocking. Hatch walked over and pulled it open. She entered the short hallway, passing a bathroom on the left and the cubicle stations for the deputies' office space located to the right. Up ahead on the left was Savage's office. Around the corner, another hall led back to the holding cells and interview rooms and down into the sally port area. In the same corridor was a small conference room used for roll call briefings.

Hatch walked up to the conference door that was partially closed. The murmur of a solitary voice came clear as she moved closer. It was the familiar deep-throated voice of Dalton Savage. "This is going to be on an assistance only basis since it's technically out of our jurisdiction. We've been given approval by the Tribal Council to assist, but we are strictly operating in a support capacity. Do you guys understand?"

Hatch, not wanting to interrupt stood in the hallway. Even though she was separated by the door, Hatch was convinced she caught a hint of Savage's distinct scent. Black licorice.

Through the gap in the door, she could see the slender frame of rookie Deputy, Kevin Littleton. He met her gaze and raised his eyebrows.

Littleton pointed toward the door where Hatch was standing. The distraction stopped Savage's speech dead in its tracks.

Hatch, figuring no point in delaying the inevitable, opened the door.

As it swung wide, Savage dropped a marker he was holding and then fumbled on the floor for a moment as he retrieved it. He came up red-faced, either from his sudden lurch forward or embarrassment. Impossible to tell. His blue eyes, salt and pepper hair and strong jawline hadn't changed a bit in her absence.

He wore the buttoned-down cream-colored shirt with the silver star badge above the pocket. A pair of neatly fitted blue jeans completed the rural lawman's uniform.

"Hatch?" Savage stammered, then looked at his watch. "I thought you weren't going to be here till tomorrow."

"Yeah, change of plans." Hatch figured at some point she'd explain, but didn't feel here and now was the time, or maybe there wouldn't come a time at all. She arrived early would be a good enough explanation for now. "I just got settled in back home. Sorry to interrupt."

"No need to apologize. I was just finishing up. We're helping out the Southern Ute Reservation. They've had an incident and we're going to be assisting."

"An incident?" Hatch asked.

"A death."

"Murder?"

Savage shrugged. "I don't know yet. I have very little to go on."

"Then why are you being called in? Don't they have their own police?"

"They do," Savage said. "The victim is their police chief."

Hatch's eyes widened just a bit. Then she scanned the room.

Littleton and Becky Sinclair were present, but she didn't recognize the third man. There was a new face in a sheriff's uniform. He had jet black hair and tan skin along his taut jawline that pulsed with each clench of his teeth. His arms were tightly folded, the muscles of his exposed forearms were like coiled rope. Hatch guessed him to be in his early 20s, but the young deputy had a seriousness to him that made him seem much older.

"Hatch, meet our newest member. This is John Nighthawk."

Hatch nodded. "Like the Lake?"

"My people," Nighthawk said quietly, with a reserved confidence.

Nighthawk Lake held a different significance for Hatch. It was where her dead sister's body had been dumped. She pushed the thought from her mind.

"Nice to meet you, John."

"Likewise."

Hatch turned to Savage. "I'll leave you to it. I just wanted to let you know I was in town."

"No. Wait," Savage said. "Seriously—I was just finishing up. We're going to be heading out to the reservation shortly, but I've got a couple of minutes."

Savage then turned back to the trio of deputies. "Make sure that you have plenty of gloves and bags for collecting evidence. We're going to assist in any way we can. Be prepared for anything that's asked of us."

The group started to clear the room, the three deputies and Savage making up the entire law enforcement contingent of Hawk's Landing.

Littleton, a little less sheepish than she'd remembered passed by and gave her a pat on the back. Sinclair gave a quick hug. Nighthawk was the last to pass by. He gave Savage a solemn nod before moving out into the main space.

Once alone in the conference room, Savage whispered. "The other reason we're helping, the dead tribesman is Nighthawk's father."

"I come back into town and things go all topsy-turvy."

"Well, hopefully it's not a homicide," Savage said. "There's no gunshot or stab wounds. We're going to be looking at other possible causes. Maybe it was a heart attack? They want to be thorough and being that he's law enforcement, they wanted us to oversee it to make sure that they didn't miss anything. I think they're just really kind of caught off guard by it and are looking for us to be a sounding board."

Savage made his way past her, brushing his arm against hers. The gentle warmth of his body reminded her of the time she'd fallen asleep next to him.

Hatch followed him, bathed in the sweet smell of licorice trailing him.

They sat down in his office and before Hatch could say anything, Savage opened a drawer and pulled out a badge. The same badge he had given her as a temporary assignment when he had deputized her to assist in her sister's death investigation.

"I told you when you left, this badge would be here for you when you got back. Is this something you're still interested in? I know on the phone you didn't give me an answer. Do you have one now?"

Hatch looked at the badge and then at the man holding it.

"I don't. I wish I did, but it's not that simple."

"One thing I've come to accept, is with you, nothing's ever simple," Savage said, a smile creasing the corners of his eyes.

"I know you were hoping for one, but I—"

Savage held up a hand stopping her. "No need to apologize. I told you there's no expiration on my offer. As long as I'm Sheriff, it stands."

"Well, it looks like you filled Cramer's position."

He nodded. "Nighthawk's been a great addition. Smart kid. Probably, and don't repeat this, he's the best person I have on my team right now. He's got that natural talent for seeing details others miss. I've got high hopes for that one."

Hatch was silent. She heard Savage but was still in a mental deliberation about the offer. She had thought about it a lot since it was first made.

"I don't know about the badge. Let me get settled in and then I'll have an answer for you."

"Fair enough. I don't want to push, but if you take this badge this time, it can't be on a temporary basis. You'd have to go through the academy and when you finish, which I will have no doubt that you would pass with flying colors, then you'd be assigned here with me." He put the badge back in the drawer. "How about we talk more about it when you have some time? Let me get a feel for this situation over on the reservation, and then I'll give you a call later. Maybe we can meet up tonight or sometime tomorrow."

Hatch stood. "I'd like that. I'd like that a lot."

As Hatch walked toward the front door, the deputies made their way out the back. She said goodbye to Barbara and left.

Hatch sat in the Astro van, lost in a moment of thought. As she pulled out, the caravan of Suburban police vehicles pulled out of the rear lot, heading off in the opposite direction.

Hatch watched them go, disappearing from her rearview mirror's view as Savage and his team headed off to fight crime and Hatch headed home to her new, normal life.

Order your copy of *Smoke Signal* now:

https://www.amazon.com/Smoke-Signal-Rachel-Hatch-Book-ebook/dp/B089KT6VCV/

Join the LT Ryan reader family & receive a free copy of the Rachel Hatch story, *Fractured*. Click the link below to get started:

https://ltryan.com/rachel-hatch-newsletter-signup-1

ALSO BY L.T. RYAN

Find All of L.T. Ryan's Books on Amazon Today!

The Jack Noble Series

Never Go Home

Beyond Betrayal (Clarissa Abbot)

Noble Judgment

Never Cry Mercy

Deadline

End Game

Noble Ultimatum

Noble Legend

Noble Revenge

Never Look Back (Coming Soon)

Bear Logan Series

Ripple Effect

Blowback

Take Down

Deep State

Bear & Mandy Logan Series

Close to Home

Under the Surface

The Last Stop

Over the Edge

Between the Lies (Coming Soon)

Rachel Hatch Series

Drift

Downburst

Fever Burn

Smoke Signal

Firewalk

Whitewater

Aftershock

Whirlwind

Tsunami

Fastrope

Sidewinder (Coming Soon)

Mitch Tanner Series

The Depth of Darkness

Into The Darkness

Deliver Us From Darkness

Cassie Quinn Series

Path of Bones

Whisper of Bones

Symphony of Bones

Etched in Shadow

Concealed in Shadow

Betrayed in Shadow

Born from Ashes

Blake Brier Series

Unmasked

Unleashed

Uncharted

Drawpoint

Contrail

Detachment

Clear

Quarry (Coming Soon)

Dalton Savage Series

Savage Grounds

Scorched Earth

Cold Sky

The Frost Killer (Coming Soon)

Maddie Castle Series

The Handler

Tracking Justice

Hunting Grounds (Coming Soon)

Affliction Z Series

Affliction Z: Patient Zero

Affliction Z: Abandoned Hope

Affliction Z: Descended in Blood

Affliction Z : Fractured Part 1

Affliction Z: Fractured Part 2 (Fall 2021)

Love Hatch? Noble? Maddie? Cassie? Get your very own L.T. Ryan
merchandise today! Click the link below to find coffee mugs, t-shirts, and even
signed copies of your favorite thrillers! https://ltryan.ink/EvG_

Receive a free copy of The Recruit. Visit:

https://ltryan.com/jack-noble-newsletter-signup-1

ABOUT THE AUTHOR

L.T. Ryan is a *USA Today* and international bestselling author. The new age of publishing offered L.T. the opportunity to blend his passions for creating, marketing, and technology to reach audiences with his popular Jack Noble series.

Living in central Virginia with his wife, the youngest of his three daughters, and their three dogs, L.T. enjoys staring out his window at the trees and mountains while he should be writing, as well as reading, hiking, running, and playing with gadgets. See what he's up to at http://ltryan.com.

Social Medial Links:

- Facebook (L.T. Ryan): https://www.facebook.com/LTRyanAuthor

- Facebook (Jack Noble Page): https://www.facebook.com/JackNobleBooks/

- Twitter: https://twitter.com/LTRyanWrites

- Goodreads: http://www.goodreads.com/author/show/6151659.L_T_Ryan

Made in the USA
Monee, IL
30 August 2023